PARNUCKLIAN

FOR

CHOCOLATE

PARNUCKLIAN
FOR
CHOCOLATE

∘ ∘ ∘

B.H. JAMES

A NOVEL

RED HEN PRESS | *Pasadena, CA*

Book design and layout by David Rose

Library of Congress Cataloging-in-Publication Data

James, B. H., 1978–
  Parnucklian for chocolate : a novel / B.H. James—1st ed.
    p. cm.
  ISBN 978-1-59709-790-1 (alk. paper)
  1. Domestic fiction. I. Title.
  PS3610.A4275P37 2013
  813'.6—dc23
                            2012033560

The Los Angeles County Arts Commission, the National Endowment for the
Arts, the City of Pasadena Cultural Affairs Division, the Los Angeles Depart-
ment of Cultural Affairs, the Dwight Stuart Youth Fund, and Sony Pictures
Entertainment partially support Red Hen Press.

First Edition
Published by Red Hen Press
www.redhen.org

ACKNOWLEDGMENTS

Thanks to *Leaf Garden* for publishing "Parnucklian for Chocolate," a short story version of the opening two chapters, and *Seahorse Rodeo Folk Review* for publishing "Alien Abductions, Typically Speaking," a version of chapter five.

Much of this novel was written during my time in the University of Nebraska Low Residency MFA program. I would like to thank the program's directors, Jenna Lucas-Finn, Art Homer, and Richard Duggin, as well as all of the UNMFAW faculty, especially my workshop facilitators: Pope Brock, Brent Spencer, Allison Adele Hedge Coke, Patricia Lear, and Richard Duggin, with special thanks to Leigh Allison Wilson and Karen Shoemaker, their kind encouragement being greatly appreciated. Thanks also to my fellow UNMFAW students, in particular my comrades in arms Stephanie Austin, Terry Kelley, Jen Lambert, and Natalia Trevino.

Deserving much gratitude are my four MFA mentors, Lee Ann Roripaugh, Jim Peterson, Kate Gale, and Amy Hassinger, all of whom were instrumental in the development of this novel. I would like to particularly thank Kate—for seeing and believing in what I couldn't—along with Mark Cull and all of the wonderful staff at Red Hen Press.

Finally, thanks to my lovely Liz, for her eye, her ear, her encouragement, and her love.

ONE

T HREE WEEKS BEFORE his sixteenth birthday, Josiah was allowed to move back in with his mother, who had been impregnated with him during an alien abduction her freshman year of college. Josiah did not move back into the home he had grown up in—the home he had lived in with his mother—but rather Josiah moved into the home of Johnson Davis, his mother's new fiancé. Johnson Davis, with whom Josiah's mother had been living for the past four and a half months, also had a child: a girl, seventeen, fully-human, named Bree, who also lived in the home of Johnson Davis, but only on the weekends.

o o o

When Josiah first saw Bree, he thought she was pretty. He thought her hair was shiny, and he liked the way she looked in her soccer uniform. When she looked at him for the first time, she smiled. He looked away.

o o o

Growing up, Josiah ate nothing but chocolate. He ate chocolate for breakfast, lunch, afternoon snacks, and, of course, he ate chocolate for dinner. Chocolate ice cream, chocolate brownies, chocolate do-nuts, chocolate candy bars and cake and mousse and pudding and his very favorite: chocolate cream pie.

Josiah's beverages consisted of chocolate milk, chocolate milk-shakes, hot chocolate, and chocolate flavored drinks such as Yoo-Hoo. The only beverage, and for that matter, the only nourishment whatsoever, that Josiah ever ingested that had not been made with chocolate or covered with chocolate, had been the occasional glass of ice water.

Josiah, however, was in perfectly good health. He had a relative-ly fast metabolism, and, more importantly, was not fully-human, thereby making him insusceptible to many of the nutritional laws that typically affect the human race.

"Other children, Josiah," Josiah's mother would often say, from the time he was very young, "cannot eat all of the chocolate they want. If they did, they would get sick and they would get fat. But your body is different. Your body is part-Parnucklian, and Parnuck-lians eat nothing but chocolate. It is their only food. Of course, they do not call it chocolate, because they speak Parnucklian, and the word 'chocolate' is an Earthling word. They call it Boboli, which is Parnucklian for chocolate.

"The planet Parnuckle," Josiah's mother would often continue, "which is the home planet of your father, and therefore is your home as well, will always be your home, even though you have never been there, and possibly never will, but it will always be there as your home, because it is the home of your father, just like this home, which is my home, and also your home, is also your home, even if you grow up and move far away, as long as you live, or unless I move to another home, but then that home will also be your home. Your father, on the other hand, will never leave Parnuckle, so that will not be an issue. Of course, that's not quite fair, as it's comparing a house on a planet to a planet. I, likewise, will never leave this planet, nor will this house, or any house I may be living in, either in the future or whenever."

o o o

As Johnson Davis, Josiah's mother's new fiancé, pulled into the driveway of his home, Josiah's mother leaned over the front seat to address Josiah, who was sitting in the back, and said, "Josiah, this is Mr. Davis's home. This is where we will be living from now on."

The home of Johnson Davis was larger than the home that Josiah and his mother had lived in. The home of Johnson Davis was blue and had two stories and unlike the home that Josiah had lived in with his mother, the home of Johnson Davis did not look exactly like the other houses on the same street. The home of Johnson Davis also had a large front lawn with green grass.

o o o

Once, when Josiah was around five years old, he had gone with his mother to the grocery store to shop for groceries. Josiah had often gone with his mother to the grocery store because Josiah's mother was a single mother and could not leave him home alone at that age, and also because Josiah was very attached to his mother and loved her very much. While in the bread aisle, shopping for little Boboli donuts, Josiah saw a plastic bag containing round bread with the word *Boboli* printed on it. Later, when he and his mother were in the car on the way home, Josiah told her about the bag. He was going to ask her if the bag that said *Boboli* could possibly mean that there were other people on this planet that spoke Parnucklian, maybe even part-Parnucklians like him, and he was also going to ask why the bag that said *Boboli* had some kind of round bread in it and no Boboli at all, but before he could ask, Josiah's mother reached across the cab of the car and grabbed Josiah by the forearm, spearing her fingernails into his skin.

"Never interrupt Mommy while Mommy is driving," Josiah's mother said. When Josiah's mother let go, Josiah watched as the little white half-moons on his arm turned pink and disappeared.

o o o

Johnson Davis and Josiah's mother led Josiah through the doorway and into the home of Johnson Davis. Inside the doorway was a square section of linoleum. The linoleum was white with blue checkered lines and was just big enough for Johnson Davis and Josiah's mother and Josiah to all stand on at once, which they did after passing through the doorway. Johnson Davis and Josiah's mother each lifted one foot and began taking off their shoes.

Johnson Davis encouraged Josiah to take off his own shoes by saying to Josiah, "Josiah, this is where we keep our shoes," and stepping toward a corner of the square of linoleum next to the door and bending down onto one knee and placing his shoes, a pair of dark blue loafers, very carefully side by side in the corner and twisting his torso halfway around to receive the shoes of his fiancée, a green slip-on shoe with no heel which she handed to Johnson Davis already carefully aligned side-by-side and which Johnson Davis received two-handed, maintaining their alignment as he turned back toward the corner and placed the pair neatly beside his own. Johnson Davis then looked with anticipation toward Josiah, his two hands raised in Josiah's direction.

Josiah took off his right shoe and then his left shoe. He held the two shoes side by side and handed them to Johnson Davis, who further aligned the pair before carefully placing them beside the other two. Johnson Davis then stood and extended his arm, waving it slowly across the space in front of him.

"Welcome home, Josiah," Johnson Davis said as Josiah's mother placed her hands on each of Josiah's arms, just below the shoulders, and squeezed.

o o o

Earlier that day, Josiah had been led to a room in the group home that he did not remember ever having been in before. Josiah had been living in the group home for the previous two years. The room that Josiah was led to was the lobby, and waiting in the lobby for Josiah was his mother and a man who had his hand on Josiah's mother's back. As Josiah entered the lobby, Josiah's mother stepped forward and hugged him and started to cry a little bit and told him that she was so happy to see him and that she was so happy that they were going to be together again.

Josiah's mother then stepped back and stood next to the man. The man again put his hand on Josiah's mother's back. Josiah's mother, who was thirty-five years old, looked much older than Josiah had remembered her. She was wearing a light green sundress with a short white sweater over it. The man next to her looked even older than she did. He wore a brown sweater and had a grey beard.

"Josiah," Josiah's mother said, "I'd like you to meet someone very special. This is my new friend, Mr. Johnson Davis."

Johnson Davis, whom Josiah's mother had met at a church that she had begun attending shortly after Josiah had moved into the group home, and who taught Latin American History at the local community college, stepped forward and took Josiah's hand. He shook Josiah's hand very deliberately.

"Mr. Davis is my fiancé, Josiah," Josiah's mother said. "We are engaged. We are going to be married."

Josiah nodded.

o o o

The previous night, at the group home, Josiah had written a letter to his father on Parnuckle telling him that tomorrow his mother would be coming to take him back home and that he really really didn't want to go back and live with his mother and at the end of the letter Josiah asked his father, as he had done numerous times since being sent to the group home, if he could please come and live with him on the planet Parnuckle, and if possible could he be there before ten the next morning to pick him up.

o o o

Throughout Josiah's childhood, Josiah's mother had encouraged Josiah to write letters to his father. Josiah would write a letter to his father every week, usually writing the letters on Sunday afternoons.

Josiah would write to his father about the things he had been doing, both at home and at school, and he would also ask his father
questions about life on Parnuckle and what he had been up to. The
letter Josiah wrote to his father the week of his seventh birthday,
which was his third letter overall, went like this:

> *Dear father*
>
> *thank you for reeding my letter i hope you are haveing a good
> day how is the planet Parnuckle i hope the wether is nice maybe
> some day i will be abel to visit you there yesterday i turned seven my
> mother made me a choclate cake you would call it a boboli cake she
> allso gave me new socks*
>
> *love josiah*

The next Saturday, Josiah's mother delivered to Josiah the following letter in response:

> *Dear Josiah,*
>
> *This is your father. Thank you for your letter. You are a very
> good writer, though you should work on your capitalization and
> punctuation.*
>
> *I am very happy to hear that you have turned seven.
> Congratulations. New socks! My, what a wonderful gift. What a
> wonderful mother you have. You must be so pleased. By the way, the
> Parnucklian word for socks is toasties.*
>
> *The weather on Parnuckle is beautiful all year long. Even when
> it is raining or storming, it is beautiful. We do not have the nasty
> seasons that you have on most parts of your planet.*
>
> *Well, I must be getting back to work now. It is very busy here.*
>
> *I miss you and love you very much. Please tell your mother that I
> miss her and love her very much, as well.*
>
> *Love,*
> *Your father*

Josiah would always receive responses to his letters, delivered
to him by his mother, on the following Saturdays, and his father's

kind words always made him feel happy, no matter what kind of mood he may have been in.

One week, when Josiah was eleven years old, he wrote a letter that went like this:

> *Dear Father,*
> > *Will you please come live with us in our home?*
> > > > *Love, Josiah*

Twenty minutes after Josiah gave the letter to his mother to send to his father, Josiah's mother returned to Josiah's room. "Josiah," Josiah's mother said, "your father is not going to come live with us."

"Why not?" Josiah asked.

"He lives far too far away."

"He could visit."

"He is very busy, Josiah."

"Does he love us?"

"Of course he does."

"How do you know?"

"What do you mean, how do I know, Josiah? He's your father. Of course he loves us."

After a few seconds, during which Josiah and his mother were both silent, Josiah asked his mother, "How do they say 'love' on Parnuckle?"

"I'm not sure, Josiah," Josiah's mother answered. "Why do you ask?"

"I don't know. How?"

"I'm not sure. How do you think, Josiah?"

"'Home.'"

"'Home'?"

"Yes."

"Why 'Home'?"

"I just think it is."

Josiah then decided that if he ever grew up and had people that he loved, other than his mother, of course, and his father, whom he had never met, such as a wife and maybe children of his own, he would live with them, all together, in his home, wherever that may be, and none of them would ever have to leave that home.

o o o

Josiah's first day in the group home had its ups and it had its downs. He did not know anyone at the group home, it being his first day, so Josiah, who was thirteen years old at the time, spent part of the day sitting alone on a rug in an area near a corner of the rather large common room, staring at comic books, of which there was a stack containing various titles.

The day before, Josiah had woken up in the home he had lived in with his mother and instead of walking into the bathroom, as he normally would have done, he walked into the kitchen and peed onto the kitchen linoleum. Josiah's mother walked into the kitchen shortly thereafter to find Josiah standing triumphantly in a pool of shiny urine. She responded by storming toward Josiah—her sneakers, which she always wore to work because she spent so much time on her feet, splashing in the pee as she crossed the kitchen floor—and grabbing the part between his neck and his right shoulder and squeezing. Josiah's mother then forced Josiah, through further squeezing and a series of shouts, to get down on his hands and knees and clean the pee up, dropping a white and red checkered kitchen towel onto the linoleum next to him. She then insisted that Josiah accompany her on the daily errands without allowing him to wash his hands or change his clothes.

The next incident occurred that very night when Josiah stood and peed on the sofa while he and his mother were watching the *CBS Evening News with Dan Rather*, whom Josiah's mother thought was lovely. Josiah's mother responded by chasing Josiah around the house and into his room, inside which he locked himself and, over the course of the evening, peed in three times: twice onto the bed and once into the dresser drawer in which he kept his socks and underwear.

The next morning, Josiah's mother asked their neighbor, Martin, whose wife had been a good friend of Josiah's mother and who was handy with tools and had a good many of them, to help her bolt and lock Josiah's bedroom door from the outside so that she could keep him from drinking any more liquids and thus he would not be able to pee in the house anymore, and also to allow her a way to starve him as a punishment for having peed in the house prior, to which Martin obliged before returning home and promptly phoning Child Protective Services.

Josiah had been told to wait in the rather large common room of the group home by someone who had had to finish filling out a few papers and who would be back to take Josiah to his new room and show him around and discuss the rules and procedures. The person who had had to go and finish filling out a few papers and whom Josiah was waiting for had led Josiah to the room with the comic books, which also included three beanbag chairs, which Josiah at the time did not know were chairs, and some board games, and told Josiah that he could read some of these comic books while he was waiting and it would just be a minute.

Nearly an hour after Josiah was left in the room, a short boy with glasses came over to where Josiah was sitting and sat down on the opposite side of the stack.

"Hi," said the boy. "Are you reading those comic books? I've read most of those already. In fact, I've read all of them. I used to be a big comic book fan."

Josiah stopped staring at the comic book he was holding and stared at the boy.

"I don't read comics anymore," the boy continued. "I only read novels. I have a shoebox full of them in my room. If you want, I can let you borrow some. Then if you read them, we can talk about them."

Josiah stared at the boy.

"I'm thinking of starting a novel club, here," the boy said, "where we can read the same books at the same time and talk about them. Do you think you want to join?"

Josiah set the comic book back onto the stack, stood up, peed on the boy, and left, leaving the boy sitting alone and crying.

o o o

Johnson Davis and Josiah's mother showed Josiah the living room of the home of Johnson Davis, which they were in after taking a few steps off of the linoleum square and onto the beige carpet, as well as the kitchen and the dining room, which Josiah thought was dark, even though the lights were on, and which was decorated so that it resembled the dining room on a boat or ship of some kind, with a thick rope running along the top of the four walls and an old ship's helm hanging from one wall, similar to one Josiah had seen in a movie about children who had had to battle against pirates on a pirate ship. The home that Josiah had lived in with his mother had not had a dining room. Josiah and his mother had eaten most of their meals at a yellow table in their kitchen.

Johnson Davis and Josiah's mother also showed Josiah the laundry room and the back porch and the garage, which was full of brown boxes, and the backyard, which, like the front yard, was also large and filled with green grass, until finally reaching the upstairs, where, after first being quickly shown the bedroom of Johnson Davis, which, as Josiah's mother explained to Josiah, was also now the bedroom of Josiah's mother, Josiah was shown his own bedroom.

o o o

Josiah's bedroom in the home he had lived in with his mother had been filled with posters of Mark Harmon, who, at the time that the posters were purchased, had been the star of a popular television program that took place in a hospital. Josiah's mother told Josiah, once he was old enough to understand, that the reason his room was filled with posters of the television actor Mark Harmon was that Mark Harmon was the one Earthling male, of the Earthling males that Josiah's mother was familiar with, that most closely resembled Josiah's father on Parnuckle, and since Josiah's mother understandably had no actual photographs of Josiah's father on Parnuckle, and since Josiah's mother very much wanted Josiah to feel a closeness and a kinship with his father and to be surrounded by his image and his presence, and since Mark Harmon himself was an exceptionally gifted actor and accomplished individual that would be an inspiration to any young man, Josiah's mother thought it fitting that she should fill Josiah's bedroom with various images of Mark Harmon, including one of Mark Harmon walking on a beach in only his shorts with a dog jumping nearby and one of Mark Harmon wearing the white lab coat and serious look of his character on television and one of Mark Harmon wearing a suit and looking nonchalantly over his shoulder and a half a dozen others.

o o o

At the group home, unlike the home he had lived in with his mother, Josiah did not have his own room. Josiah shared a room at the group home with three other boys. Two of the boys' names were Joey Simms and Eli Koslowski. The other boy was the boy Josiah had peed on earlier. His name was Patrick.

After Josiah peed on Patrick and left the room he had been told to wait in, he walked down a hallway and into a bathroom. The bathroom had a picture of a boy on its door. Josiah went into the bathroom and into one of the stalls and shut the door of the stall and locked it and sat down on the toilet seat. Josiah had never sat down on a toilet seat with his pants up before. It felt unusual. He started to cry.

A few minutes later someone else came into the bathroom. It was Patrick. He had gone to his room and gotten a change of clothes and now was going to clean himself up. He was also crying. Josiah could barely hear Patrick's crying over the running water in the sink and his own crying. The same was true for Patrick, in regards to Josiah's crying.

"I won't tell anyone," Patrick said. Josiah was startled when Patrick began speaking, and being startled caused Josiah to suddenly stop crying. Patrick had stopped crying just a few seconds before he spoke.

"Why did you do it?" Patrick asked. Josiah did not say anything. Josiah had not known that Patrick had known that he was in the stall and now that Josiah did know that Patrick knew he wished very much that Patrick didn't know.

"Why?" Patrick asked again. "I didn't do anything to you."

Josiah did not respond to Patrick. He began to cry again. Patrick turned off the water in the sink. The room was silent other than Josiah's crying.

"I was just trying to talk," Patrick said. "You looked lonely."

Josiah began to cry more.

"I thought you might want to be friends," Patrick said.

Josiah again did not respond but instead stayed inside the locked bathroom stall until Patrick finished cleaning himself up and finished changing his clothes and left. After Patrick had finally gone, Josiah began to cry very loudly, and did so for several minutes, until the person who had had to go and finish filling out some papers and whom Josiah was supposed to have waited for in the large room he had been told to wait in, a man named Clay who smelled like a car, came into the bathroom looking for Josiah and heard Josiah crying, which Josiah stopped doing almost immediately after hearing Clay come through the door, and Clay knocked lightly on the door of the locked stall and asked Josiah if he was okay in there and told Josiah that it was alright and it was not so bad and he knew Josiah probably missed his old home and his friends and his parents and whatnot but that for the time being he was in the very best place and even though he was sad at the moment it would only get better and would he like to see his new room?

o o o

Josiah's new room in the home of Johnson Davis had no posters of Mark Harmon in it. It did, however, have one very large framed poster that took up most of one wall of the room and featured a black and white photograph of a man in shorts and a tank top running toward the camera and sweating profusely. Below the man, in big letters, was the word BELIEVE.

As Johnson Davis and Josiah's mother led Josiah into Josiah's new room, Josiah began to stare at the poster of the man who was running and sweating, mostly because it was a very big poster and took up most of the wall facing Josiah. Johnson Davis saw that Josiah was staring at the poster and said, "Isn't it wonderful?" Johnson Davis stepped across the room and stood before the poster, facing it, but still addressing Josiah across the room behind him, his hands, made into fists, not so much rested as pressed into the area of his ribs. "You're probably wondering who it is," Johnson Davis said, and then, before Josiah could respond, "The truth is, I don't know. I have no idea. It's been so long since I've been involved in competitive running."

Johnson Davis turned and faced Josiah and Josiah's mother, who still stood near the door. "I was once very involved in competitive running," Johnson Davis said to Josiah.

"He was quite accomplished," Josiah's mother added.

"I was nearly an Olympian. Twice," Johnson Davis said.

"Isn't that wonderful?" Josiah's mother asked.

Josiah nodded.

Johnson Davis shifted his gaze slightly to address Josiah's mother. "Does Josiah play any competitive sports?"

"No," Josiah's mother responded, "but he's very active."

"Fine. Fine," Johnson Davis said. As Johnson Davis turned back to the poster, it occurred to Josiah that if his father was in fact coming to get him and take him back to Parnuckle, and if he had not arrived to the group home in time and had missed him, he would be looking for him at the home that Josiah had lived in with his mother, where he had sent Josiah his letters, and would have no idea where the home of Johnson Davis was.

"It's certainly an Olympic runner," Johnson Davis continued. "I don't know the name. But he's impressively strong. Impressively fluid. You can see that."

"It's certainly a lovely image," Josiah's mother said. "Don't you think, Josiah?"

Josiah nodded.

"And inspirational, don't you think?" she added.

Josiah nodded.

"Probably from an African country," Johnson Davis said, still staring at the poster. "Or South America. Could be South America."

TWO

JOSIAH FIRST MET Johnson Davis's daughter Bree four days after moving into the home of Johnson Davis. Having decided at eleven years old that if he ever grew up and had people that he loved he would live with them all together in his home, Josiah thought that Bree, whom he thought was pretty, liking the way that she looked in her soccer uniform, may be someone he could love and have a family with and live all together with in a home, and by the end of that night, he was sure of it.

That evening, Josiah and his mother waited, with dinner ready in the kitchen, for Johnson Davis to return from picking Bree up from her school. On weekdays, Bree lived with her mother in a town forty-six miles away from the town where Johnson Davis lived. Bree was on her high school's Girls Varsity soccer team, and the team happened to have had a game that afternoon, putting Johnson Davis and Bree's arrival at well after seven o'clock in the evening.

o   o   o

When Bree was eleven and a half years old, her art teacher Mr. Adlinson had told her that she was a very special girl and that he was going to show her what a man's penis looked like.

"You're going to have to see what one looks like some day, aren't you, if you're going to be a mommy?" Mr. Adlinson had said to her. "This way you'll be prepared."

Later that afternoon, in the home of Johnson Davis, Bree had asked Johnson Davis if she could see his penis, and when Johnson Davis responded with abundant bewilderment and concern and anger, Bree had explained that she wanted to see if they were all the same.

When Bree's mother, the former wife of Johnson Davis, finally returned home from the grocery store, she went to speak with Bree in Bree's room, inside which Bree had been locked for the last hour and a half and inside which she had been told she would be locked for the rest of her life. Bree convinced her mother, the former wife of Johnson Davis, that she had wanted to compare the penis of her father to a picture of a man's penis that she had seen in a textbook at school.

Bree was fifteen years old the first time that she was suspended from school. That week, Manny Bowler and Freddy Carson were caught smoking marijuana behind the science building of the high school that they and Bree attended. Manny Bowler and Freddy Carson were very worried that they would get into a lot of trouble when their parents found out that they had been caught smoking marijuana, so they were relieved when the Assistant Principal, Mr. Dawes, informed them that their parents might not necessarily need to find out as long as Manny Bowler and Freddy Carson were willing to reveal to Mr. Dawes where they had gotten the marijuana.

When Mr. Dawes informed Bree that selling illegal substances on campus was grounds for expulsion as well as involving local law enforcement, Bree informed Mr. Dawes that she would not tell anyone that Mr. Dawes's brother-in-law, Mr. Adlinson, who was an art teacher at the nearby elementary school, had shown her his penis when she was in the sixth grade as long as her selling illegal substances on campus was grounds for suspension rather than expulsion and not grounds for involving local law enforcement at all and as long as she was able to remain on the Girls Junior Varsity soccer team.

o o o

Shortly after Johnson Davis and Bree arrived at the home of Johnson Davis, after Bree was allowed to put her bag into her room and to use the restroom and after Johnson Davis had made a formal introduction of Bree to Josiah and likewise Josiah to Bree, during which Bree, whose hair Josiah thought was shiny, smiled at Josiah and Josiah looked away, Johnson Davis and Josiah's mother and Josiah and Bree all sat down in the dimly-lit dining room resembling the interior of a pirate ship and began their dinner. Johnson Davis and Josiah's mother and Bree were each having a pork chop and some steamed vegetables that Josiah's mother had spent the earlier part of that evening preparing. Josiah was having a piece of chocolate cream pie. Josiah's slice of chocolate cream pie was so large that the slice constituted between one-quarter and one-half of the pie itself, which Josiah's mother had purchased at the local grocery store earlier that day while shopping for pork chops and vegetables.

As Bree sat down to the table, the dishes holding the pork chops but not yet the vegetables having already been set out, and Johnson Davis and Josiah having already been seated, Bree looked at the plate set before Josiah, Josiah and the plate both having been set directly across from Bree, and asked, "Is that your dinner?"

Josiah, who had spent the past several minutes sitting in silence at the table with Johnson Davis as they had both waited for either Josiah's mother to emerge from the kitchen or Bree from the bathroom, answered, "Yes."

"You're having pie?" Bree asked.

"Yes," Josiah responded.

"For dinner?" Bree asked.

Josiah was again going to answer "Yes" to Bree when Johnson Davis interrupted and told his daughter, "Oh, yes. Pie—chocolate pie—is one of Josiah's favorite meals."

"Is it?" Bree asked.

"It certainly is. Josiah, you see, has a very unusual diet," Johnson Davis said.

"Consisting of pie?"

"Not just any pie."

"*Chocolate* pie?"

"Correct. Or chocolate cake or chocolate ice cream or chocolate whatever-have-you."

"Chocolate?" Bree asked.

"Oh, yes," Johnson Davis said, "It seems Josiah does not eat anything other than chocolate. Isn't that right?" Johnson Davis turned to Josiah. Josiah nodded.

Bree also turned to Josiah. "You eat nothing but chocolate?" she asked.

Josiah again nodded.

"Oh no," Johnson Davis said. "Nothing but chocolate."

o o o

Four days earlier, on the way back to the home of Johnson Davis after having picked Josiah up from the group home, Johnson Davis, whom Josiah had just met and whom Josiah had just learned was going to be the husband of his mother, decided that they should stop and have some dinner as it was getting late.

Johnson Davis pulled into the parking lot of a restaurant and parked, and as he and Josiah's mother and Josiah entered the restaurant, Johnson Davis holding the door open for the other two, Johnson Davis told Josiah's mother and Josiah that this place had the best taco salads anywhere on God's green Earth, the absolute best, and they absolutely had to try one, and when they were all three seated and the hostess asked if she could take their drink orders, Johnson Davis informed her that they already knew what they would be having and they were ready to order right away and they would all three be having the taco salad, which was the absolute best on God's green Earth.

When the hostess stepped away after telling Johnson Davis that she would go right away and get their server, Destini, and Destini would be happy to take their order, Josiah's mother told Johnson Davis that while she was quite intrigued by this taco salad that he seemed to be so fond of, Josiah would probably not enjoy it as much and would probably rather have something else. When Johnson Davis, somewhat disappointed, asked Josiah's mother what she thought Josiah would like better than the best taco salad on God's green Earth, Josiah's mother opened the menu and scanned the inner side of the first flap and responded that Josiah would probably enjoy either the Triple-Layer Chocolate Truffle Cake or the Triple-Layer Dark Chocolate Mousse. When Johnson Davis responded by asking, "For dinner?" Josiah's mother responded by saying to Johnson Davis, "Didn't we discuss this?" to which Johnson Davis responded, "Oh, yes. Of course."

"And I thought that there was no problem."

"No, no problem. I just . . ."

"Forgot?"

"No, I remember you telling me."

"But you didn't believe me?"

"No, no, I believed you. I just . . ."

"What?"

"I didn't think you were . . . serious."

"You didn't think I was serious?"

"I just . . . Well, take my Uncle Francis. We used to say all he ate was potatoes. We meant that he ate a lot of potatoes."

o o o

"Is that healthy?" Bree asked, sitting at the dining room table, shifting her eyes from Josiah to Johnson Davis and back as she spoke, so as to direct the question at either. Josiah was unsure how to answer this question, other than to repeat what he had heard his mother say numerous times, that he was a perfectly healthy boy, and Johnson Davis, along the same lines, was about to say to his daughter, "Doesn't he *look* healthy?" when Josiah's mother, pushing the door open with her shoulder, entered the dining room from the kitchen, carrying a bowl of steamed broccoli, cauliflower, and carrots in one hand and a pitcher of ice water with two slices of lemon floating at the top in the other.

"Dear," Johnson Davis said to Josiah's mother as Josiah's mother set the bowl and the pitcher onto the table, "Bree was just asking if it is healthy for Josiah to eat chocolate cream pie for dinner."

Josiah's mother paused, plunging a large spoon into the bowl of vegetables as she held one hand out in search of a plate. "Why would she ask that?"

"I was just curious," Bree said.

o o o

When Josiah was five years old and the time had come to send Josiah to school, Josiah's mother had decided to send Josiah to a local private school, explaining to Josiah that the local private school would be a more accepting environment for a boy that was special—a boy that was part-Parnucklian—than the local public school would be, and that the children of most important people, such as senators or mayors or news anchors or business owners, went to private schools such as the local private school, and it should be no different for the son of an important official of the planet Parnuckle. However, private school was somewhat expensive. The parents of children who went to private school had to pay tuition every month for their child to continue attending the private school, and also had to buy books and uniforms. The uniform at the private school that Josiah's mother decided to send Josiah to consisted of a white polo shirt and a pair of navy blue pants, along with a navy blue sweater for days when it was cold. Josiah's mother bought Josiah's uniform at a store that the woman in the school's office had recommended. The store, the woman told Josiah's mother, often carried school uniforms that the parents of former private school students no longer needed and had sold.

Josiah's mother knew that it would be difficult to pay the private school's tuition each and every month, but at the same time it was very important to Josiah's mother that Josiah be somewhere where he would be treated as special.

"For a child such as yourself, Josiah," Josiah's mother said, "not just any school will do. It is important that you go to a school that recognizes your differences. That will see how special—how important—you are."

On the first day of kindergarten at the local private school, the children were asked to walk to the front of the classroom and tell the teacher and the other children about themselves and their family.

"I'm Josiah," Josiah said when it was his turn, "and I live with my mommy in our house. My mommy cleans other people's houses. My daddy lives far, far away on the planet Parnuckle." When Josiah said that his father lived far, far away on the planet Parnuckle, the other students began to giggle, which made Josiah embarrassed and upset. Josiah went back to his seat and did not say another word until snack time.

At snack time, when Josiah pulled from his bag a chocolate pudding cup and a chocolate brownie and a chocolate wafer snack, the teacher, a woman named Mrs. Swain, asked Josiah if he had anything to eat other than chocolate.

"No," Josiah replied.

"Do you think it's a good idea to eat nothing but chocolate?" Mrs. Swain asked.

Josiah shrugged, wrestling with the clear plastic wrapper that surrounded the chocolate brownie.

"Do you think that's very nutritious?" Mrs. Swain asked.

"Parnucklians eat nothing but chocolate," Josiah answered. Mrs. Swain was unsure what to do when Josiah told her that Parnucklians ate nothing but chocolate, just as she had not known what to do when Josiah had told her and the other children that his father lived far, far away on the planet Parnuckle, or what to do when the other children had giggled at Josiah's story and obviously embarrassed him, but on the fourth day of that week, when Josiah for the fourth day brought nothing but chocolate to eat for snack time, Mrs. Swain informed the principal, who called a meeting with himself and Josiah and Josiah's mother and the school's nutritionist.

"It has come to our attention, ma'am," said the principal to Josiah's mother, after pleasantries and introductions had been exchanged, "that your son Josiah has been bringing to school, for snack time, nothing to eat but chocolate."

Josiah's mother, sitting up very straight in the chair in front of the principal's desk, answered, "Yes."

Josiah's mother was twenty-four years old at this time. She had an ad in the yellow pages and people would call her and have her come and clean their houses. Josiah's mother was very good at cleaning houses. Her own mother, Josiah's grandmother, who was dead and whom Josiah had never met, had kept a very clean house, and Josiah's mother and her sisters had spent most of their spare time as children cleaning it. Josiah's mother had about seven houses that she cleaned. Usually Josiah's mother would go to each of the houses once a week.

"Were you aware of this, ma'am?" asked the school principal.

"Of course," answered Josiah's mother.

"You were?"

"Of course."

"Could you explain, please?"

"Explain?"

"Yes."

"Explain what, sir?"

"Well, ma'am," interrupted the school nutritionist, who was tall and had a clipboard and leaned against the wall over by the window, "we worry that such a diet is not in Josiah's best interests."

"In what way?" asked Josiah's mother.

"We feel it could be harmful," said the principal.

"It just isn't healthy," said the nutritionist.

"Gentlemen," said Josiah's mother, "Josiah simply loves chocolate. It is his favorite thing. And as you can see, he is a perfectly healthy boy."

While Josiah's mother, at the time, was only twenty-four years old, she was not incredibly pretty. She was not ugly, either. She was neither pretty nor ugly. She almost always wore sundresses.

When the weather was not sunny, she usually wore sweaters over the sundresses.

"Yes," said the principal, "he certainly is healthy now."

"Yes, we can see that," said the nutritionist.

"But," said the principal.

"But," said the nutritionist, "it would simply be irresponsible of us to allow Josiah, while he is in our care, to indulge in a diet that we know to be harmful to him."

"How do you know?" asked Josiah's mother.

"Excuse me?" said the nutritionist.

"How do you know that Josiah's diet is harmful to him?" asked Josiah's mother.

"Such a diet simply lacks the ideal balance of nutrients," said the nutritionist. "It lacks the ideal nutritional value."

"It's simple science," said the principal.

"Are you saying that I am trying to harm my son?" asked Josiah's mother.

"No, no," said the principal.

"No," said the nutritionist.

"We are simply trying to make you aware," said the principal.

"Aware," said the nutritionist, "of the potential dangers."

"Are you saying I'm a danger?" asked Josiah's mother. "A danger to my son?"

"No, no," said the principal.

"No," said the nutritionist, "but you must be advised that, though Josiah appears healthy now . . ."

"*Appears* healthy?" asked Josiah's mother.

"Appears," said the principal, "and no doubt is."

"Yes, certainly," said the nutritionist. "No doubt. But you must be advised that, though Josiah is clearly healthy now, the diet that we are observing may have long-term adverse effects."

"May we ask," asked the principal, "what Josiah's diet consists of at home?"

"I should say not," answered Josiah's mother.

The principal then informed Josiah's mother that the bottom line was that they, as school officials, must insist that Josiah, while he is in their care, shift to a more suitable and nutritional diet, and Josiah's mother thanked the men and took Josiah and left, saying to Josiah, on the car ride home, "Although private schools, Josiah, such as this one, as we discussed, are for important people and the children of important people, such as yourself, this particular private school is not ready for a student as important—as special—as you are. Clearly, Josiah, you are far too special to go to this school," and the next day Josiah's mother removed Josiah from the local private school and placed him in the local public school, from which she never heard anything about Josiah's diet again.

At Josiah's new school, the local public school, on Josiah's first day, Josiah was asked, as he had been on his first day at the local private school, to go before the class and introduce himself and give his new classmates and his new teacher information about himself and his family.

Josiah stood at the front of the class, wearing a pair of navy blue pants and a white polo shirt. Josiah's mother had made it clear that she most certainly was not going to purchase a whole new set of clothes for Josiah to wear to school when she had just purchased him a perfectly good set the week before.

"I'm Josiah," Josiah said to the class, "and I live with my mommy in our house. My mommy cleans other people's houses. My daddy lives far, far away on the planet Parnuckle."

The other students in the class stared at Josiah. One picked his nose.

"On the planet Parnuckle," Josiah continued, after staring back at the staring students for several seconds, "no one ever has to take baths, or showers, because there is no dirt, and no one ever goes to sleep, because no one ever gets tired, and no one ever has to go shopping, because everyone has everything already in their house."

The students continued to stare at Josiah. One of them, the one that had picked his nose, whispered, "Wow."

Josiah's teacher at his new school, who had asked Josiah to go before the class and introduce himself, would have thought that Josiah's story was strange, and would have wondered why a boy would make up such a story, and possibly would have notified someone, such as a principal or a counselor, and another meeting might have been called, but the teacher, who was not a real teacher but rather a long-term substitute teacher who was filling in for the real teacher and who had only had Josiah go before the class to introduce himself because he had been instructed to do so by a book about teaching, specifically titled, *What I Will Do on the First Day of School*, had not been listening at all to Josiah, but rather had been reading a magazine article about fishing.

Three months later, the long-term substitute teacher was forced to leave because long-term substitute teachers can only teach for so many days before the school has to pay them more money, and he was replaced by a new long-term substitute teacher who, having read the same book that the previous substitute had read, and, in fact, that Mrs. Swain at the local private school had read, asked Josiah and the other members of the class to once again go before the class and introduce themselves.

When it was his turn, Josiah once again told the class his name and told them where he lived and with whom and what his mother did for work and where his father lived, along with several details about the planet Parnuckle, the same details—all of which Josiah had learned from his mother and from his father's letters—that he had shared with the class previously.

The new long-term substitute teacher found Josiah's story so imaginative and so creative that he decided to call Josiah's mother immediately after school, partly because *What I Will Do on the First Day of School,* the book that had instructed him to ask the students to go before the class and introduce themselves, had also instructed him to establish positive early contact with parents.

Josiah's mother was vacuuming when the phone rang. Once the long-term substitute teacher finished telling Josiah's mother just how imaginative and creative he found Josiah's story to be, Josiah's mother responded by saying, "Please don't ever call here again."

o   o   o

"Curious?" Josiah's mother repeated, not so much to Bree as to Johnson Davis, as she spooned a scoop of vegetables, unevenly rationed so that the carrots were in clear majority, onto the plate of Johnson Davis, which Johnson Davis had placed into the out-held hand. "Is she normally so curious about other people's health?" she said to him.

"It just seemed strange," Bree said.

"You should ask her," Johnson Davis said, addressing Josiah's mother's question as if Bree had not spoken.

"It just seemed strange to me," Bree repeated.

"I see," said Josiah's mother. She was wearing a purple sundress with small, navy-blue pinstripes.

"It's just a little strange," Bree said, "don't you think?" She again passed her eyes over the other three in the room, addressing the question to all.

"To each his own," Josiah's mother said.

"I guess so," Bree said, sarcastically.

Josiah's mother paused, as if to allow all to take note of her recognition of Bree's tone and her lack of appreciation for it. "I guess so," she said back at Bree.

o o o

Johnson Davis and Josiah's mother had been dating for a week and a half when Johnson Davis announced to Josiah's mother that he would like her to meet his daughter, Bree, who lived with him on weekends. This seemed a natural progression in the relationship, as after a week it had seemed inevitable that Johnson Davis and Josiah's mother would be spending time together on the very weekends that Bree would be visiting. Johnson Davis usually picked Bree up from school on Friday afternoons and drove her the forty-six miles to his home where she still had her own room and where she would spend the entire weekend with Johnson Davis before Johnson Davis drove her back, usually on Sunday evenings after an early dinner.

Johnson Davis and Josiah's mother met for lunch that Friday, having grilled cheese sandwiches and French fries at a local diner, remaining at their table long after finishing their meal, Johnson Davis having no classes on Friday and Josiah's mother having no house-cleaning jobs, and they drank refills of Coke and discussed the lessons of History before returning to the home of Johnson Davis where they spent four minutes kissing and twenty-two minutes watching television before it was time for Johnson Davis to leave. Johnson Davis and Josiah's mother decided that it would be best if Josiah's mother waited at the home of Johnson Davis for he and Bree to return, giving Johnson Davis time to discuss with Bree the fact that he had now entered into a new relationship, the first he had entered into since his wife, Bree's mother, had left him, and to discuss Bree's feelings about this and to make clear to Bree that Johnson Davis's new girlfriend, Josiah's mother, had no intentions of replacing Bree's mother, who was a fine woman—in her own way—and a fine mother.

Initially, there were no problems between Josiah's mother and Johnson Davis's daughter, Bree. Johnson Davis introduced Bree to Josiah's mother and Josiah's mother smiled and said "Hello" and Johnson Davis introduced Josiah's mother to Bree and Bree smiled and said "Hi," after which all three went out for pizza at the local pizza parlor. At one point during their dinner, Bree said "Excuse me for reaching" as she reached across Josiah's mother for another piece of pizza. Based on the meal as a whole, but particularly on this one moment, Josiah's mother had decided that Bree was a very pleasant young lady.

The problems began shortly after dinner, in the parking lot of the local pizza parlor, when Bree wanted to go to see some of her friends from her previous school. In the entire two-and-a-half-month period that Bree had been visiting Johnson Davis on the weekends, ever since moving forty-six miles away with her mother, Bree had not spent any time nor asked to spend any time with any of her friends from her previous school, until she and Johnson Davis and Josiah's mother were in the parking lot of the local pizza parlor, walking pleasantly to the car after their very pleasant meal.

"Which friends?" Johnson Davis asked, stopping his own progress toward the car and therefore that of the others, leaving all three standing still and facing one another in the center of an aisle of parked cars.

"Just some of my friends. From school. I haven't seen them," Bree replied.

"Which ones?" Johnson Davis asked again.

"Just a few of my friends. I don't know."

"Which ones?"

"I don't know. Jessica."

"Where are you meeting?"

"I don't know."

"Have her over. I'd love to see her."

"We were going to go do something."

"What?"

"I don't know."

"Have her come pick you up." A set of headlights turned into the aisle of the parking lot in which the three were standing and began to come their way. They all shifted to the same side of the aisle and lined up in a row. The car passed and Johnson Davis broke rank and continued toward his own car. Bree and Josiah's mother followed.

Inside the car, with Johnson Davis in the driver's seat and Josiah's mother beside him in the front passenger's seat and Bree behind her in the back seat, Johnson Davis asked, "Who else?"

"I don't know," Bree said. "Just some friends."

"Ariel?"

"No."

"What friends? Who?" Johnson Davis's tone, at that moment—his tone at that moment being unlike any tone Josiah's mother had heard him use—surprised Josiah's mother, and even began to make her feel apprehensive.

"You don't know them," Bree said.

"What do you plan on doing?" Johnson Davis asked.

"Not decided. Just hanging out."

"Hanging out?"

"Yes."

"I'm going to need to see your purse."

"What?"

"Your purse. I need to see your purse."

"No. No way."

"What's that?" Johnson Davis said.

"No way," Bree repeated.

"Then I guess we'll just head home."

"What?"

"I said I guess we'll just head home."

"You can't hold me hostage."

"Prisoner."

"You can't hold me prisoner."

"Of course I can."

"Dear," Josiah's mother said, "please calm down."

"Let me tell you, my dear," Johnson Davis said, re-shifting his shoulders to now address Josiah's mother, "about what Bree and her little friends like to do when there are no parents or figures of authority around. They like to smoke marijuana—"

"Oh, Jesus," Bree interrupted.

"They like to smoke marijuana," Johnson Davis repeated, "and to drink alcohol, and talk to boys and go to bed with boys . . ."

"What the hell?"

"And go to bed with boys . . ."

"Fuck you."

"Young lady," Josiah's mother said to Bree, in spontaneous reaction to Bree's choice of words.

"What?" Bree responded.

"That's no way," Josiah's mother said slowly, "to talk to your father."

"That's none of your business," Bree said to her.

"Do not speak to her that way," Johnson Davis said to Bree.

"Don't involve her in my personal life," Bree answered back.

"Of course it's her business," Johnson Davis said, ignoring Bree.

"Why?" Bree asked. "Because you've been seeing her for a week?"

"There's no need for you to be rude to me," Josiah's mother said.

"Then don't tell me what to fucking do," Bree said.

"She'll tell you whatever she wishes," Johnson Davis said to Bree.

"Is it necessary to use such language?" Josiah's mother said.

"Yes," Bree said.

"She's a saint," Johnson Davis said.

"She should mind her damn business," Bree said.

"Please don't use that language," Josiah's mother said.

"A goddamn saint," Johnson Davis said.

"Your father," Josiah's mother said, "is only concerned about your safety, and because I love your father, I'm concerned, too."

"You don't even know me," Bree said.

"You're not going anywhere," Johnson Davis said, "and that's the end of it."

"That isn't fair," Bree said.

"Trust was broken long ago," Johnson Davis said.

"This is bullshit," Bree said.

"Show him your purse, then," Josiah's mother said.

Bree paused momentarily, staring at Josiah's mother with a blank expression. "Show him yours," she finally said.

"Do not address her," Johnson Davis commanded, holding up a finger.

"Do you look in *her* purse?" Bree asked. "You've known her a whole week."

"Do not address her," Johnson Davis said again, finger still up.

"I'm asking *you*," Bree said. "Do you look in her purse?"

"She hasn't broken my trust."

"And I have?"

"Certainly."

"Right back atcha."

"Young lady," Josiah's mother said.

"What?" Bree responded.

"You have no respect for your father."

"I have no respect for my father?"

"Clearly not."

"Who *are* you?"

"Your father's friend. A concerned adult."

"Well maybe you should mind your own business."

"Enough," Johnson Davis said. "Do not address her."

"Tell her not to address me," Bree said.

"Enough," Johnson Davis said.

"I can address who I please," Josiah's mother said.

"Screw you," Bree said.

"Excuse me?" Josiah's mother said.

"Enough," Johnson Davis said, shouting. "Enough. That will be all. Goddamnit. You've made a mockery of the entire evening. You won't be going anywhere. Nowhere, and that's it."

"Bullshit," Bree said.

"Young lady!" Josiah's mother said.

"Goddamnit enough! The end," Johnson Davis said, starting the ignition and pulling out of the parking space to begin the silent drive home.

When Bree came down to eat her breakfast the next morning, she was startled to find Josiah's mother already standing in the kitchen, drinking a cup of coffee and wearing a yellow sundress with light blue floral print. Bree hadn't even considered this new woman or when she would be leaving or whether or not she would be leaving at all. Bree asked Josiah's mother if she had stayed the night, delivering her question in such a way that at once clearly demonstrated both her disapproval, if the suggestion were to be true, as well as her indifference either way.

Josiah's mother did not respond to Bree's question, but rather waited, leaning against the counter and drinking her coffee while Bree collected from the cupboards and drawers cereal, bowl, milk, and spoon and then combined these into her breakfast which she then sat down at the table to eat. Josiah's mother approached the table and sat, setting her coffee cup down but not letting go of it. Josiah's mother then told Bree that she felt that the two of them had gotten off on the wrong foot, to which Bree did not respond and after which both Bree and Josiah's mother were silent for nearly a minute, other than Bree's crunching and Josiah's mother's sipping, until Josiah's mother continued by saying that she simply wanted Bree to know that while the previous evening was certainly unpleasant and that she was certainly not proud of either of their behaviors, she believed in fresh starts, in fact she believed fresh starts were one of the most important things in existence, and in fact both Christianity and America would be nowhere without fresh starts, if you think about it, and that she sincerely hoped that she and Bree, despite the rockiness of the previous evening, could have a fresh start, because Josiah's mother, though it had been only a week—nearly two weeks, actually, not just one week as Bree had declared the night before—Josiah's mother was falling more in love with Bree's father each and every day, in fact each and every minute, and that she could tell, she could just sense, that they would be together for a long time, forever even, whatever that means, however one chose to view that, but that she truly believed that they were meant to be together and would be for a long, long time, and therefore it is very important that she and Bree, whose father loves her very much and says so often—Isn't that nice to hear?—become good friends and learn to trust each other and maybe even someday love each other, and then Josiah's mother finished by saying that she believed this all must begin by erasing the bad feelings from the night before.

Bree stood and carried her bowl to the sink and as she left the room responded, through a final mouthful of cereal, "You got it."

From that point forward, over the course of the next four-and-a-half months, until the night that Josiah first met Bree, conversations between Bree and Josiah's mother were limited to no more than three words per participant at a time.

o o o

Josiah's mother finished serving Josiah and Bree and Johnson Davis, each handing over their plate and then receiving it back with a serving of steamed vegetables, before serving herself and sitting. As they all four began to eat, the table was silent until after nearly two minutes when Johnson Davis set his fork down next to his plate, swallowed the last bite of carrot still in his mouth, and announced to all, "Quite a game today."

Josiah and Bree and Josiah's mother each looked up—still chewing and/or swallowing their food—in acknowledgment, Josiah's mother making eye contact with Johnson Davis, Bree with Josiah, and Josiah—briefly, before turning away when she smiled at him—with Bree.

"Did they win?" Josiah's mother asked.

"They certainly did," Johnson Davis answered, "thanks to Bree."

"Did she do well?" Josiah's mother asked, turning her head toward Bree but still addressing Johnson Davis.

"They would be nothing without her," Johnson Davis said. "They would be hopeless."

"I don't think that's true," Bree said, turning toward Johnson Davis.

"Anyone can see it," Johnson Davis said. "She scored five goals today."

"Three," Bree said.

"Whichever. And that one that that one girl scored may as well have been yours," Johnson Davis said.

"No," Bree said.

"Anyone can see it," Johnson Davis said.

"We have really strong defense," Bree said to everyone.

Johnson Davis turned to directly address his fiancée. "Bree is modest," he said, "which is good, but she should be proud of her soccer play. It is something she excels at. Something she has worked at and seen results. It gives her direction. Young people need direction. They need something important in their lives. Something to work at. For me, it was running. For Bree, it is soccer. Everyone has their own interests. But what's important is the path. The focus."

"Do you play any sports?" Bree asked Josiah.

"Josiah does not play any sports," Johnson Davis answered. "In fact, he is homeschooled."

Bree, who had turned toward her father when he had begun speaking, turned back to Josiah and asked him, "How long have you been homeschooled?" which Josiah's mother answered by saying, "Since seventh grade."

Bree, still facing Josiah, who was now facing her, asked, "How is it?" Josiah had just enough time to shrug before Johnson Davis answered that homeschooling certainly had its own strengths and its own shortcomings, and Johnson Davis was about to begin listing those strengths and those shortcomings, beginning with the shortcomings, when Bree interrupted him to say, "Why don't you let him answer?"

"Excuse me?" Johnson Davis said.

"You don't have to talk for him," Bree said. "Why don't you let him answer?"

"Josiah is very shy," Josiah's mother said.

"So?" Bree asked. Unsure how to respond, Josiah's mother simply stared at Bree.

"Perhaps she has a point, dear," Johnson Davis said to Josiah's mother. "Of course Josiah can speak for himself. Let's let Josiah answer the question."

Johnson Davis leaned toward Josiah. "Josiah," he said, "the question was, 'How was it?'—*it* being *homeschooling*. How is homeschooling, Josiah?"

"It's okay," Josiah said.

"Do you like it?" Bree asked.

"I guess," Josiah said.

"Don't you miss regular school?" Bree asked.

Josiah shrugged.

"Do you have any friends?" Bree asked.

Josiah shrugged.

"Do you or don't you?" Bree asked.

"Patrick," Josiah said.

"Who's Patrick?"

"My friend."

"How do you know him?"

"From the group home."

"The group home?"

"Okay, that's enough," Josiah's mother said.

"You were in a group home?" Bree asked.

"That's enough," Josiah's mother said.

"Yes, yes," Johnson Davis said to Bree, "Josiah spent a period of time in a group home."

"Why?" Bree asked.

"That's none of her business," Josiah's mother said.

"We're not discussing that," Johnson Davis said. "This is not the time to discuss that."

"Why not?" Bree asked.

"We'll discuss it later," Johnson Davis said.

"It's none of her business," Josiah's mother said.

"We can all discuss everything later," Johnson Davis said. "Now let's change the subject. Let's talk about something else."

Everyone stopped talking and stared toward the center of the table. After several seconds, Johnson Davis said, "Talk about something else."

Bree again looked at Josiah. Josiah looked back at her. "Does Patrick know that you only eat chocolate?" Bree asked.

"Yes," Josiah said.

"What's he think about that?" Bree asked.

Josiah shrugged.

"Do you have any other friends?" Bree asked.

Josiah shrugged.

"Do you have a girlfriend?" Bree asked.

Josiah's mother stopped chewing and stared at Bree. She swallowed. Josiah shook his head.

"Have you ever had a girlfriend?" Bree asked.

"Dear," Josiah's mother said to Johnson Davis.

"Bree," Johnson Davis said to Bree, "I'm not sure that's appropriate."

"Why not?" Bree asked.

"I just don't think it's appropriate," Johnson Davis said.

"Why would you ask him that?" Josiah's mother said to Bree.

"It just came to mind," Bree said.

"Well let's just stop it," Johnson Davis said.

"Stop what?" Bree asked.

"We just think it's inappropriate, so that will be that," Johnson Davis said.

Josiah and Bree and Johnson Davis and Josiah's mother continued in silence—both Josiah's mother and Bree poking at their respective pork chops with their forks, Johnson Davis dragging his last bite of broccoli through the juice left on his plate from the meat, and Josiah breaking into bite-size pieces the soft part of his pie's crust, smeared with the last traces of the chocolate filling, leaving the hard crust from the pie's edge—until Bree looked up from her plate and asked Josiah, "Do you *want* a girlfriend?"

The next several seconds involved everyone but Josiah shouting at everyone but Josiah, Johnson Davis purposely and dramatically knocking over his water glass and repeating the words "goddamn" and "travesty," and Josiah's mother calling after Bree as Bree left the room, "You are not going to fuck my son!"

Later that night, after everyone had gone to bed, Bree did indeed try to fuck Josiah.

o o o

Once, when Josiah was nine years old, he had been sitting quietly alone in his room with the light off on one of the evenings when his mother had made him sit quietly alone in his room with the light off because she was going to have a special friend over for dinner. This particular night, Josiah began to feel very hungry. He decided to go into the kitchen and be very quiet and not bother anyone and find some cake or some donuts and quickly take them back into his room and turn out the light.

Josiah made it only a few steps down the hall when he stopped. The lights in the living room, through which he would need to pass to get to the kitchen, were also off, as were the lights in the kitchen itself. The entire house was dark, and Josiah could hear voices—quiet voices—coming from the living room. Josiah crouched down and crawled on his hands and knees to the end of the hall and peeked around the corner. In the darkness, he could see what looked like the shape of his mother and what looked like the shape of Josiah's mother's special friend, or at least what Josiah imagined to be the shape of his mother's special friend, whose name Josiah did not know and whom Josiah had not met because Josiah had already been in his room with the light off when the special friend had arrived, and the shape of the special friend and the shape of Josiah's mother seemed to be sitting on what looked like the shape of the couch.

Josiah could now hear what the quiet voices were saying, or at least one of the quiet voices. The quiet voice that Josiah assumed belonged to his mother's special friend, because the voice was a man's voice, was saying, "Fuck me, baby." The special friend's quiet man voice said "Fuck me, baby" two times, or at least two times that Josiah could hear. Josiah could not hear what his mother's quiet voice was saying. Josiah listened for a few minutes more before returning his room, where he spent the rest of the night thinking about what he had seen and heard and about chocolate cake.

The next morning, at breakfast, sitting at the yellow table, eating his bowl of Cocoa Puffs, Josiah turned to his mother, who was eating a single piece of unbuttered bread with a knife and fork, and asked her what it meant to fuck someone. When she asked what he had just said, Josiah repeated his question. Josiah's mother responded by again asking Josiah what he had just said, only louder, and before he could respond she asked again, equally as loud, and before he could respond to that she stood and grabbed Josiah's bowl and her own plate and tossed them several feet into the sink, the plate breaking, as she left the room.

o o o

Lying in his bed, several hours after dinner, Josiah having been told by his mother, shortly after Bree had left the dining room, that dinner was over and to go to his room and go to bed, Josiah was having a dream in which he and his mother were at the zoo and his mother was pushing a shopping cart and was desperately searching for something and he was desperately trying to keep up with her when he was awoken by the weight of Bree, who had climbed on top of him in his bed. "Shh," she said, lowering her face close to his so that her hair brushed over his eyes. "I can't sleep." There was enough light coming through the window for Josiah to see that Bree was still wearing her high school soccer jersey but not any pants. She began to move and rub the part of her body that was not wearing any pants back and forth over the same part of Josiah's body, his part being covered by pajama pants and covers, and then she pushed her mouth onto his mouth and opened his mouth with her tongue and used her tongue to lick his tongue. At some point during all of this, Josiah first began to feel movement and sensations in the area of his Andre Agassi, which was Parnucklian for dick.

o o o

Josiah first learned the meaning of the Earthling word "dick" while at the group home, having up to that point known it only as an Andre Agassi, the Parnucklian word for "penis." He came to this knowledge when one of the other boys at the group home, a boy named Eli Koslowski, drew a picture of Mr. Donaldson, the resident counselor at the group home, on the wall of the bathroom. In the picture, Mr. Donaldson's head was replaced by a large Andre Agassi, and the picture was labeled, Mr. Dickhead. Josiah had been wondering what the Earthling term "dick" meant for quite some time, as it was often used by the other boys in the group home in various contexts, and eventually Josiah was able to assign meaning to other terms commonly in use at the group home, such as cock or prick or Johnson, all of which were Earthling words for Andre Agassi.

o o o

Josiah felt his Andre Agassi stiffen, as it had done before, and it seemed that Bree must have felt it, too, as her rubbing became more focused in that area. Josiah then felt a rush of something that he had not felt before and then it felt like he had peed, but not quite exactly like he had peed, but similar. In embarrassment, Josiah tried to reach down to either move Bree, whose rubbing had not ceased, or maybe to cover his Andre Agassi with his hands, but he was unable to do either of these things as Bree's weight on his bed covers, which were spread over him, had his arms and his hands pinned down. The stiffness in Josiah's Andre Agassi went away and Bree, who had begun rubbing harder and faster, looked down at him and asked, "Did you come?" to which Josiah simply stared back at her with wide-open eyes. She turned her head to the side and continued to rub, now even faster and even harder and Josiah began to feel pain in the area of his Andre Agassi and Bree covered her mouth with her hand and continued to rub, now even faster and even harder and Josiah's eyes began to tear up and he wanted to push her away but could not because of the aforementioned pinning by the bed covers, but then Josiah heard a sort of squeal from behind the hand that covered Bree's mouth and she stopped rubbing and dropped her head down onto the bed right next to Josiah's head, her hair once again brushing over his eyes, and she whispered into his ear, "Put your sheets in the machine before your mother gets up," and then she was gone.

THREE

FOR AN ENTIRE week while in the seventh grade, less than
a year before he would move into the group home and less
than three years before he would meet Bree, Josiah would
not speak any words other than, "I'm Vince Clortho, Keymaster
of Gozer. Are you the Gatekeeper?" Sometime during the sixth
day that Josiah said nothing other than, "I'm Vince Clortho, Keymaster of Gozer. Are you the Gatekeeper?" Josiah's seventh grade
teacher, whose name was Mrs. Lorrence, tried to force Josiah
to say something other than, "I'm Vince Clortho, Keymaster of
Gozer. Are you the Gatekeeper?" Specifically, she wanted him to
say his real full name, which was Josiah Westcott Ryan. "Josiah,"
Mrs. Lorrence said to him, "I want you to say, 'My name is Josiah
Westcott Ryan.'"

"I'm Vince Clortho, Keymaster of Gozer. Are you the Gatekeeper?" said Josiah in response, to which Mrs. Lorrence in turn
responded, hovering over Josiah's desk, "No, Josiah, I don't want
you to say that. I want you to say, 'My name is Josiah Westcott
Ryan.'" Josiah again responded by saying, "I'm Vince Clortho,
Keymaster of Gozer. Are you the Gatekeeper?" after which Mrs.
Lorrence leaned even closer to Josiah and said to him, "Josiah, I
want you to listen to me. You are not Vince Clohtho, Keywhat's-it
of Gozer, and I am not the Gatekeeper. I am Mrs. Lorrence, and

you are Josiah—Josiah Westcott Ryan—and I am only going to ask you one more time, please tell me your name. Say, 'I am Josiah Westcott Ryan.'"

Before Josiah could finish saying, "I'm Vince Clortho, Keymaster of Gozer. Are you the Gatekeeper?" Mrs. Lorrence slammed her palms down on Josiah's desk and put her face very close to Josiah's and said to him in a voice louder and more angry than she had used before, "Josiah Westcott Ryan, if you do not say, 'My name is Josiah Westcott Ryan' right now, you are going to be sorry," but before she could finish saying this, Josiah clamped down on her nose with his teeth. Mrs. Lorrence tried to pull away, but Josiah would not let go. Mrs. Lorrence began to bleed and then to scream, and then the other students began to scream and then to cry.

Having heard the screaming, two eighth-grade boys ran over from the room next door. One of the eighth-grade boys began hitting Josiah on the left side of the head with a two-inch-three-ring binder. The other eighth-grade boy began hitting Josiah on the right shoulder with Mrs. Lorrence's rain stick, a hollowed-out stick with little bitty seeds inside of it for the purpose of making a sound that sounded like rain, but only when the rain stick was shaken lightly. When the eighth-grade boy was swinging the rain stick and using it to hit Josiah in the right shoulder in an attempt to persuade him to let go of Mrs. Lorrence's nose, the sound coming out of it did not sound like rain.

The two eighth-grade boys were able to hit Josiah enough times with the two-inch-three-ring binder and Mrs. Lorrence's rain stick to free Mrs. Lorrence's nose from Josiah's clamped teeth just as the school janitor, having also heard the screaming, came running into the room. Despite Mrs. Lorrence's escape, Josiah's violent fit was not over, as he began to attack other sixth graders, snapping his teeth at one and then another, forcing the school janitor to tie Josiah up with an extension cord until higher authorities arrived. After Josiah's release two weeks later, he began home-schooling.

o o o

One year earlier, after the father of one of Josiah's classmates, a Certified Public Accountant, had come to Josiah's sixth-grade class to explain what it was like to be a Certified Public Accountant, Josiah had asked his mother what his father did for a job on the planet Parnuckle. Josiah and Josiah's mother were sitting at the yellow table in their kitchen, eating dinner. Josiah was having chocolate cupcakes, which Josiah's mother had removed individually from their packaging and placed on a small plate, and Josiah's mother was having hot chicken broth with saltine crackers. Josiah's mother answered that she would tell him what his father did on the planet Parnuckle in ten minutes. Josiah and Josiah's mother sat silently, Josiah eating his cupcakes and Josiah's mother eating her broth and crackers, until six minutes had passed, when Josiah's mother told Josiah that his father was the Keymaster of Gozer, and that Gozer was the President of Parnuckle, and that the Keymaster of the President of Parnuckle was a very important position in the Parnucklian government.

o o o

Six days before he bit the nose of Mrs. Lorrence, on the day that Josiah began saying, "I'm Vince Clortho, Keymaster of Gozer. Are you the Gatekeeper?," Josiah had come running into the kitchen, where his mother was preparing dinner, from the living room, where he had been watching a movie on television. "Mom," Josiah said to his mother, "guess what the people in the movie are saying?" Josiah's mother momentarily stopped stirring the large metal bowl full of milk, two eggs and chocolate pudding mix and asked her son, "What are they saying, dear?" to which Josiah responded that a man in the movie had said that he was Vince Clortho, Keymaster of Gozer, which Josiah's mother had told Josiah was his father's job on the planet Parnuckle, and he was going to ask her if this meant that something had happened to his father, or if maybe the man in the movie knew his father, but before Josiah had a chance, Josiah's mother handed him the bowl and slapped him on his right cheek, causing him to drop the bowl onto the kitchen linoleum. Josiah's mother turned and left the kitchen and went into her room and did not emerge until late that evening—well after she and Josiah's normal dinner time—to tell Josiah that it was time for him to go to bed, Josiah having stood waiting for her in the kitchen the entire time and having eaten the contents of the dropped bowl.

The next morning, when Josiah's mother asked Josiah if he wanted a chocolate chip muffin or a Ho-Ho for breakfast, Josiah responded, "I'm Vince Clortho, Keymaster of Gozer. Are you the Gatekeeper?"

"Suit yourself," Josiah's mother responded as she put both the muffin and the Ho-Ho into the wastebasket under the sink. "Go get in the car."

o o o

The place from which Josiah was released two weeks after trying to bite off the nose of Mrs. Lorrence was a psychiatric facility located thirty-two miles from the home of Josiah and his mother.

Josiah, who was twelve years old at the time, had his own room at the psychiatric facility—unlike his room in the group home he would be sent to in less than a year, which he would have to share—and each day a tall woman who smelled weird came to Josiah's room and led him down a long hall and a flight of stairs and another long hall to a room where Josiah met with a man who would ask Josiah a lot of questions. The room where Josiah met with the man was much different from Josiah's room at the psychiatric facility. Josiah's room at the psychiatric facility had only a bed, a dresser, a table, a lamp, and a chair, but the room where the man asked the questions was filled with photographs of people hugging and photographs of people smiling—all in different settings, such as sandy settings and grassy settings and snowy settings—and some of the people in the photographs were the man who asked the questions and some of the people were not, and on one wall was a picture of an old house in a rainstorm and on another wall was a picture of a pink tree, and there were also several different types of chairs in the room, and two different couches, one long and one shorter, and both couches were the color of the walls, which were the color of wet wood. Many more things in the room seemed to be made of wood, or to be the color of wood, unlike Josiah's room, where more things seemed to be made of metal and plastic, and the room where the man asked the questions was not as bright and not as cold as Josiah's room.

In one corner of the room, behind a tall, soft chair on which the man usually sat, and behind the large wooden desk behind the chair, on a long counter that ran along one wall of the room, was a framed picture of a woman. The woman in the picture stared directly at Josiah. She had a long face and was not smiling. Her arms were held up in the air and her hands could not be seen, as the woman was running them through her long, black hair, creating the illusion that the arms grew from or were an extension of the thick hair that clouded over her head. The woman wore nothing other than what looked like a bathing suit. The bathing suit was black, and parts of it were transparent. The parts that were not transparent were made up of designs that resembled clumps of black flowers. Two silvery lines hung from each of the woman's ears.

A few weeks prior to Josiah biting her, Mrs. Lorrence had taught Josiah's class about the people of Greece and their customs. Josiah had learned about the Greek gods and goddesses. Mrs. Lorrence had passed around a picture book with pictures of paintings and sculptures of the gods and goddesses. Josiah thought that this woman in the photograph was probably one of those goddesses.

The man who asked the questions would usually ask Josiah the same questions over and over again. The majority of Josiah's answers would consist of "Yes" or "No" or "I don't know" or "Maybe," Josiah paying little attention to the man and his questions. All of Josiah's attention, other than what it took to deliver one of the aforementioned responses at the appropriate moment, was instead focused on the photograph of the goddess woman.

The photograph of the goddess woman was actually a photograph of the singer and songwriter and actress Cher. The man who asked the questions had received the autographed picture of Cher at a Cher concert, the tickets to which he had purchased for his wife for her birthday, mistakenly remembering that his wife was a huge fan of Cher and spent a great deal of time talking about her. The man's wife opened her gift and revealed that she was actually a huge fan of the singer and songwriter and actress Madonna and not Cher, the man's wife throwing the tickets, which did little more than flutter to the floor, at the man and then crying through the remainder of her birthday dinner, after which the man instead took his secretary, now former secretary, who turned out to *actually be* a fan of the singer and songwriter and actress Cher, to the concert. The man and his former secretary had had to wait outside for several hours to obtain the autograph, and after the former secretary slapped the man when he tried to kiss her later that night, he kept it for himself.

In the picture, Cher was wearing nothing but a black negligee with purple trim and dangly silver earrings and was running her fingers through her hair. The picture was signed by Cher, herself, the final stroke of the "r" running through one of her bare legs. Josiah did not know who the singer and songwriter and actress Cher was, but Josiah could not stop looking at the photograph.

Once the three hour session was over and the tall woman took Josiah back to his room, Josiah picked up the white pencil and yellow pad of paper that had been placed upon the desk in his room, the pencil and pad having sat dormant up to that point, and Josiah began to draw a picture of the photograph that he had spent the day staring at.

Despite the fact that Josiah had spent so much time staring at the photograph of the goddess woman, the picture that he drew on the yellow pad, while it shared the basic shape of the goddess woman, did not look like the actual photograph in the room of the man who asked the questions. Josiah then remembered having seen a program on television about a man who painted little circles and lines in little squares and when he was done and you looked at all of the squares at once, it looked like a person's face. Josiah decided that beginning the next day, he would study the photograph of the goddess woman in parts, memorizing a small portion of it each day and then perfectly reproducing that memorized portion onto his yellow paper that evening.

Josiah ripped the page from the pad that contained the disappointing picture he had just drawn and slid the page to the corner of the desk. He then carefully ripped the next page, a blank sheet of yellow paper, from the pad and laid it flat, using the edge of the pad as a guide as he lightly produced three evenly-spaced pencil lines across the sheet and seven down it, creating, when finished, a barely visible grid of thirty-two boxes.

The next day, when Josiah visited the room where the man asked the questions, Josiah imagined that same grid as he stared at the photograph, and began to focus in and concentrate on the upper left hand square. It was blue. In fact, now that, in his mind's eye, Josiah applied his grid of thirty-two squares to the photograph itself, he found that the top row of squares and the first and last column of squares contained nothing but the photograph's light blue backdrop, which delighted Josiah as it meant that his task would potentially require fewer than the thirty-two days he had calculated the previous evening in his room.

As the man began to ask Josiah questions about how he was feeling the morning of the day that he bit the nose of Mrs. Lorrence, including questions about what he had had for breakfast and how he felt about having to wake up early in the morning and what his mother says to him when she wakes him up and how that makes him feel—Does he feel excited? Does he feel annoyed?—all of which Josiah responded to either with "Yes" or "No" or "Maybe," Josiah, in his mind's eye, moved down a row of squares and over one column to the first square of the imagined grid that contained a portion of the image of the goddess woman, that square containing a part of the woman's arm and a lot of her hair and a little bit of forehead. Josiah began by studying the arm part, paying close attention to its shape and its position and proportion in relation to the hair and the little bit of forehead.

Two and a half hours later, by the time the man was done asking questions, Josiah had accomplished no more than having carefully studied the one piece of arm, firmly memorizing its shape and size and position in the square but failing to study the hair, particularly its contours and the parts that shined and the parts that didn't, and certainly not focusing any time on the little bit of forehead.

Josiah returned to his room and very accurately reproduced the arm part into the appropriate square on his pad, realizing that his task was actually going to take much longer than he had thought.

Despite this slow start, by Josiah's sixth day in the room with the man Josiah had completed most of the goddess woman's face, other than a small piece of chin in an adjoining square, and was becoming quite pleased with the image that was forming on the pad.

The next day, the tall woman who smelled weird did not come to Josiah's room to take him to the other room where the man asked the questions. She did not come the next day, either. Nor did anyone come to Josiah's room during those two days to tell Josiah why the tall woman was not coming to take him to the man's room.

That evening, Josiah began to worry that he would not be able to finish reproducing the photograph of the goddess woman, having only completed four of the fourteen squares that contained the woman's image—the four squares that contained most of the woman's face, other than the small piece of chin.

Josiah sat in the chair at the desk in his room for nearly eighteen minutes, wondering what to do, before reaching for the sheet of paper with his unfinished image and the pad of paper and pencil. Josiah ripped another sheet from the pad and once again used the edge to gently draw two lines, one splitting the page in half each way, creating a grid of four squares on the new sheet of paper.

It was 6:20 in the evening, shortly after dinner time, when Josiah began to reproduce larger versions of the four squares that contained the woman's face, other than the piece of chin, onto the new sheet. By ten after three in the morning, the enlarged image of the goddess woman's face was complete, and Josiah began to gently erase the two lightly drawn lines.

The tall woman came the next day and led Josiah down a different hallway to a different room that was much smaller and had white walls along which were several bookshelves and several file cabinets of various sizes, so that only small portions of the white walls were actually visible, mostly the portions near the ceiling. The room had a lot of books and papers in it. The bookshelves were stuffed with books and papers and some of the file cabinets had papers sticking out of the tops of open drawers. The room also contained a desk, which was covered with books and papers, and a table, which was also covered with books and papers, and a man. The man was larger than the man who had asked questions in the room the color of wet wood had been, and this larger man, unlike the man who asked the questions in the room the color of wet wood, had a beard. The tall woman introduced the man as Dr. Simon and left. The tall woman had never told Josiah the name of the man in the room the color of wet wood, who had gone on vacation to The Bahamas with his new secretary, nor had the man. Dr. Simon asked Josiah to sit, and Josiah sat in the chair near the table while Dr. Simon sat in the chair near the desk.

"First of all, Josiah," Dr. Simon said, "I want you to feel as comfortable as possible during our time together. In fact, there is no need for you to call me Dr. Simon. That's not very comfortable, is it? I'd like you to call me Bob. Is that okay with you?"

Josiah nodded.

"Great," said Bob. "I also want you to feel comfortable enough to say anything you want to say. Anything at all, and not be afraid that I or anyone else is going to judge you or get mad at you or that you are going to get into trouble. You won't get into trouble over anything you say here, is that okay?"

Josiah nodded.

"Finally," Bob continued, "I want you to know that I am on your side. And I am not mad at you and I do not blame you for what happened between you and Mrs. Lorrence. Obviously, you reacted the way you did and did the thing you did because you felt uncomfortable. Let's be honest. You and I both know that what happened happened because Mrs. Lorrence did something that caused you to feel threatened. Does that sound right?"

Josiah shrugged.

"Come on Josiah, does that sound right?"

"Yes."

"Great. It's great to hear you admit that. And it's totally under-standable. It's totally natural for one to protect oneself when one feels threatened. No one is judging you for that. Certainly not me, anyway. All I'm concerned with, Josiah, is exploring other ways to deal with those same feelings, or similar feelings. Other ways of dealing with similar situations. Better ways. Does that sound okay?"

"Okay."

"Great. Because while no one is mad at you and no one is judging you, it is important that we realize that reacting the way that you did, doing what you did, was hurtful. Not only to Mrs. Lorrence, who had to go to the hospital, but also to your classmates, who probably were very scared at the time and maybe are still scared, a little. And then of course we have to think of Mrs. Lorrence's family. Her husband, who probably loves her very much and was very sad and worried, and her own children, if she has any, which she probably does. We have to consider how our actions may have affected all of these people. And you! We can't forget you. Think of how all this is affecting you."

When Bob was speaking about Mrs. Lorrence's children, Josiah felt himself almost begin to cry.

"So, then," Bob said, "let's begin by discussing other ways that a person such as yourself might have reacted to Mrs. Lorrence's threatening behavior. Sound okay?"

"Yes."

"Good. Okay, Josiah. Imagine that we are back in your class-room on the day of the incident between you and Mrs. Lorrence. Imagine yourself in the exact spot you were in just before the inci-dent occurred."

"What do you mean?"

"I mean, Josiah, where in the classroom were you just before Mrs. Lorrence made you feel threatened."

"At my table, in my chair."

"Who else is at the table?"

"Sally Donald and Brian Martinez."

"Okay, Josiah, imagine yourself sitting at your table, in your chair, next to Sally Donald and Brian Martinez, just before you felt threatened and bit Mrs. Lorrence. Are you imagining it, Josiah?"

"Yes."

"Where is Mrs. Lorrence?"

"Standing over the table."

"Describe it."

"What do you mean?"

"How is she standing? What is she doing? What is she saying?"

"She is very close to me."

"Yes. And?"

"She is very close to my face."

"What is she saying?"

"She is telling me to say my name."

"To say your name?"

"Yes."

"And are you saying it?"

"No."

"And what is Mrs. Lorrence doing?"

"Yelling."

"Yelling?"

"And getting close to my face."

"And what are you feeling?"

"What do you mean?"

"Are you angry? Are you threatened?"

"Angry."

"Why?"

"She won't stop."

"And what do you want to do?"

"Make her stop."

"And how?"

"I'm going to bite her nose."

"And STOP! Stop there Josiah, and begin to think. Hold on to the feelings that you felt—the anger—but think. What else can you do, other than bite Mrs. Lorrence's nose?"

"I don't know."

ob, determined that while Josiah was clearly either delusional or pathological liar or something to that effect, and that he seemed to have numerous unresolved issues with his mother that probably sulted in the incident in question, Josiah had clearly learned new ays to deal with his feelings and was no longer a danger to anyone.

hen Josiah returned home from the psychiatric facility, for the en months before he began to pee whenever and wherever he nted, Josiah did not say anything to his mother. He did not ak to her when she asked him why the hell he did what he did what the hell he was thinking and if he knew how close they e to taking him away and how many awful questions she had to ver and how much awful bullshit she had to listen to. He did speak to her when she told him that if he had nothing to say to hen he could get his own damn dinners out of the damn pan-or did he speak to her when she told him to clean the kitchen an the bathroom or mow the lawn or wash the car—all of h he did, without speaking—and he did not speak to her on evenings, when Josiah's mother would have Josiah sit down yellow table with his homeschooling workbook and fill in swers as she read them from the instructor's key.

"Think."

"I don't know."

"Think, Josiah."

Over the course of the next two days, Josiah and Bo
various things Josiah could have done other than bitir
rence's nose, such as Josiah asking her to please back a
she is very threatening or Josiah closing his eyes and
ten or closing his eyes and imagining that he is in
threatening place or laying his head down on the
tending he had fallen asleep or crying uncontrollably
to garner sympathy or simply snapping at Mrs. L
rather than actually biting it, which would not have
which would have captured Mrs. Lorrence's atten
certainly have been better than actually biting her

On the third day, Bob began to ask questions
to some of the questions that the man in the r
wet wood had asked. These questions had to do
life was like at home and what his relationship
mother. When Bob started asking Josiah what h
like with his mother, Josiah told him, "She's no

"She's not your mother?" Bob asked in respc

"No."

"What do you mean, she's not your mother

"She's not my real mother."

"She isn't?"

"No."

"Who is your real mother, Josiah?"

"My real mother is a goddess," Josiah
then asked Josiah why he believed his mo
what particular goddess he believed hi
reached into his pocket and pulled out a
per and handed it to Bob.

"Josiah, this is a picture of Cher," Bob

"My real mother is the goddess Cher,

Two days later, on a Friday, Fridays
at the psychiatric facility were most o

FOUR

WHEN JOSIAH FINALLY woke the morning after Bree came into his room, he found that his sheets and comforter were missing. He was simply lying in his pajamas on the bedspread and mattress. Josiah remained lying in bed, or as is the case when one has no sheets nor any covers, remained lying *on* his bed later than usual for a Saturday morning, in large part due to a level of apprehension at the thought of facing Johnson Davis's daughter Bree, given that he was still uncertain as to what exactly had happened the previous night—other than the fact that he sort of liked parts of it and hoped those parts would happen again—and what exactly he would or should say to Bree when he saw her.

Nevertheless, Josiah did eventually venture downstairs after showering and changing clothes, having had to unstick, in a somewhat painful maneuver, his Andre Agassi from his pajama pants, which he would have usually worn downstairs on a Saturday morning, along with his pajama top.

When Josiah, having changed into a t-shirt and pair of shorts, finally made his way down to the kitchen of the home of Johnson Davis, which was also now his home as well as the home of his mother and, on the weekends, Bree, with whom Josiah had had some sort of sexual encounter that he found himself unable at the moment to define, he discovered the kitchen full of activity, in-

cluding the creation of various aspects of breakfast and the forma-
tion and storage, for purposes of transport, of lunches and snacks,
as Johnson Davis and his fiancée, Josiah's mother, had decided that
it would be good for their newly-established family to spend a day
all together at the local fun park.

o o o

That morning, between the time that he had woken up with no
sheets and covers and the time that he had made his way downstairs to the kitchen of Johnson Davis, shortly after un-sticking his
Andre Agassi from his pajama pants, Josiah had written a letter to
his father. The letter went like this:

> Dear Father,
>   I am sorry that we missed each other. I hope you didn't wait too
> long for me or spend too much time looking. We don't live where we
> used to live anymore. Now we live with Johnson Davis. He is going
> to be my other mother's husband.
>   If you can't make it here to get me, that's okay. I met a really nice
> girl named Bree. She is very pretty. Her hair is shiny.
>   Talk to you soon.
>
>   Love,
>   Josiah

o o o

Josiah had never—either in the home he had lived in with his
mother or at the psychiatric facility or the group home or in the
home of Johnson Davis for the four days he had lived there before
the night Bree arrived—shared his bedroom with a girl. In fact,
other than at the group home, Josiah had always had his own room.
At the group home, as mentioned, Josiah has shared a room with
three other boys, whose names were Joey Simms and Eli Koslowski
and Patrick.

After sharing his room with Bree, Josiah, though also confused, was much more excited—unable, in fact, for several minutes after, to breathe, and unable for several hours to sleep—than he had been about sharing his room with Joey Simms and Eli Koslowski and Patrick.

o o o

As Clay, after finding Josiah sitting in a stall of the boy's bathroom and crying, had led Josiah down a hallway of the group home on the way to Josiah's new room, Josiah had wondered if his new room at the group home would be similar to his room at the psychiatric facility, but when Clay opened the door to Josiah's new room and said to Josiah that here was his new room, Josiah was surprised to find that there were already three other boys in his new room, and was even more surprised to find that one of the boys was the boy that Josiah had peed on and who had spoken to Josiah in the bathroom and whose name, Josiah found out, when Clay introduced Josiah to the boy as well as to the other two boys, was Patrick.

Clay left and Josiah was alone with the three boys. Eli Koslowski walked up to Josiah and said, "Who are you?" Twelve seconds earlier, before leaving, Clay had said to Joey Simms and Eli Koslowski and to Patrick that this was Josiah and he would be their new roommate. Joey Simms walked up and stood next to Eli Koslowski, who was standing in front of Josiah. Both Eli Koslowski and Joey Simms were taller than Josiah, and Eli Koslowski was taller than Joey Simms.

"Didn't you just hear?" Joey Simms said to Eli Koslowski. "His name's Josiah."

"Well what's he do?" Eli Koslowski asked. Eli Koslowski's face looked flat. Patrick sat on his bed behind them, staring into an open book.

"He's our new bunk buddy," Joey Simms said. The beds in Josiah's new room were bunk beds. There were two sets of bunk beds, placed perpendicular to one another. The bed Patrick was sitting on, staring into a book, was a bottom bunk.

"Well he's not getting a top bunk," Eli Koslowski said to Joey Simms.

"No shit," Joey Simms said.

"He gets the other bottom bunk," Eli Koslowski said.

"No shit," Joey Simms said. "The top bunks are ours."

"That's right," Eli Koslowski said.

"Why would we give him one of our bunks?" Joey Simms said.

"Well we're not," Eli Koslowski said, and turning to Josiah, added, "You get that one," and Eli Koslowski pointed to the other bottom bunk, the one Patrick was not sitting on, the two sets of bunk beds having been placed perpendicular to one another.

Josiah walked to the bottom bunk that Eli Koslowski had pointed at. A thin red sheet covered the bed and was tucked tightly under the mattress. A folded purple blanket lay at the bottom end. Josiah sat down. Patrick, on the bunk perpendicular to Josiah, only a few feet away, did not look up. The book he was reading had a picture of a very tall and bumpy person, whose skin was the color of tapioca pudding and who had one eye, standing over a man holding a gun in one hand and a small book in the other. The man, with the tall, bumpy, one-eyed tapioca man standing over him, was standing over a girl, who was wearing a nightgown and held one hand over her face. She was not touching her face, just suspending the hand over it. The title of the book was *Cyclops Island*. Patrick, the boy Josiah had peed on and who was now Josiah's roommate, did not look up from the book when Josiah sat down. His eyes were red and puffy. So were Josiah's.

Joey Simms walked across the room and stood before Josiah and Patrick. "So what's your story?" he said to Josiah.

Josiah shrugged. Joey Simms imitated Josiah's shrug and asked, "What are you doing here? How'd you get here?" Josiah was about to again shrug when Eli Koslowski, who had approached them from across the room and stood next to Joey Simms, interrupted, saying, "Look at their eyes."

"What about them?" Joey Simms asked.

"They're all red," Eli Koslowski said, "like they've been crying."

"Well we know this one's always crying," Joey Simms said. As he spoke, Joey Simms kicked Patrick's foot, causing Patrick to lose balance and drop his book as he extended one hand to brace himself against the bed.

Eli Koslowski laughed as Patrick, without looking up, retrieved his book from the floor, which was covered with short orange carpeting, and resumed his prior position.

"Let's go shoot hoops," Joey Simms said as both he and Eli Koslowski left the room. "Let the babies cry."

Josiah and Patrick sat silently for only a moment before Patrick, still holding his book open with one hand, the other hand resting on the mattress, suggested to Josiah that he could read some of his book to him. It was three o'clock in the afternoon. It had been one thirty when Josiah was dropped off at the group home by a woman in a police uniform who had told Josiah to call her Officer Melissa. Officer Melissa had kissed Josiah on the cheek and said "Good luck" before leaving Josiah with Clay. It was the first time a woman other than Josiah's mother had kissed him. Josiah's mother had often kissed Josiah on the cheek, usually doing so over and over.

"Okay," Josiah responded.

"And if you like it," Patrick said, "you can borrow it."

"Okay."

"I won't go back to the beginning. I'll just read from where I'm at."

"Okay."

"But I'll tell you what's happened so far. So it makes sense."

"Okay."

Patrick, sitting on the bottom bunk next to Josiah, then proceeded to tell Josiah the story of *Cyclops Island*, which consisted of Dutch Lucas—who had also been the hero of *Rapier's Bait* and *Mirror of Death* and who between adventures worked as a used-car salesman, which ironically, because he was such a successful adventurer, he was terrible at and he only kept the job because the lot's owner, Simpson Shavies, had been such close friends with Dutch's father, Snap Lucas, now deceased and former Chief of Police but also, secretly, world adventurer who, like Dutch, also operated in secrecy for the protection of both himself and those he served—being approached by this guy named Lang who had recently bought an island off the coast of somewhere down in South America and wanted to hire Dutch to go to the island and search for Lang's associate Bo Jeffries, whom Lang had sent to assess the newly-acquired island's resources, as well as Lang's son, Lawrence Lang, whom Lang had sent to both retrieve Jeffries and to carry out and complete the same assessment.

Dutch, who at the beginning of his adventures always seems to be just in it for the money but then by the end does it out of love and goodness and stuff, agrees to take the job for no less than one hundred thousand dollars, which Lang agrees to. Then Dutch offers to carry out the assessment of the island's resources that Lang's associates had both failed to accomplish for a twenty-five percent interest. Dutch and Lang go back and forth about this for a while and then Lang agrees.

So Dutch has his pilot, Sandy Smiles—who also works at the used car lot and there's always this scene where Dutch and Sandy have to convince their boss Mr. Griffin, who is very gruff and doesn't like Sandy or Dutch and thinks they're losers even though in real life they're great adventurers, to give them time off—has him fly him to this island and they have some close calls along the way, like they do in all their adventures, usually involving a shortage of fuel and Dutch yelling at Sandy, but they get there eventually and Sandy drops Dutch off and they discuss when to rendezvous and whatnot and then Sandy leaves and Dutch takes off on his search.

So he walks around for a while through the trees and finds weird footprints and stuff and strange carvings until after a while he hears a woman scream and takes off running. He finds the woman and her clothes are all torn and her hair all messed up and she's yelling, "They're coming! They're coming!" and Dutch can see the trees moving but can't see what's coming but they take off running and go through the trees and have to jump some rivers and stuff and Dutch keeps looking back but he can't see what's after them and then they slide down this mud-slide thing and they're safe, and that's when Dutch asks the woman—they're hiding under this rock ledge at the bottom of the hill they slid down and huffing and puffing and covered in mud—asks the woman what on Earth they were running from and she tells him all about the Cyclopses, which he doesn't believe at first—he never believes in the weird, supernatural stuff at first even though he's been on all these adventures and has seen dragons and talking rocks and stuff—and then he asks her who she is and how she got on this island and that's when we find out that she's Bo Jeffries and Bo Jeffries was a girl all along and she's this island expert, and the next part is the part that Patrick was at in the book, and so Patrick suggested that he start reading, and told Josiah that in this part they've washed up and built a fire and it's dark so it's safe because the Cyclopses can't see anything in the dark unless they're in their own lair, which is enchanted, and we're about to learn that Bo Jeffries is Lang's fiancée, which is okay because she doesn't really love him she's just being forced to marry him because Lang has this agreement with Bo's father, but by the end Bo will fall in love with Dutch and we'll find out that Lang is evil.

Patrick read to Josiah for nearly an hour, stopping at the point in which Dutch had to decide between saving Bo Jeffries and retrieving the probably very valuable and ancient Diary of King Nuvela, which the Cyclopses had been bred to protect, that also being the point when Patrick's voice began to get tired. Patrick offered to loan the book to Josiah if he liked it and wanted to finish it—Patrick had already read it and knew what would happen—as well as any of his others, he could just pick through them, showing Josiah the two large shoeboxes under his bed in which he kept the paperbacks.

o o o

After breakfast in the home of Johnson Davis, as instructed, Josiah went into his room and changed into clothes suitable for a fun park, specifically a pair of jeans and a t-shirt and a sweat-shirt, and packed a plastic bag with his swimming trunks and a towel.

Josiah had just pulled on his jeans and was fully clothed when Bree walked through the door, which Josiah had left open, from the hallway and closed the door behind her.

"Hi," Bree said to Josiah.

"Hi," Josiah said to Bree.

"What are you doing?" Bree asked.

"Nothing," Josiah answered.

"How did you sleep?"

"You took my sheets."

"Yeah."

"You told me to put them in the machine."

"Changed my mind. Did it myself. Did you like it?"

"What?"

"Did you like what we did?"

Josiah shrugged. "I guess so."

"What part did you like best?"

"What do you mean?"

"Did you like the kissing part best? Or the other part?"

"I don't know. The kissing part."

"Do you want to do it some more?"

Josiah nodded. Bree walked up to Josiah and put her hands on his arms and put her face up to his face, with her eyes closed, and once again she pushed her mouth onto his mouth and opened mouth with her tongue and once again used her tongue to lick his tongue. Josiah's Andre Agassi stiffened.

Bree stopped and said to Josiah, "Use your tongue, too."

"What do you mean?" Josiah said.

"Move your tongue, too. Like I'm doing," and Bree again put her mouth onto Josiah's, and when she began to lick his tongue with her tongue, Josiah began to lick her tongue as well. Josiah's Andre Agassi stiffened further.

After several seconds, Bree again stopped, and she let go of Josiah's arms and stepped back and smiled at Josiah. "What about the other parts?" she asked.

Josiah shrugged.

"Did you like the other parts?" Bree asked again.

"Did you fuck me?" Josiah asked. One day at the group home, while Patrick had been reading to Josiah, Josiah, who had first heard his mother's special friend use the word "fuck" when he was seven years old, again heard the word "fuck"—not in one of the Dutch Lucas novels, but in an intense espionage thriller involving Russians that Patrick had been given one year for his birthday. In fact, Josiah heard the word several times that same day, as Patrick read from the same book, and at one point Josiah asked Patrick, having not received a complete answer eight years earlier when he had asked his mother, what the word "fuck" meant, to which Patrick had replied that fucking was what men and women—such as husbands and wives or boyfriends and girlfriends—did to one another in bed.

"Do you know what that means?" Bree asked.

"Yes," Josiah answered.

Bree sat down on the edge of Josiah's bed. "You do?"

"Yes," Josiah said.

"I didn't fuck you."

"Did I come?"

"Yes. So did I. That's why I took your sheets."

"What does that mean?"

"You came all over your sheets. So did I."

Josiah stared at Bree.

"Maybe this is something your mother should explain," Bree said.

"She's not my mother."

"She's not your mother?"

"No."

"Who is she then?"

Josiah shrugged.

"Who is she if she's not your mother?" Bree asked again.

"The woman I was left with," Josiah said.

"By whom?"

"By my real mother."

"Who's your real mother?"

Josiah unzipped the front pocket of the black duffel bag he had carried his clothes home in and pulled from the pocket a folded sheet of yellow paper which he unfolded and handed to Bree.

o o o

On the morning of Josiah's twelfth day in the group home, Patrick having read every one of his Dutch Lucas paperbacks aloud to Josiah, Josiah sitting and listening intently, wondering what Dutch Lucas really looked like and what Cyclops Island or the Mists of Terror or any of the other settings of Dutch Lucas's adventures looked like, which led Josiah to wonder, as he often did, what his real father looked like and what the planet Parnuckle looked like, Josiah handed to Patrick a folded sheet of yellow paper. Patrick asked, as he unfolded the sheet, "What is it?"

"A picture," Josiah answered.

"Of what?" Patrick asked

"My mother."

o o o

"This is your mother?" Bree asked.

"Yes."

"It looks like Cher."

"Yes."

"Cher is your mother?"

"She is a goddess."

"A goddess?"

"Yes."

"Your real mother is a goddess who looks like Cher?"

"Yes."

"Where is she?"

"She lives on a planet far, far away."

"She lives on another planet?"

"Yes. With my father."

"What's it called?"

"Parnuckle."

"So your parents live on a planet far, far away. Called Parnuckle."

"Yes."

"That's pretty weird."

"I guess."

"So how'd you get here?"

"She had to send me away."

"Your real mother?"

"Yes."

"Why?"

Josiah then explained to Bree, as he had explained to Patrick, the day that Josiah had shown Patrick the drawing of his mother, about Parnuckle—that Parnuckle was a planet far, far away where they spoke their own language, called Parnucklian, and that Parnuckle was the home of his father, whom he had never met.

Josiah then told Bree, as he had told Patrick, that when he was very little his mother had told him that he was part-Parnucklian, but now he knew that his mother was not his real mother, that his real mother was Parnucklian, like his father, and was a beautiful goddess, named Cher, and that he was not part-Parnucklian, but all Parnucklian.

When Patrick had then asked Josiah how he had gotten here, to Earth, Josiah had responded that he didn't know, to which Patrick had responded, "Well, obviously she had to send you away."

"Why?" Josiah had asked.

After a pause, Patrick had answered, telling Josiah, as Josiah now told Bree, that Josiah's mother—real mother—had probably sent him away for his own protection. "And to save the planet, of course."

"Sounds important," Bree said, and as she handed the sheet of yellow paper, unfolded, back to Josiah, Josiah said to Bree, "Are you my girlfriend?"

"I don't know," she answered. "Do you want me to be?"

"I don't know."

"Well, shouldn't you decide?"

"I guess."

"You guess?"

"I guess."

"Well, I'm not going to be your girlfriend if you're not sure."

"Okay."

"Okay, what?"

"I'm sure."

"Sure, what?"

"You're my girlfriend."

"Just like that?"

"I guess."

"Now you *guess* again?"

"I don't know."

"Okay, Josiah," Bree said, standing. She walked to Josiah and stood close. She moved one hand, hanging at her side, and put it around one of his hands, hanging at his side, her hand feeling cold but soft, and continued, "But if I am going to be your girlfriend, and you are going to be my boyfriend," and she moved her face closer to his, lowering her voice to a whisper, "then we have to be secret boyfriend and girlfriend, and never tell anyone," and she moved her face away and released his hand and turned and walked out his door.

The fun park that was local to the home of Johnson Davis and Josiah's mother and Josiah and on the weekends Bree included a rather comprehensive video arcade along with a well-kept miniature golf course and a fairly extensive water park made up of a number of slides of various complexities, an artificial flowing canal that ran around the perimeter of the park for the purposes of relaxed floating, and one of those wave-pool/lagoon things which had recently re-opened after having been closed down for a year and a half for repairs.

In Johnson Davis's car on the way to the local fun park, Johnson Davis said, "Now, listen. The purpose of this little trip is that we can all get to know each other and be a family and so forth.

"So," he continued, looking in the rearview mirror at the reflection of his daughter, Bree, who was sitting next to Josiah in the back seat, the exposed skin of Bree's right leg and Josiah's separated only by the slightly-short-of-a-foot expanse of the empty middle seat, "that means we all need to stick together and not run off all over the place," to which Bree rolled her eyes and, after waiting for her father Johnson Davis to turn his own eyes from the mirror and back to the road, she turned slightly and smiled somewhat mischievously at Josiah, causing him to quickly turn away and causing his Andre Agassi to slightly stiffen.

Before arriving at the local fun park, during a conversation held in the front seat which Josiah—though not Bree, who had put into her ears a set of earphones—could hear, Johnson Davis and his fiancée, Josiah's mother, had decided that the newly-established family should begin its day at the miniature golf course portion of the park.

As Johnson Davis and Josiah's mother and Bree and Josiah crossed the parking lot of the local fun park, Johnson Davis and Josiah walking behind and slightly slower than Josiah's mother and Bree, as Josiah and Johnson Davis were each carrying one end of the ice chest that Johnson Davis had led the newly-formed family in packing, Josiah's mother turned to Bree and said, "I want to apologize for last night."

"Me too," Bree said in response.

"I apologize," Josiah's mother said.

"Me too," Bree said.

"Thank you," Josiah's mother said.

"Thank *you*," Bree said.

The miniature golf game began with Johnson Davis announcing that they would be playing "Boys against Girls!" and then demanding that both Josiah and Bree, as the representatives of their teams and in order to determine which team would go first, engage in a match, best two out of three, of Rock-Paper-Scissors, which Josiah had never actually played before, though he had seen other boys, such as Joey Simms and Eli Koslowski at the group home, play Rock-Paper-Scissors, usually at the start of a game of kickball or basketball, all of which Johnson Davis learned upon asking Josiah before the match with Bree began if he had ever played Rock-Paper-Scissors, leading Johnson Davis to provide Josiah with a short tutorial which included a basic outline of the rules and a brief history of the game's genesis and a slightly less brief discussion of the irony of the fact that though Rock-Paper-Scissors is itself a game it is often used, as the current situation shows by example, in the facilitation of other games, and a practical demonstration of the proper hand movements and positions required, at the end of which Johnson Davis took Josiah aside, placing a hand upon his shoulder, and whispered into his ear that a strategy that had served him well over the years was choosing the same object—either rock, paper, or scissors, it doesn't matter, any of the three would do—in all three turns, turning traditional strategy on its head and thereby often confusing the opponent, a strategy that proved unsuccessful in Josiah's match against Bree, Josiah choosing scissors in each turn, given that Bree, as a member of the family of Johnson Davis, had had extensive practice in the playing of Rock-Paper-Scissors, Rock-Paper-Scissors having been used throughout Bree's childhood not only to determine order of competition but as a mediator in nearly all decisions, and thus Bree had equally extensive exposure to the favored strategy of Johnson Davis and easily defeated Josiah with a volley of rocks.

Johnson Davis then announced that, "Okay, the girls won, that means they go first," to which Bree immediately responded, "No, it—" but was cut off by Josiah's mother, who said, "Actually, dear, I believe that by winning we get to choose to go first or second," to which Bree added, "We want to go second," turning and nodding her head up and down, seeking confirmation, at Josiah's mother, who said, "Yes, second." So Johnson Davis and Josiah stepped forward to the first hole, which consisted of a narrow red-carpeted lane which dropped abruptly into a red-carpeted circle set at a lower level than the lane, the hole being set in the middle of the circle. Johnson Davis suggested that Josiah go first, and as Josiah approached the tee, Johnson Davis once again placed a hand upon Josiah's shoulder and suggested to Josiah that he not take direct aim at the hole given that the abrupt drop at the end of the carpeted lane would undoubtedly send the ball off course, but rather Josiah should aim the ball at a twelve- to fifteen-degree angle to either the hole's left or right, allowing the ball to curve back in the hole's direction once it reached the carpeted circle.

Josiah placed his red ball on the tee and, once Johnson Davis had risen after outlining Josiah's intended course, which he did very meticulously on his hands and knees with his own club, and had put a stop, by lifting his hand, to Bree and Josiah's mother's conversation, which had been about Bree's shoes, Josiah hit the ball in the direction Johnson Davis had instructed him, and the ball rolled forward down the lane, dropped into the red-carpeted lower level circle, continued in a straight line, passing the hole, two-and-a-half feet to its left, ricocheting off the six-inch high cement wall at the back of the circle, rolling back to the right and stopping about a fourth of the distance from the wall to the hole.

"Well, okay," Johnson Davis said, "we have to start somewhere," and Johnson Davis stepped forward and placed his blue ball on the tee, held his club in the air, its handle even with his belt and the head with his shoulders, took a step back, announced, "A bit softer, I think, is the ticket," stepped forward, lowered the club's head and tapped the little blue ball, which rolled between half and three-quarters of the way down the lane and stopped.

Bree and Josiah's mother finished the first hole with six strokes and Josiah and Johnson Davis with nine, and when, after the second hole, which consisted of a green-carpeted lane and a green-carpeted circle—the carpeted lane on this hole including two bumps which ran along its width and the carpeted circle featuring a three-inch high hill in its center, the top of which being flat and containing the hole—Bree and Josiah's mother's total was sixteen strokes and Josiah and Johnson Davis's was twenty-two, Johnson Davis began to quiz Josiah's mother as to the previous miniature golf experience of both her and her son, reporting that he and Bree both had ample experience, as the two of them, along with Bree's mother, who never really took to the game, had spent many a Sunday afternoon at the local miniature golf course, which had recently closed and which, though it was perhaps not as elaborate or as clean as this one—referring to the miniature golf course at the local fun park—had been much closer and much more convenient. Josiah's mother reported that while Josiah had never actually played miniature golf before, she herself had played quite often, at least once every two weeks from the age of six to the age of seventeen, her childhood friend and later college roommate Becky Simpson's father being the owner of a course, and being that it was Becky's father who drove Josiah's mother and Becky to school and later picked them up—Josiah's mother's mother dropping Josiah's mother off at the end of Becky's driveway each morning—Becky and Josiah's mother spent many an afternoon amongst the holes of Becky's father's miniature golf course, passing the time until the close of business when Becky's father would drop Josiah's mother off at home, at which point she would begin her vacuuming and dusting before doing her homework.

When Becky went to a different high school than the school that Josiah's mother attended, Becky and Josiah's mother often rendezvoused Saturday afternoons at Becky's father's course, on those Saturdays when Josiah's mother's mother decided that Josiah's mother had cleaned their home sufficiently enough to take an afternoon off.

Johnson Davis then declared that perhaps it was unfair that two players such as Bree and Josiah's mother, who clearly had a great deal of miniature golf experience, should be matched against he and Josiah, Josiah having none. Johnson Davis suggested, then, that the teams be reformed and play re-started at the initial hole.

"That makes no sense," Bree said.

"What do you mean it makes no sense?" Johnson Davis said.

"Dear," Josiah's mother said, "no matter how the teams are reformed, wouldn't there still be one team with two experienced players and another team with only one experienced player?"

"Exactly," said Bree.

Josiah said nothing.

"Yes, of course," said Johnson Davis, "But being that I am the player—of the four—with the most total experience with the game—both the miniature version and the not-miniature, my father staunchly believing golf—generally in reference to the not-miniature version—to be the one true test of both mind and body, and it being one of the several sports—the non-miniature, that is—that I competed in in high school, before track and field became my sole focus—I would then be the most able to precisely modify my own play to match the deficiencies of the opposing team, thus making it a truly even contest."

"If you are the most able player," said Bree, lifting the scorecard from the hand of Josiah's mother and studying it before finishing her sentence, "then why are thirteen of your team's twenty-two strokes yours and only nine Josiah's?" Bree smiled at Josiah, not mischievously, but Josiah still looked away.

"Well, if you must know," Johnson Davis answered, speaking more loudly than he had been previously, "my attention was so directed toward guiding and lending support to Josiah here, who I could immediately see was at a disadvantage, that I neglected, during those two holes, to focus on my own play."

After the game of miniature golf was over, the game having been restarted from the first hole with the newly-formed team of Josiah and Bree competing against and eventually beating, by one stroke, after Bree pulled off an impressive double-bogey on the eighteenth hole, the newly-formed team of Johnson Davis and Josiah's mother, Johnson Davis decided that it was time for lunch. The miniature golf area of the local fun park featured both a restaurant and a food stand. Johnson Davis, who was noticeably more grumpy than he had been at the start of the miniature golf game, also decided that in the interest of keeping the cost of the newly-formed family's trip to a minimum, especially given the price of the admission tickets, which were a whole hell of a lot more expensive than Johnson Davis remembered them being, Johnson Davis and his fiancée, Josiah's mother, would go into the restaurant and have lunch while Josiah and Bree went to the food stand, for which Johnson Davis gave Josiah and Bree each a five dollar bill.

As Bree and Josiah sat at one of the fiberglass tables near the food stand, Bree with her basket of French fries and Josiah with his cup of chocolate ice cream, Bree asked Josiah, "So what's with the chocolate?"

Josiah said nothing, simply stared back at Bree.

"Why only chocolate?" Bree asked.

"Parnucklians eat nothing but chocolate," Josiah answered.

"Nothing?"

"No. But they call it Boboli."

"Like the bread? For pizza?"

Josiah said nothing.

"Weird," Bree said.

Josiah shrugged. Bree placed a French fry into her mouth and chewed and swallowed it. Josiah swallowed a spoonful of his ice cream.

"So is everybody fat?" Bree asked.

"Our bodies are different," Josiah answered.

"How convenient."

"Yes."

"So you've always eaten chocolate?"

Josiah nodded.

"Have you ever eaten anything else? Ever?"

Josiah nodded again. "At the group home."

"Did they make you?"

"Yes."

"Why were you there?"

Josiah shrugged.

"Did you do something?"

"I peed."

"What do you mean you peed?"

"I peed in my room. And in the kitchen."

"Why?"

"I don't know."

"So you were sent away? For peeing?"

Josiah nodded.

"What was it like, the home?"

"I don't know."

"Was the food good?"

"I guess."

"What did you like best? What food?"

"I don't know. French fries."

"Really?"

"Yes."

"What kind? The skinny kind, or this kind?" Bree held up one of her French fries. It was thick, with ridges. The crinkly kind.

"That kind," Josiah said.

"Yeah?"

Josiah nodded.

"Eat it," Bree said, and she held the French fry close to Josiah's face. Josiah took the French fry in his mouth, his lips touching the two fingers with which Bree held the fry, and began chewing it.

"Is it good?" Bree asked.

Josiah nodded, chewing.

"Good," Bree said.

Once Johnson Davis and Josiah's mother and Josiah and Bree had all finished their lunch and all reunited, it was decided amongst the newly-established family that the next step would be to change into their bathing suits and enjoy the water park portion of the local fun park, and after nearly forty minutes of floating together in a small clump inside the artificial flowing canal, Josiah and Bree on inner tubes, Josiah's mother on a raft, and Johnson Davis not actually floating but treading water the entire time and sort of leading the way around and around the perimeter of the local fun park, Josiah's mother and Johnson Davis agreed that, despite Johnson Davis's command that the newly-established family spend its day at the local fun park all together and getting to know each other and being a family and so forth, Josiah and Bree could in fact ascend the ten stories of the park's newest water slide attraction and then partake in said attraction, dubbed The Suicide Mission, without Johnson Davis and Josiah's mother.

As Josiah and Bree began to climb the stairs to the top of The Suicide Mission, at around the second story, Josiah asked Bree, "Why a secret?"

"Why do you think?" Bree said in response.

"I don't know."

"We're like brother and sister."

"Not really."

"No. But sort of. Our parents are getting married. That would be weird."

"Why?"

"It would just be weird."

"Why?"

"It just would. Trust me."

Shortly after Josiah and Bree arrived, a bit winded, at the state-mandated break area for weary climbers on the fifth story, they were approached by two teenage boys, who were already at the break area, named David and Isaac, David walking slightly ahead of Isaac.

David and Isaac were both wearing swim trunks similar to those Josiah was wearing, but their bodies were bigger and darker than Josiah's.

"Hi," David said to Bree.

"Hi," Bree said to David.

"I'm David."

"I'm Bree."

"This is Isaac," said David to Bree, causing Isaac to nod his head upward at Bree.

"This is Josiah," said Bree to David, causing both David and Isaac to look in the direction of Josiah, causing Josiah to look away.

"Are you guys friends?" asked David.

"We're brother and sister," answered Bree.

"Cool," said David.

"Are *you* guys brother and sister?" asked Bree.

"We're friends," answered David, smiling slightly.

"I like your bathing suit," said David to Bree, referring to her bikini, which was green and covered with little white swirlies.

o o o

When Bree had emerged from the locker room of the water park portion of the local fun park wearing the green bikini with little white swirlies, Josiah had begun to stare at it and then to stare at the parts of Bree that he had never seen before or had not seen under ample light and not while pinned down—until she wore the green bikini with white swirlies—causing his Andre Agassi to stiffen and causing Bree, when she caught Josiah staring at the green bikini with white swirlies and at her parts, to smile at Josiah mischievously, causing Josiah to turn away.

o o o

"Thanks," said Bree to David. "I like your tan."

"Thanks," said David. "Are you guys by yourselves?"

"Our parents are here," answered Bree.

"Well, if it's alright with your parents, maybe we can all hang out for a while later," said David to Bree, causing Bree to smile mischievously at David in the way that she often smiled mischievously at Josiah, often causing Josiah to look away.

"I guess we have to get to the bottom of this slide first, don't we?" asked Bree.

"I guess we do," replied David, and the four of them continued up the stairs.

o o o

Bree had been thirteen and eight months when she began dating Steven Caldwell, the boy who lived in the house next door to the house of Johnson Davis and Bree's mother. Bree began dating Steven Caldwell the week that Carter Caldwell, Steven Caldwell's father, drove Bree home from school each day because Johnson Davis and his former wife, Bree's mother, were spending their afternoons that week in the office of Viola Rubinaugh, provider of professional marriage counseling with care. On Tuesday of the week that Carter Caldwell drove Bree home from school each day, Bree gave Steven Caldwell a blow job in his room while Carter Caldwell used the leaf blower in the front yard. On Wednesday, Bree gave Steven Caldwell another blow job in the TV room during an episode of *Duck Tales* while Carter Caldwell took a nap in the upstairs master bedroom.

Steven Caldwell spent Thursday of the week that Carter Caldwell drove Bree home from school each day following Bree around the campus of their middle school and offering to carry her books or her backpack and opening classroom doors for her, and by lunchtime Bree would not speak to or acknowledge Steven Caldwell at all. That afternoon, at the home of Carter Caldwell, when Carter Caldwell asked Bree and Steven Caldwell if they wanted to come to the neighborhood grocery store with him to buy ice cream and orange juice, Steven Caldwell told his father that he had too much homework and could not go with him. Steven Caldwell had hoped that this might be an opportunity to get another blow job from Bree, but instead Bree told Carter Caldwell that she had no homework at all and would love to go with him, so Bree and Carter Caldwell got into the car of Carter Caldwell and left Steven Caldwell all alone.

During the drive to the neighborhood grocery store to buy ice cream and orange juice, Carter Caldwell asked Bree, "So how's school?" to which Bree responded, "It's okay," to which Carter Caldwell further asked, "Get good grades?" to which Bree responded, "Sometimes."

"Get into a lot of trouble?"

"Not really."

"How about Steven?"

"No, not really."

"Are you guys going steady?"

"Who?"

"You and Steven."

"No, not really."

"Got *any* boyfriends?"

"Not really."

Besides buying both ice cream and orange juice at the neighborhood grocery store, Carter Caldwell also bought a pack of cigarettes, which he opened as he and Bree returned to his car, taking from the pack of cigarettes a cigarette which he lit and began smoking as he and Bree pulled out of the parking lot of the neighborhood grocery store.

"Can I have one of those?" Bree asked Carter Caldwell about a quarter of a mile down the road.

"What? You smoke?"

"Yeah."

"Really?"

"Yeah, so?"

"I don't know. You're a little underage, I guess."

"Am not. Everyone smokes at school."

"Everyone? Steven, too?"

"No, he doesn't. But a lot do."

"Yeah?"

"Yeah."

"I don't know. I can't give you a cigarette."

"What's the difference? I already smoke."

"I don't know. I guess," and Carter Caldwell held the pack of cigarettes out to Bree, his hands shaking, and Bree pulled from the pack of cigarettes a cigarette and took from Carter Caldwell the cigarette lighter, the tips of her ring and middle fingers making contact with the knuckles of his same two fingers. Tilting her head but still keeping her eyes on Carter Caldwell, Bree lit the cigarette and began smoking it, blowing the smoke out in a slow, smooth, steady stream.

Carter Caldwell's cigarette was nearly gone but Bree's cigarette was only half-gone when the car turned onto the street on which Carter Caldwell and Johnson Davis lived.

"You should probably put that out before we get too close to the house."

"Or we could pull over and smoke another one."

"I don't know."

"I only got to smoke half of mine."

"I guess. I guess I wouldn't mind another one."

As Carter Caldwell and Bree each smoked their second cigarette in the car of Carter Caldwell, parked about a mile or so from
their homes, Bree asked him, "So, do you want to touch me?"

o o o

The feeling Josiah felt when he reached the bottom of the ten-story-
tall water slide attraction, The Suicide Mission, was very similar to
the feeling Josiah had felt at the group home on the day that, during the period between morning activities and pre-lunch activities,
Joey Simms had approached Josiah and stated that he very much
admired Josiah's sweater and asked Josiah where he had gotten it
and if he could ever borrow it, but before Josiah had a chance to
answer, Eli Koslowski grabbed the back of Josiah's underwear and
pulled them upward very quickly and very forcefully, causing them
to stick in the middle of Josiah's Thomas Magnum and causing
Joey Simms and Eli Koslowski to run from the room laughing and
slapping hands and leaving Josiah with the feeling that he now felt
upon reaching the bottom of the ten-story-tall water slide attraction, The Suicide Mission.

As Josiah climbed out of the small pool at the bottom of the
slide and began to pull his swim trunks out of the middle of his
Thomas Magnum, Josiah saw Isaac shaking his long blonde hair
and heard him shouting, "Whoo! Whoo! That was fucking awesome! Whoo!" and near Isaac, Josiah saw David and Bree standing face to face and talking, but Josiah could not hear what David and Bree were saying to each other, as they, unlike Isaac, were
not shouting.

As Josiah approached David and Bree, Josiah could hear Bree
saying to David, ". . . locker room to get my purse," and as Josiah
came even closer, Bree turned to Josiah and said, "We're going to
the volleyball courts. Ready?"

When Bree and David and Isaac and Josiah reached the volleyball
courts adjacent to the water park portion of the local fun park,

which were different from the volleyball courts at the group home because these volleyball courts had sand covering the asphalt, they did not stop, but rather followed Bree past the volleyball courts toward the restroom facility made of large gray bricks near the volleyball courts. Again, Bree and David and Isaac and Josiah did not stop at the restroom facility nearby the sand-covered volleyball courts, but rather followed Bree behind the restroom facility to a small grass-covered area in between the back wall of the restroom facility and a tall chain-link fence that had wooden strips woven through it so that the chain-link fence was not see-through like most chain-link fences, where Bree opened her purse and pulled out a small blue instrument that was strangely shaped but shiny and that had little white swirlies, which reminded Josiah of Bree's bikini, except that Bree's bikini was green with white swirlies and the strangely shaped but shiny small instrument was blue with white swirlies.

After Bree pulled out the shiny blue instrument, she then reached back into her purse and pulled out a rolled-up plastic sandwich bag. Once Bree un-rolled the plastic sandwich bag, Josiah could see that it held in its bottom a green leafy-looking substance, some of which Bree took out of the plastic sandwich bag and put into the part of the shiny blue instrument that resembled a small, thick bowl.

Bree put the green leafy-looking stuff into the part of the shiny blue instrument that resembled a small, thick bowl, and pulled out a red cigarette lighter similar to the yellow cigarette lighter that Joey Simms from the group home had used to light cigarettes and held it upside down with one hand and held the shiny blue instrument to her lips, specifically the part of the shiny blue instrument opposite of the part that resembled a thick bowl, sucking in very hard, after which she removed the instrument from her lips and then, after making a funny face for several seconds, blew smoke out of her mouth in a way somewhat similar to the way that Joey Simms would blow smoke out of his mouth when smoking cigarettes at the group home, except that Josiah liked the way that Bree looked when blowing smoke out of her mouth.

Bree then passed the shiny instrument to David, who in turn passed the instrument to Isaac, both of them repeating the same basic actions that Bree had performed, except that both David and Isaac coughed heavily for nearly a minute after blowing the smoke out of their mouths. Isaac then held the instrument out to Josiah, but before Josiah, who was unsure if he should take the instrument, could take it, Bree grabbed the instrument and told Isaac, "He probably doesn't want any."

Bree and David and Isaac passed the shiny instrument amongst themselves once again and once again each blew smoke from their mouths, Josiah again liking the way that Bree looked when she blew smoke out of her mouth and David and Isaac again coughing, though not as heavily and for not as long.

"This is some good shit," said David to Bree as he passed the shiny instrument back to her, causing Bree to smile mischievously at David in the way that she sometimes smiled mischievously at Josiah as she put the shiny instrument back into her purse, after which she announced in David's direction, "I have to go to the bathroom," and then pausing for a few seconds before adding, "Do you need to go?" to which David responded, "Yeah," and then followed Bree around the side of the restroom facility made of large gray bricks.

"Dude, I need to sit down," said Isaac, and Josiah followed as Isaac walked around the front of the restroom facility and seated himself at a green wooden table with two green wooden benches attached to it, near the entrance of the men's restroom portion of the restroom facility. As Josiah seated himself on the green wooden bench on the side opposite the side that Isaac had seated himself on, a man in striped shorts and a striped t-shirt approached the entrance to the men's restroom, causing Isaac to stand up from the green wooden bench and step toward the man, saying, "Hey, man, there's shit and water all over in there. It must've, like, overflowed. My buddy went to find a janitor," to which the man in striped shorts and a striped t-shirt responded, "Oh, oh. Okay. Thank you, young man," before turning and walking back the way he had come. Isaac watched the man for a moment before returning to his seat on the green wooden bench, saying, "Man, I am fucking high," and pausing for several seconds before continuing, "I am so fucking high." Josiah, unsure what else to do or say, simply nodded and looked down at the green wooden table. He then looked back up and said, "I didn't really want any," before looking back down at the green wooden table, to which Isaac responded, "Yeah, man, that's cool."

Josiah and Isaac were silent for several minutes before Isaac laughed in a way that seemed like he couldn't help but to laugh and said, still sort of laughing as he said it, "You think he's fucking her?" causing Josiah to abruptly look up from the green wooden table and turn toward the entrance of the men's restroom. Josiah sat very tensely for several seconds before standing and walking toward the entrance.

Josiah was initially stopped by Isaac's hand on his arm, and then by Isaac moving in front of him, saying, "Whoa, whoa, whoa, dude, what are you doing? You don't want to go in there," to which Josiah responded, "We're all supposed to stay together," to which Isaac responded, "Dude, don't worry. They just went to the bathroom. Let's sit down," but Josiah did not move and simply stared at Isaac, who continued, "Dude, I'm sorry about what I said. About your sister. I'm just so fucking high."

"She's my girlfriend," Josiah said.

"Your girlfriend?"

"Yes."

"I thought she was your sister."

"It's supposed to be a secret."

"That's pretty weird, man."

Josiah was considering what he should say next to Isaac when Bree emerged from the entrance of the men's restroom, with David, smiling toward Isaac, following behind her. Bree looked at Josiah without expression and asked, "Ready?"

In the car on the way back from the local fun park to the home of Johnson Davis, Josiah could somehow tell that Bree was looking over at him from time to time and could somehow tell that Bree was also smiling, but not in the mischievous way that Bree sometimes smiled at Josiah and also had smiled at least twice at David, but in a different way that Josiah had not seen before. Despite the fact that Bree was smiling at Josiah, Josiah did not turn away. Josiah did not turn away because, though he could tell that Bree was from time to time looking at him and smiling at him, Josiah did not once look toward Bree the entire ride back from the local fun park to the home of Johnson Davis.

Later that night, Josiah was lying in bed awake, unable to fall asleep because he was unable to stop thinking about Bree and about Bree coming out of the men's restroom with David, and the way that Bree looked when she blew the smoke from the shiny blue instrument out of her mouth and the way that Bree looked in her Girls Varsity soccer jersey and the way that she sometimes smiled at him mischievously and the way that that would make him look away and sometimes make his Andre Agassi stiffen and the way that she also smiled at David that way at least twice and the way that she had pinned him down with her legs and the way that her hair smelled and the things that Isaac had said to him about her and the way that she had smiled at him in a different way in the car on the way home and the feeling from his Andre Agassi that was similar to peeing but not quite exactly and the way that Bree looked in her green bikini with white swirlies and the parts of her that he had never seen until she wore the green bikini when suddenly Josiah could hear someone that he could somehow tell was Bree come into his room and walk toward his bed and then walk around his bed to the side opposite of the side out from which Josiah was looking, as Josiah was lying on his side and was lying very still, and then Josiah could feel the someone that he could somehow tell was Bree climb onto the bed and crawl under the covers and then he could feel Bree's arm sliding over his arm and around his chest an instant before he could feel her hair against the back of his head and against the side of his neck and then Josiah could feel Bree's other arm push through between his rib cage and the bed and then around his stomach and Josiah could feel Bree's chest against his back and one of her legs against the back of one of his legs and he could feel his Andre Agassi stiffen but then he began to think again about the way that Bree had smiled mischievously at David the way that she sometimes smiled mischievously at him and about the things that Isaac had said about Bree and about the look on Bree's face when she came out of the men's restroom and about the look on David's face when he came out of the men's restroom behind Bree and smiled at Isaac and then Josiah began to think about the feelings that he felt while sitting on the green wooden bench attached to the green wooden table, staring at the entrance to the men's restroom, and then began to think about the feelings that he felt in the car on the way home from the local fun park, when Bree kept looking at him and smiling but in a different way, and then Josiah began to feel those feelings again, or at least feelings similar to those feelings, and Josiah decided to pull away from Bree and leave the room and go into the hallway and maybe pee on the door to her room and then never ever speak to or look at her again, but as soon as Josiah began to struggle his way free, Bree tightened her embrace, causing Josiah to struggle even harder, causing Bree to tighten her embrace even more, squeezing her arms toward each other until she was able to lock them together by grabbing the elbow of the opposite arm, causing Bree's chest to rub even more against Josiah's back and causing her hair to brush even more against the back of his neck, causing Josiah's Andre Agassi to further stiffen, but at the same time the increasing tightness of Bree's embrace further heightened Josiah's desire to break free from it, and Josiah began to struggle more and more, but Bree, in turn, squeezed harder and harder, and then Josiah began to kick at Bree with his legs, but in turn Bree quickly wrapped her legs around Josiah's legs and squeezed and Josiah could feel, in their ability to squeeze, that Bree's legs were as strong as, if not stronger than, her arms.

At this point, though for the most part unable to move, Josiah began to thrash violently in an attempt to break free from Bree, but Bree did not let go. This continued for several minutes until, finally, sweating profusely, Josiah stopped thrashing and struggling and lay still. When he fell asleep forty minutes later, Bree was still holding him.

FIVE

Josiah's first full week in the home of Johnson Davis without Bree, which began that following morning, the following morning being a Sunday, was somewhat difficult for Josiah. Despite Josiah's desire to remain lying in bed thinking about Bree or what he felt about Bree and what he would say to Bree the next time that he saw her, which he hoped—though at times when he thought about Bree he became angry or upset—would be soon, Josiah's mother woke Josiah up very early so that she and Josiah could resume Josiah's homeschooling.

Up until four weeks before Josiah moved into the home of Johnson Davis, Johnson Davis and Josiah's mother had spent their Sunday mornings at the local church, Johnson Davis having preferred a prolonged breakfast following the early service to a rushed breakfast before the mid-day service. Johnson Davis and Josiah's mother had, in fact, met at the local church. Johnson Davis had first visited the church, which was seven blocks from his house, shortly after his daughter Bree, at age sixteen, had had an abortion.

Josiah's mother had first attended the church after meeting a deacon from the church through an online dating website. The name of the website was *Perfect Match* and Josiah's mother, who had purchased a personal computer because a friend suggested that she should create a website for her maid service business, had begun using *Perfect Match* at the suggestion of the same friend, a woman named Margaret who worked part-time at the hair salon where Josiah's mother usually got her hair cut and who, at her own suggestion and mostly because she did not earn enough money cutting hair part-time to support herself and her two cats and her younger brother who had recently lost his job at an auto repair business and had moved back in with her, had accompanied Josiah's mother on a number—specifically four—of her house-cleaning jobs, helping her with some of the larger houses on Josiah's mother's list in exchange for a little extra income. Margaret claimed that she had met several nice guys, specifically three, through the website, one who had bought her a cute bracelet, and she had even set up her brother, whose name was Sean and who needed to get back out there, with an account and he had already received several hits. Margaret believed that Josiah's mother should try it. She always looked so sad all the time.

Josiah's mother and the deacon had met at a local coffee shop after spending a week answering questions that each had submitted for the other through the website's "Getting to Know You" system. The deacon had been very nervous, and at the end of a long conversation about dogs and about faith, the deacon invited Josiah's mother to accompany him to his church, where he was a deacon, the following day, the following day being Sunday.

Over the next several weeks, the deacon and Josiah's mother, besides attending the church each Sunday, went on several dates during which they talked less and less and ate more and more, usually ending with the deacon and Josiah's mother making love at the deacon's apartment, during which the deacon would stare very intently at Josiah's mother's forehead and after which the deacon would stand naked next to the bed and talk to Josiah's mother about the direction in which the country was moving and his view of the future. Toward the end of the several weeks, Josiah's mother had stopped calling the deacon and had stopped answering his calls.

After the deacon and Josiah's mother stopped going on dates, Josiah's mother did not, as one may have expected, and as the deacon himself had expected, stop attending the church on Sundays. During the time that she had accompanied the deacon to the church's Sunday services, she had become fascinated by the stories of Jesus and the Apostles and the beautiful songs and especially the image and the story of the Virgin Mary. The deacon, who had liked Josiah's mother very much, found it difficult to continue attending the church now that Josiah's mother insisted on not only attending every service the church offered, other than the Spanish service on Sunday afternoons, but also on making her presence known to all in attendance by singing more loudly than every other parishioner and sometimes even reading along—loudly—the gospels and readings, so that eventually the deacon decided to cease his deaconship and began attending another local church on the other side of town.

Johnson Davis, who had known the deacon only vaguely but had thought that he was an unimpressive individual, first noticed Josiah's mother, as many others had, because of her propensity to sing and read loudly. Johnson Davis, who usually sat not all the way in the back but in a pew near the back, often watched Josiah's mother, who always sat in a pew very near the front and was always pleasantly dressed in a pleasantly colored sundress, and often imagined approaching her and talking to her after services had ended and possibly asking her out on a date, but he never did and eventually he accepted that he never would and slowly his fantasies of ever speaking to her dissipated. Thus he was quite surprised the Sunday afternoon that he looked up to find her walking toward him at the church's potluck social.

Johnson Davis and Josiah's mother, once they began dating, attended services at the local church routinely for three months; however, two Sundays after the local church's longtime and much-beloved pastor, Father Mike, retired and was replaced by a man older than Josiah's mother but younger than Johnson Davis, named Father Tom, whom Josiah's mother, after two Sundays, found disgustingly smug, Josiah's mother, who over the course of several weeks had found her personal study of God's word to be more and more rewarding and the weekly ritual of church less and less so, had suggested—somewhat insistently—to Johnson Davis that they abandon the local church and the smug Father Tom to focus on their own spiritual growth. Besides, she had told Johnson Davis, what more did they need beyond the Word of the Lord itself, adding that she wasn't even convinced this Father Tom was a real priest anyway.

Johnson Davis, who, shortly after his daughter's abortion and his subsequent divorce, had found attending church comforting, had since lost interest and found his fiancée's somewhat insistent request convenient, as he viewed Sundays—particularly Sunday mornings, before it became too hot—to be an ideal time for catching up on yard work and household chores, and readily agreed.

At five to eight on Josiah's first Sunday morning in the home of Johnson Davis, Josiah, who had awoken at half-past-four to find that Bree had left his room and who had been lying awake since, heard knocking on his bedroom door, followed by the voice of his mother singing the words, "*Riiiise and Shiiiine.*" Though he had, over the course of the past two years, forgotten, Josiah's mother had sung these words at Josiah, through his bedroom door, every morning of Josiah's life until he moved into the group home.

When Josiah walked downstairs, he found his mother standing alone in the kitchen, wiping the kitchen table with a white cloth. Josiah, who, from the kitchen, could see into the living room and into the dimly-lit dining room, looked around for anyone else, specifically Bree. Josiah's mother, without looking up from the table, said to Josiah, "Breakfast after your shower. Then your lessons."

"Where's Bree?" Josiah asked.

Josiah's mother looked up. After a long pause, during which Josiah's mother simply stared at Josiah, she said, "Why do you ask that, Josiah?"

Josiah shrugged.

Josiah's mother stopped staring at Josiah and continued wiping the table, pushing a group of four crumbs from each direction until they joined into a small pile. "Mr. Davis took her home," Josiah's mother said. "Early. Some prior commitment with her mother."

Josiah nodded.

o o o

In the time between Josiah's removal from elementary school and his moving into the group home, the homeschool curriculum of Josiah's mother had consisted primarily of real world lessons, such as lawn maintenance, which included the mowing of grass and the raking of leaves and the trimming of hedges and the pruning of flowers and at times the cleaning of gutters, along with housekeeping, which involved the scrubbing of sinks and toilets and countertops and the mopping of floors and the washing of windows and dishes and glasses and silverware and shirts and pants and socks and towels and underwear and at times Josiah's mother's car.

From time to time, Josiah's real world lessons would involve sitting still and quiet in the kitchen while Josiah's mother watched her favorite television programs in the living room or sitting still and very, very quiet in his room, with the lights off, if Josiah's mother wished to bring a friend home for dinner and/or to watch a movie.

o o o

While in the shower very early on the Sunday morning of Josiah's first full week in the home of Johnson Davis without Bree, Josiah wondered if his real world lessons would begin inside the home of Johnson Davis—in the kitchen or maybe one of the bathrooms— or outside the home of Johnson Davis—either in the front yard or the back yard—but when Josiah finished showering and dressing and came back downstairs, he found his mother seated at the kitchen table, seemingly waiting for Josiah. In one area of the kitchen table, Josiah's mother had placed a plate with toast on it and a bowl with cereal in it and a small pitcher with milk in it and a glass with juice in it. In another area of the kitchen table, Josiah's mother had placed a large red textbook with black borders and black letters on the cover that spelled out *New Way: Christian Focused Home-Based Instruction for Today's Youth*.

Josiah looked down at the area of the kitchen table upon which Josiah's mother had placed toast and cereal and milk and juice with a look of confusion. Noticing his look of confusion, Josiah's mother said to Josiah, "Josiah, from this day forward, we will not be eating chocolate. When I say that we will not be eating chocolate, I mean that we, meaning you, will no longer eat nothing but chocolate. Some chocolate some of the time is fine, but as for the rest of the time, we need to start eating like normal people. Most, or I should say *all*, of your life, we, meaning I, have not treated you like a normal person. This is because you are not a normal person. You are special. But now I realize that I have possibly treated you too special, and now we have problems. So, from now on, we, meaning you, are going to be doing more normal things, like eating foods other than chocolate. But you mustn't think that this means that you are normal, like everyone else. You are not. You must never forget that you are special. You are more than other people. You are part-Parnucklian, which is a wonderful thing. We, or I should say, I, simply feel that it would be good for you to do normal things for the time being. So sit down and have some breakfast."

Josiah's mother began sliding plates and bowls and pitchers and glasses, saying, "Here. Here is some toast, and here is some cereal, and here is some milk to pour over the cereal, and here is some juice," and before Josiah had a chance to begin eating his toast or his cereal or pouring his milk or drinking his juice, his mother continued, "Also, real world lessons will no longer be a part of your homeschooling curriculum. Your yard maintenance and housekeeping skills have reached the Advanced Level, and it is time to move on to something else. From this point on, we will be studying the life and words of Jesus Christ. Jesus Christ was a wonderful man who changed the world and continues to change it even today. He, like you, is also special. He is the son of God. On the home planet of your father, which is also your home, they do not believe in Jesus Christ nor do they worship him, but that is forgivable because Jesus never visited the planet Parnuckle, so they would have no way of knowing about him. Jesus did visit this planet, of course, so people on this planet that do not believe in him will go to Hell. Hell is a horrible place consisting mostly of fire. That is why it is very important that we get to know Jesus."

o o o

Drew Martell had been the Sophomore Class President at the high school that he and Josiah's mother had both attended and later the Junior Class President and later the Student Body President. Drew Martell had also been the baseball team captain and the soccer team captain and the basketball team captain.

All of the girls at the high school that Drew Martell and Josiah's mother had both attended had been in love with Drew Martell. Some of the girls wrote love letters to Drew Martell, some having kept the letters in their sock drawer or under their mattress and others having been brave enough to give the letters to Drew Martell, either having passed them to him in class or having left them on his doorstep, some having signed the letters and others not. Other girls would plan their weddings to Drew Martell and think of names for the babies that they and Drew Martell might have. Some would call the home of Drew Martell and when he answered they would hang up and giggle. A few had been brave enough to stay on the line and talk to Drew Martell. Some girls at the high school had sex with Drew Martell.

Approximately each semester, one girl at the high school would get to be the girlfriend of Drew Martell. Every fall, at the beginning of the school year, Drew Martell would choose a girl to be his steady girlfriend, making that girl the envy of all of the other girls at the high school, usually breaking up with that girl sometime around winter break and then finding a new girl to be his new girlfriend, making that girl the envy of all of the other girls, usually breaking up with that girl sometime before summer break.

The girls whom Drew Martell had chosen to be his steady girlfriends, and who had become the envy of all of the other girls at the high school that Drew Martell and Josiah's mother had both attended, were seen somewhat as celebrities or as royalty. Those girls would soon develop an entourage of other girls. Way would be made for those girls and their entourages in the hallways. Lunch tables would be cleared. Lunch would be fetched. Lunch money would be loaned out. Homework assignments would be relinquished for the purposes of copying. Sluts who had sex with Drew Martell behind the back of his steady girlfriend, either in a car or at the movie theater or in the boy's locker room, would be harassed, bumped into in hallways, their books knocked to the ground, "slut" and "whore" shouted in the cafeteria. Phone calls would be made to homes proclaiming to whomever answered that the daughter of the house was a slut and a whore. The names and phone numbers of sluts would be recorded on bathroom walls.

Drew Martell had never chosen Josiah's mother to be one of his steady girlfriends. Nor had Drew Martell had sex with Josiah's mother, either in a car or at the movie theater or in the boy's locker room. In fact, it seemed that Drew Martell had had no idea who Josiah's mother was. They had had two classes together over the course of the three years that they both had attended the same high school at the same time, but Josiah's mother had never once spoken to Drew Martell and Drew Martell had never once spoken to Josiah's mother.

Despite the fact that Drew Martell had had no idea who Josiah's mother was and that Josiah's mother had never once spoken to Drew Martell and Drew Martell had never once spoken to Josiah's mother, Josiah's mother, like all of the other girls at the high school that she had attended, had been madly in love with Drew Martell, and had imagined her wedding to Drew Martell and the names of the babies that they might have had.

o o o

"Unfortunately," Josiah's mother said to Josiah, sitting at the table in Johnson Davis's kitchen, "Jesus had not yet made his way into my life at the time that I was taken onto the Parnucklian spaceship and met your father. Parnucklians would have made wonderful Christians. They are very compassionate, just like Jesus. But at the time I was lost. At the time I was just like other teenage girls out there in America, lost and in need of God's love. I was a very good girl in middle school and in high school. I did all of my homework and studied hard for my tests and was polite to my teachers. I went to bed early and always ate a good breakfast and never talked to boys. But when I left high school and went to college and moved out of my parents' house and into the dormitory, something happened, something that happens to a lot of teenagers, but especially teenage girls, when they leave their parents and go to college. I became excited. I began to feel a feeling of freedom and excitement. I began to stay up late. I began to miss some of my classes. I began to drink beer and other alcoholic beverages. I had given in to the temptations of the Devil, though at the time I was unaware of it. At the time, what I was doing felt good and felt right. I was having fun. But in reality I was being blinded by the Devil. The Devil was trying to trick me into being his servant, which no one should want to be. Luckily, even though I was being very bad, I did not begin going out with boys. This is an area, for whatever reasons, that the Devil was unable to lead me toward. Many teenage girls, when they leave their parents and go to college, begin talking to and going out with lots of boys. For example, my roommate in the dormitory, Beth, went out with most of the boys on the boys' floor of our dormitory. Beth would spend the night with a boy nearly every night. She would sleep with boys in her bed in our dormitory room. When I say that they slept together, Josiah, I mean that they had sex, which is a sin unless you are having sex with a person that you are married to."

o o o

When Josiah had been twelve years old, Josiah's mother had sat Josiah down at the kitchen table and said to him, "Josiah, the time has come for you to learn about sex. Sex is something that a man does to a woman using his Andre Agassi. On this planet, an Andre Agassi is called a penis." Josiah's mother had held up a twelve-ounce bottle of apple juice and had continued, "When a man and a woman have sex, the man takes his Andre Agassi, or penis," Josiah's mother had then held up a coffee cup and had put the twelve-ounce bottle of apple juice, lid first, inside of it, "and puts it inside of the woman's vagina, which is located in the same place that a man's penis is located. There is no Parnucklian word for the woman's vagina. To the Parnucklians, the woman's vagina is a very special and very secret place, and therefore no name is given to it and it is rarely spoken of. On this planet, the woman's vagina has been given many names. At any rate," and Josiah's mother had begun moving the twelve-ounce bottle of apple juice in and out of the coffee cup, "the man puts his penis into the woman's vagina until he is able to have an orgasm. This can be painful for the woman and can cause her to become pregnant and have a baby, so only people who really, really love each other should try it. Josiah, you should not put your penis, or Andre Agassi, into any woman's vagina until you know it is the right time, which will be a long time from now." Josiah's mother had then set the twelve-ounce bottle of apple juice and the coffee cup down on the kitchen table and left the kitchen and went into her room and shut the door.

o o o

"But I was not like Beth in that way. I stayed up late like Beth and went to parties and drank beer and missed classes like Beth, but I did not have sex with boys like Beth did. I did not have sex with boys because somehow I always knew that there was something special out there waiting for me. All of my life, from the time I was a little girl, I always felt, always knew, that there was something special out there, and I just had to wait until I found it or it found me."

o o o

She had seen him, from across the room, but had never imagined that moments later he would notice her, let alone approach her, let alone talk to her, let alone have any idea who she was.

"I can't believe you recognized me. I didn't even think you knew my name."

"How could I not know your name? We went to school together for like three years." He stood close, but not too close.

"I know, but . . ." The house was well-furnished, and as her hand casually searched the space behind her in search of support to combat the feeling of tipping that she was experiencing at that moment, it conveniently came into contact with what, without looking, felt like an oak side table. She kept her right hand flat against the table, which was nearly the height of her waist, and held a bottle of beer in her left.

"We even had a couple of classes together. Didn't we?" He held a plastic glass in his own right hand. His left was shoved halfway into his jean pocket.

"Yes, but . . ."

"And now here we are. So how are you liking State?" Though it had been only a year, he was different, she thought. Different, but the same, as if he had been added to but also subtracted from.

"It's great. I mean . . . it's amazing."

"Is this your first Kappa Chi party?"

"Yeah. I mean . . . my roommate and I were going to come last week . . . but, well . . . she got sick."

"But you guys made it this time."

"Well . . . yeah," she responded, remembering her beer and taking a sip, hoping that this behavior would somehow hide her awkwardness. "Actually, she still isn't feeling that well. But she dropped me off."

"And is she picking you up?" The surrounding noise in the room, while it did not stop, seemed to quiet itself. She watched his eyes gaze into hers.

"Yeah . . . I'm supposed to call her . . . when . . ."

"Do you need another beer?"

She let go of the table behind her and shifted the weight of her upper body forward, toward him.

"Sure. Sure."

"I'll get it. Be right back."

He had already stepped away, grabbing the empty bottle, quickly but gently, from her hand as she said, "Okay. Thanks," to his recently departed back.

o o o

"There are three days, Josiah, that I consider to be the most important three days of my life. Of course there are other days that are also very important, but if I had to choose three days that are the most important, these would be those three. Those three days are, not in chronological order, the day that you were born, the day that I found Jesus Christ, and the day that your father came into my life."

o o o

She could feel the upper parts of her arms and the back part of her legs begin to shake. She had, other than the brief period she had held on to the oak side table behind her, been holding her beer bottle close to her body, one hand at its base and two fingers of the other hand on its neck. Without it, her hands now felt awkward. She pushed half of each into the pockets of her jeans, as she had seen him do. She looked around the room.

"Beer's out, I guess," he said upon finally returning. "I brought you something else."

"Oh, okay."

"Cheers."

"Cheers. This tastes good. What is it?"

"I don't even know."

"Oh."

"Like it?"

"Yes. It tastes really good."

" . "
. . .

" . "
. . .

"Want another one?"

"Okay."

"Be right back."

o o o

"Alien abductions, typically speaking, Josiah, are seen as scary, trau-matic events. But there was nothing scary or traumatic about my alien abduction experience. Your father, who was my alien abduc-tor, and who was on a research mission for the planet Parnuckle, which is one of the job duties of the planet Parnuckle's Keymaster of Gozer, was very kind and very gentle throughout the entire event."

o o o

"Here you go. Cheers."

"Cheers. What is that you're drinking?"

"Oh, this is 7-Up. I have a soccer match tomorrow, so I'm taking it easy."

"A soccer match?"

"Yeah."

"Where?"

"Here."

"Oh."

"..."

"..."

"Ready for another?"

"Can we maybe sit down first?"

"Sure."

"Great. That's better."

"..."

"I..."

"What?"

"Nothing. I... nothing."

"..."

"..."

"Ready now?"

"Okay."

"Okay. Be right back."

o o o

"There was no pain or discomfort. I didn't feel a thing. One moment I was in my dorm room, studying for a biology midterm, and the next moment I was asleep, though I didn't know, of course, at that moment, that I was asleep, because we are never really aware that we have fallen asleep, it's just something that happens. And then I woke up."

o o o

"Here you go."

"Thank you."

"No problem. I was just thinking."

"What were you thinking?"

"How crazy it is seeing you here."

"Yeah."

"Yeah. When I saw you, I didn't really believe it. I was like, 'It can't be her.' But then it was you. It's all sort of . . . I don't know . . . surreal."

"Yeah?"

"Yeah."

"Can I ask you something?"

"Okay."

"How come you never talked to me like this in high school?"

"What do you mean?"

"I mean, you never talked to me like this in high school. You talked to lots of other girls, but never really me at all. Why is that?"

"I don't know."

"You don't know?"

"Not really. I guess I was just shy."

"You didn't seem shy."

"I didn't?"

"No. You had all those girlfriends. And all the girls liked you."

"*Allll* the girls?"

"*Yeeeeahhhh*. I mean . . . you seemed so confident."

"I don't know. I guess . . . around those girls, it was easy to be confident. It was like . . . I didn't care what they thought. You know?"

"Sort of."

"Girls like you were different."

"Girls like me?"

"Yeah. You know, like . . . pretty . . . but smart."

"Yeah?"

"Yeah. With girls like you . . . it was like you could see through me."

"I never thought you even noticed me."

"I noticed you."

"You did?"

"Of course I did."

"Yeah?"

"Yeah."

"Come here."

o o o

"When I woke up, I was on the Parnucklian spaceship. As I said, I hadn't felt a thing. The spaceship, or the room I was in on the spaceship, was warm and dark. But it was not scary. It was dark, but there was a glow. At first, I could only hear his voice, but as my eyes got used to the dark glow, I could see him, first just his shape, and, eventually, everything. He was very handsome. Like you. Parnucklians look just the same as Earthlings. They are built exactly the same, but they are often more handsome."

o o o

"You're a good kisser."

"I am?"

"Yeah."

"Thanks. You're a good kisser, too."

"Thanks. Ready for another drink?"

"Actually, I feel really tired."

"Oh. Do you want to lay down for a while?"

"Yeah. That sounds good."

"You can lay down for a while and then we'll call your room-mate."

"Okay."

o o o

"Because he was on a research mission for the planet Parnuckle, he asked me many questions about the planet Earth. He started by asking me what we called different things, such as trees and water and rocks. He spoke perfect English. Communication was not at all difficult. He was also interested in our education system."

o o o

"Mmm. What are you doing?"

"It's okay."

"Mmm."

"You like that?"

"I . . . yeah. Mmm."

"Oh, baby."

"I . . ."

"You're so fucking hot."

"I . . ."

"I want you so fucking bad."

"I . . . Mmm."

"You like that, baby?"

"Yes. I . . . Mmm."

"Do you want me inside you baby?"

"I . . . I don't know."

"I want to be inside you, baby. I want to fuck you so bad."

"I . . ."

"Do you want me to fuck you?"

"I . . . I don't know."

"Do you want me to make you come?"

"I . . . Mmm . . . I don't know."

"Tell me you want me to fuck you."

"I . . . Mmm. Mmm. I want you to fuck me."

"Tell me you want me to make you come."

"I . . . I want you to . . . I want you to make me come."

"Tell me you love me."

"I love you."

"Oh, baby."

"Mmmm."

"Ohhhh."

"Do you . . . Do . . . Should you use a condom?"

"I don't have one. Ohhh."

"But . . ."

"Is it your first?"

"It . . ."

"Ohh. Is it?"

"Mmm. Yes."

"Then it's okay."

"I . . ."

"Okay?"

"I . . . Okay."

"Ohhhh."

"Mmm. Ah! Mmm."

"Oh. Oh. Oh."

"Ah. Ow. Ah."

"Oh, baby."

o o o

"Then, he began to tell me about his home planet, Parnuckle. He came closer to me and told me, in a tender voice, to close my eyes and be still. He placed his hand on the top of my head, and when he did I could see a vision, in my mind, with my eyes closed. I could see a vision of beautiful fields and mountains and lakes. But these were not beautiful golden fields or beautiful purple mountains or beautiful shimmering blue lakes as we are used to, and which are beautiful enough as it is, but rather these fields and mountains and lakes, and whatever else I was shown, as there were other things, it's just that these are the examples that I can remember, keeping in mind that visions, like dreams, are very abstract and difficult to remember, were filled with all colors all at once, all the colors of the rainbow, but even more, as there seemed to be colors that we are unaware of and cannot comprehend with our limited minds, and there were cities vibrant with life and color and people who were all smiling and happy and handsome."

o o o

"Do you need a ride home?"
"Oh . . . uh . . . yeah . . . yeah, I guess."
"Be right back."

o o o

"He then removed his hand from the top of my head and placed it on my chest. He told me to open my eyes and when I did he told me that I had been chosen. I had been chosen to be the one person on this planet with knowledge of the beautiful planet of Parnuckle with its beautiful people, and this gift was something that was to be cherished and to be protected because it was something wonderful but also something dangerous, though he didn't explain that part all that thoroughly, but I suppose it has something to do with the destructive nature of man's insatiable desire for consumption, and I expressed my thanks for this gift by thanking him over and over and telling him how honored I was to be the one to receive this gift, and then he leaned in close and told me that I had one gift yet to receive and I started to tell him that that was unnecessary as he had done enough already but he silenced me by adding additional pressure from his hand to my chest and once again told me to close my eyes."

o o o

"Who are you?"

"I'm Mark."

"What are you . . . what do you want?"

"Drew asked me to give you a ride home."

SIX

BEFORE JOSIAH COULD learn about the life and works of Jesus Christ, he first had to learn about God, who was the father of Jesus Christ, otherwise the life and works of Jesus Christ would be out of context. So Josiah spent his first day of home-schooling in the home of Johnson Davis, which began shortly after Josiah finished his breakfast, which his mother believed to be his first breakfast consisting of food other than chocolate, though it was not, and during which he could think about very little except Bree, learning about how God created the world and all of the plants and the animals and even the dinosaurs and eventually the people, beginning with Adam and Eve, who were naked. Josiah's mother told Josiah that Adam was a man and was also the very first man and therefore he was the only man like himself on the planet, making things very lonely for Adam. There were birds and there were sheep and there were lions and tigers and probably bears and even bugs and fish but there was no one else or no thing else that looked like Adam, even though Adam, unlike the other animals, was made in God's image, meaning that Adam looked similar to what God would look like if he were able to see him, however Adam, like us, could not see God, only hear his voice, which was a great and intimidating voice, so that all that Adam could see, when looking around, was that he was the only one of his kind.

Josiah's mother also told Josiah that, after some time, God decided to create a woman for Adam, to be friends with and marry and have children with, so he waited until Adam was asleep and took out one of his ribs, magically, so that it did not hurt Adam, and turned that rib, magically, into a woman, similar to a man but different, named Eve, who, just as Adam was the first and only man, became the first and only woman. Josiah's mother told Josiah that Adam, who was a good man, loved Eve very much, but that Eve, who was not a good woman, had tempted Adam to do something very wrong; had corrupted him, and Josiah's mother told Josiah that he should be careful and immediately tell his mother if anyone ever tried to tempt him to do something he shouldn't be doing.

Josiah nodded repeatedly as his mother said this, though his thoughts were focused on Bree, as they had been ever since Josiah's mother had mentioned Eve being naked, which reminded him of times when Bree had been naked, or partially naked, such as the time that she had come into his room with a soccer jersey and no pants and the time that she had worn the green bikini with white swirlies, which were the only two times that Bree had been naked or partially naked that Josiah was aware of or had witnessed firsthand.

Josiah thought about Bree throughout the remainder of the day's lesson, his thoughts—other than those about Bree being naked—mostly dealing either with what had happened between he and Bree two nights earlier, which, when Josiah thought about it, mostly confused him, or Josiah's thoughts dealt with what would happen between he and Bree during the coming weekend, when Bree would return to the home of Johnson Davis.

On Wednesday evening of that week, while Johnson Davis and Josiah's mother and Josiah were sitting at the dinner table, Josiah's mother asked Johnson Davis if he would like it if she and Josiah were to come with him to pick up Bree from her school that Friday, but Johnson Davis informed Josiah's mother that Bree would not be coming to stay with them for the next two weekends, as she had gone with her mother, the former wife of Johnson Davis, to visit various family members in Chicago.

Since the previous Saturday, when Josiah had last seen Bree— despite the fact that when he thought about Bree he sometimes became angry or upset—Josiah had missed Bree very much and was very much looking forward to seeing her again and possibly speaking to her about the things that had happened between them and what they meant, so after hearing that Bree would not be coming back for the next two weekends, meaning that Josiah would not be able to see Bree for sixteen days, Josiah no longer felt hungry for his dinner, which consisted of a cheeseburger and a large pickle.

o o o

That morning, Josiah had written a letter to his father. It went like this:

Dear Father,

I am writing to ask you for help. I think I am in love with the girl I was telling you about. I think about her all day long. I hope maybe someday we can be married and come and live with you. But I don't know if she loves me and I don't know what to say to her when I see her. Also, I don't think my other mother likes her. What would you do?

Hope everything is okay there. Say hello to my real mother.

Love,
Josiah

o o o

Josiah felt a very empty feeling in his stomach when he went to bed that night, to the point that he did not feel like doing anything, including brushing his teeth or washing his face or getting into bed, but rather Josiah sat in a chair in his room and stared at a picture that he had drawn the day before on a piece of binder paper of Bree kicking a soccer ball. Josiah stared at the picture for several hours until he eventually fell asleep and then later woke himself up by falling out of the chair onto the floor and then dragged himself into his bed and fell asleep until the next morning, which was the beginning of the fifteenth day before he would see Bree again.

On the fourteenth day before Josiah would see Bree again, which was a Friday, during the three-hour period between Josiah's morning lesson and his afternoon lesson, Josiah was sent to the bedroom of Johnson Davis to retrieve a pair of gloves while Johnson Davis, who had no classes on Fridays, was pruning roses in his yard. As Josiah passed through the bedroom on his way to the closet, Josiah saw a stack of magazines sitting on top of a small table against one wall of the bedroom. The magazine on top of the stack had a picture of a man wearing a suit on its cover and next to the picture of a man wearing a suit were large yellow letters that spelled out, "Ten Tips to Make Her Go Home With You." This made Josiah think of Bree, and Josiah very much liked the idea of making Bree go home with him, even though he was not precisely sure what that meant, and Josiah very much desired to read what the magazine had to say about making Bree go home with him, but Josiah needed to bring to Johnson Davis the pair of gloves, as Johnson Davis often became angry and frustrated while pruning roses and would want his gloves right away, so Josiah left the magazine on top of the stack of magazines on the small table.

On the thirteenth day before Josiah would once again see Bree, he returned to the bedroom of Johnson Davis while Johnson Davis was taking a nap on the couch, which he often did on a Saturday, and Josiah's mother was taking a midday shower. Josiah lifted the magazine from the top of the stack of magazines and carried it into his bedroom where he began to flip through the pages until he found the article that provided the Ten Tips to Make Her Go Home With You. Josiah quickly read the ten tips, which were as follows:

Tip #1: Take a bath or shower
Tip #2: Arrive on time

Tip #3: Give her a thoughtful gift
Tip #4: Be a gentleman
Tip #5: Listen to her and ask questions
Tip #6: Compliment her
Tip #7: Prepare for the conversation
Tip #8: Pay for the date
Tip #9: The Goodnight Kiss
Tip #10: I'll call you

On the eighth day before Josiah would see Bree again, after a lesson that several times mentioned Eve being naked—Josiah's mother choosing to spend a great deal of time lingering on the topic of Adam and Eve and the Garden of Eden—Josiah drew another picture of Bree, on the back of the paper on which he had drawn the picture of Bree kicking a soccer ball, which he kept hidden between the mattress and the box spring of his bed, where Josiah also kept the letters that he wrote to his father. In this picture, Bree was not kicking a soccer ball, but instead was sitting in a chair. In the picture, Bree was naked. Josiah had never actually seen Bree completely naked, but he drew what he thought Bree would look like if she were completely naked, based on the two times that Josiah had seen Bree partially naked. In fact, for each of the eight days until Josiah again saw Bree, he drew a picture of Bree naked, usually drawing the pictures in the afternoons after his lessons. In one picture, Bree was lying naked on a bed. In another, Bree was naked and jumping. In the last picture Josiah drew, Bree was standing naked next to Josiah, Josiah having also drawn himself. In the picture, Josiah was also naked, and was holding Bree's hand.

Johnson Davis woke Josiah up very early on the fifth day before Josiah would see Bree again and told Josiah to get ready for a big day. Josiah put on a pair of jeans and pulled a sweatshirt over his t-shirt and went downstairs, where Johnson Davis told him that he couldn't very well do much in an outfit like that and to go back up and change. Josiah, noticing that Johnson Davis was wearing a t-shirt and a pair of shorts, went back upstairs and took off his sweatshirt and took off his jeans and put back on the pair of shorts he had been wearing in bed and went back downstairs, where Johnson Davis asked him if he was going to change out of his loafers, to which Josiah responded that they were the only shoes he had. Johnson Davis grunted and told Josiah to follow him and walked through the living room and out the front door and down the front steps. Josiah followed, passing through the door as Johnson Davis, having descended the steps, made his way down the front walkway, calling to Josiah to shut the door behind him. Johnson Davis, having reached the sidewalk, then took off running, his legs stretched long, his shoulders arched back, calling to Josiah, "No dilly-dallying."

Josiah began to run, running down the front walkway and turning and running along the sidewalk in the direction Johnson Davis had gone. By the time Josiah had reached the sidewalk and began to gain momentum, Johnson Davis was almost to the next block. Josiah began to tire almost immediately. He had never run more than a few hundred feet at a time, and those times had been few and far between.

By the time Josiah reached the next block, Johnson Davis was nearly two blocks away, and was clearly getting further and further ahead. Josiah stopped, out of breath, and watched as Johnson Davis looked back, saw Josiah, and then turned and began sprinting, his shoulders no longer arched back, his head down, his arms swinging, and then turning at the end of the block and disappearing from sight.

Josiah began to again jog, but stopped and walked after only a few yards. He walked to the end of the block and crossed the street to the next. He had walked on for only a moment when he heard Johnson Davis's footsteps coming toward him. Josiah turned in time to see Johnson Davis round the corner of the block from which Josiah had just come, still sprinting. Johnson Davis sprinted past Josiah, slowing slightly and reaching out with the intent of ruffling Josiah's hair, but Josiah, seeing Johnson Davis's outstretched hand, stepped back quickly, stumbling and nearly falling.

"No walking now," Johnson Davis said, turning to face Josiah, kicking his knees up and running in place. "This isn't a holiday."

Johnson Davis, knees still kicking, then began to slowly and deliberately jog a circle around Josiah, exclaiming, "You see what I did? I went around the whole block and caught back up. Came up behind you." Josiah stood still, turning his head over his shoulder as far as possible in one direction and watching Johnson Davis as he crossed in front of him, following as far as he could turn his head over the other shoulder and losing sight of him as he passed behind. "Come on now, we're nearly there," Johnson Davis continued, adding, "We'll make a man of you, yet," as he broke from his circle and continued down the sidewalk in the same direction.

Johnson Davis ran along, slower this time, noticeably adjusting his speed, keeping Josiah, who jogged laboriously behind, consistently between 100 and 120 feet to his rear. They traveled four additional blocks before Johnson Davis again turned, this time to his left, crossing the empty street and entering the parking lot of a local diner.

Johnson Davis waited for Josiah at the entrance to the diner and then led him inside, Josiah loudly struggling to breathe, bent with abdominal pain, and Johnson Davis, breathing heavily himself and glistening with sweat but beaming with delight. Josiah followed Johnson Davis, who followed the hostess, who led them to a booth along the wall of the diner, where Johnson Davis and Josiah sat and where Johnson Davis, after ordering both coffee and toast for he and Josiah, began to speak to Josiah about the most important thing besides a healthy mind.

"Do you know, Josiah," Johnson Davis asked, "what is the most important thing other than a healthy mind?"

Josiah shrugged.

"A healthy mind is important, no doubt," Johnson Davis continued. "Vital. We couldn't function. In fact, we wouldn't be who we are—wouldn't be human—without a healthy mind. Do you agree?"

"Yes," Josiah answered.

"But beyond that. Beyond a healthy mind, what is the most important thing? What might it be?"

"Love?" Josiah guessed.

"A healthy body," Johnson Davis said. "Without a healthy body, we're just as useless as we are without a healthy mind. Wouldn't you say?"

Josiah shrugged.

"You know, Josiah," Johnson Davis said, "that I was nearly an Olympian?"

"Yes."

"Twice."

"Yes."

"There was a time in my life when I put all of my time and effort into athletics. Into being physically fit."

Johnson Davis paused and looked at Josiah, as if waiting for agreement before moving on. Josiah simply stared back.

"At this time of my life, Josiah," Johnson Davis continued, "as a professor of Latin American history—you are aware, Josiah, that I am a professor of Latin American history?"

"Yes."

"At the community college, here in town?"

Josiah nodded.

"She told you this, your mother?" asked Johnson Davis

Josiah nodded.

"Good, I'm glad," said Johnson Davis. "At any rate, at this time of my life, as a professor, most of my time and effort is devoted to academics. To the mind."

Johnson Davis again paused and looked at Josiah. Josiah stared back.

"But I still find the time," Johnson Davis continued, "to culti-vate the healthy body. To remain physically fit. In fact, I see the two—mind and body—as interconnected. Very deeply and care-fully interconnected. Without one, the other would suffer."

Johnson Davis looked at Josiah. Josiah stared back.

"That, Josiah," Johnson Davis continued, "is why I've woken you up this morning and had you follow me to this diner. While your mother sees to your academics, if that's what she wishes to call it, I will be seeing to your physical education. To the cultivation of your healthy body."

Johnson Davis bit off a chunk of one of his pieces of toast and began to chew it as he spoke. "You see, Josiah, while it's a fine thing that you receive your studies at home, there are certain things that you miss out on by not attending a traditional educational institution. One of those being structured daily exercise. So from this point on, you and I will be getting up early in the morning—at least some mornings—and doing things like we did today. Like running, or other various forms of exercise.

"Now you may be wondering, Josiah, if this means that you will have less time during the day to spend on your studies, with your mother, and it does not. Your mother and I have put our heads together and modified your schedule. You will simply have to work longer into the evening on certain days."

Johnson Davis paused to finish chewing and swallow another chunk of toast and continued, "Besides physical exercise, Josiah, by not attending an educational institution you are missing out on the opportunity to participate in organized sports. Are you interested in sports, Josiah?"

Josiah shrugged.

"Have you ever played a sport?"

"No."

"Do you have a favorite sport? One that you like to watch on television?"

"No."

"I'll tell you, Josiah, when I was your age, I loved sports. I couldn't get enough of them. I played every sport offered at my high school. Baseball, basketball, badminton, track, tennis, football, soccer, you name it. I sometimes went to two practices a day. It wasn't until college that my focus became more specifically track. It's track and field, you know, that I was nearly an Olympian in?"

"Yes."

"I was a sprinter. I ran the 100- and 200-meter events."

"Yes."

"Anyway, what I'm getting at, Josiah, is that by missing out on these opportunities, by not attending a traditional educational institution and missing out on the opportunity to participate in organized sports, you are missing out, in my opinion, on the opportunity to be a well-rounded individual."

Johnson Davis looked at Josiah. Josiah stared back.

"And a well-rounded individual," Johnson Davis continued, "is one that is successful." Johnson Davis took a sip of his coffee and added, "In most cases. Usually."

After Johnson Davis finished his first cup of coffee and his second cup of coffee and his two pieces of toast, during which time Josiah drank half of his own cup of coffee, which he thought tasted terrible, and ate most of one piece of his toast, all but the crust, Johnson Davis paid the bill and led Josiah out of the restaurant where he once again took off running, shouting "This way!" at Josiah behind him, who began jogging in the direction Johnson Davis had gone and whose abdominal pain was still present, causing Josiah to jog in a strange, hunched-over, off-center position.

Johnson Davis led Josiah to a local park. The local park included a small playground area. The small playground area consisted of a sandbox and a slide and monkey bars and swings and a merry-go-round. Johnson Davis and Josiah spent the next two hours at the playground area. There were no children playing because it was so early in the morning. Johnson Davis, over the course of the two hours, put Josiah through a training regimen utilizing the various attractions of the playground area, beginning with the slide, which Johnson Davis forced Josiah to run up. Johnson Davis stood on the platform at the top of the slide and Josiah stood at the bottom and Johnson Davis shouted, "Run up that slide!" at Josiah, which Josiah attempted several times to do, sliding back down before reaching the top—the metal slide with the morning dew on it being very slippery and the loafers that Josiah's mother had returned to Josiah after being released from the group home and which still fit him having very little sole left—with Johnson Davis shouting exclamations, "Up, Nancy-pants! Get up that slide!" or "Come on, Sissy-Susan! Show some effort!" until Josiah finally, on the eighteenth attempt, made his way up the slide and onto the platform, where Johnson Davis patted Josiah on the shoulder and told him, because he appeared so exhausted, that he could go and rest on one of the swings for five minutes before beginning the next challenge.

The next challenge involved the sandbox, inside which Johnson Davis stood, facing Josiah, who sat slumped in one of the three swings hanging from the crossbar of the swing set. Johnson Davis stood with his feet apart and with one fist pressed against his ribs, the other hand holding his watch, which Johnson Davis had removed from his wrist and now stared at. After Josiah had been sitting in the swing for five minutes, Johnson Davis shouted, "Time's up! In the sandbox! Now!" Josiah pushed himself out of the swing, dropping a few inches to the ground, and began walking toward the sandbox.

"Let's go! On the double!" Johnson Davis shouted. Josiah stopped walking and stared at Johnson Davis. "Now! Let's move! Shake a leg!" Johnson Davis added. Josiah then jogged the twenty or so feet to the sandbox, where Johnson Davis, once Josiah was inside, instructed Josiah to bury himself in under ten minutes. When Josiah simply stared at Johnson Davis, Johnson Davis repeated, "Ten minutes! Let's go! All but the head!"

It took Josiah seventeen minutes to bury himself. During the final seven minutes, Johnson Davis, who had done little more than count down the minutes expired during the first ten minutes, shouted things at Josiah such as, "You're over the time! You're dead! Never stop! You're dead!"

The remainder of Josiah's training regimen for the day was more conventional, consisting of crossing the monkey bars and doing chin-ups on the monkey bars and doing push-ups in the sand and sit-ups in the sand, other than the final twenty minutes, which were split between Johnson Davis standing on the merry-go-round and having Josiah hold on to one bar and spin Johnson Davis around by running in a circle, and Johnson Davis having Josiah push him on the swing, incessantly demanding that he be pushed, "Higher! Higher!"

The third day before Josiah would see Bree again was also Josiah's sixteenth birthday. On Josiah's sixteenth birthday, Johnson Davis gave Josiah the gift of one hundred dollars that he could spend on anything he wanted. When Josiah had first seen the Ten Tips to Make Her Go Home With You, he had been worried, as two of the ten tips, specifically Tip #3 and Tip #8, would require money, and Josiah had no money of his own. Josiah had worried that this would hurt his chances of making Bree want to go home with him, so he was relieved when he received the one hundred dollars that he could spend on whatever he liked.

Tip #3 To Make Her Go Home with You had suggested that Josiah give Bree a thoughtful gift. Before receiving the one hundred dollars, Josiah had been imagining how he could possibly make a thoughtful gift to give Bree using unwanted items around the house, such as burned-out light bulbs or empty toilet paper rolls, but after receiving the one hundred dollars, Josiah quickly asked his mother to please drive him to the local mall so he could look for things to possibly spend his money on.

As Josiah and Josiah's mother drove to the local mall, in the car of Johnson Davis, as Johnson Davis had persuaded Josiah's mother to sell her own car and simply use his when she needed it, Josiah's mother asked Josiah what he might like to buy with his one hundred dollars.

"I don't know," responded Josiah, staring straight ahead through the windshield.

"Do you have any ideas?" asked Josiah's mother, giving quick glances Josiah's way but keeping, for the most part, her eyes on the road and both hands on the wheel, as the car of Johnson Davis was much wider and much longer than her car had been and made her nervous. "Anything you've had your eye on?"

"No."

"No? Nothing you've been thinking about?"

"No."

"Okay. Any store in particular you'd like to try first?"

"I don't know." But Josiah did know, and did have an idea as to what he might spend his money on, but he was not precisely sure where such a store was precisely located, nor did he want to ask his mother where such a store was precisely located or discuss with her what on Earth he would possibly want to spend his money on at that particular store. Rather, Josiah simply directed his mother toward the mall in general.

After arriving at the local mall and parking Johnson Davis's car and making their way inside, Josiah and his mother walked slowly along the mildly crowded mall, looking from side to side at the various storefronts, with Josiah's mother incessantly suggesting that they go into this store or that store but Josiah continuing forward, shaking his head and showing little interest in her suggestions, until finally they arrived at Ted's Sporting Goods. Through the windows of the store Josiah could see a variety of clothing and equipment intended for use in various sporting activities, such as skies and ski poles and baseball bats and baseball gloves and biking helmets and running shoes and cleats and jerseys but Josiah was not interested in any of these items or the sports that they were associated with. Josiah crossed over the threshold and made his way inside the store, his mother following closely behind, her face skewed in confusion as she asked, "Is this the store you'd like to look in?" to which Josiah merely nodded his head, leading Josiah's mother to continue, "But dear, you don't play any sports."

"I know."

"And you've never really shown any interest in playing sports."

"I know."

"I mean, you never were that type of child. The sport type."

"I know."

"Not that I wouldn't support your involvement in sports, dear. You've just never shown an interest. Sports can be a good thing for a boy. They were very important in Mr. Davis's development, as you know."

Josiah nodded his head in acknowledgement.

"They," Josiah's mother continued, "meaning sports, specifically running, in Mr. Davis's case, track and field, as they call it, but any sport would apply, gave him a sense of direction, as you know. You, it just happens, never seemed to show an interest in that area. You, of course, as we've discussed often, are different."

Josiah again nodded his head in acknowledgement.

"However, as we've also discussed, more recently, in fact, the time has come for you to begin doing more normal things. Perhaps pursuing a sport can be good for you. I'm sure it will delight Mr. Davis."

Josiah's mother, still behind him, leaned forward over his shoulder so that he could see her face from the corner of his eye and asked, "Does this mean that you've taken an interest in playing sports? Any sport in particular?" but without answering Josiah walked toward the corner of the store.

The corner of the store to which Josiah led his mother was filled with various sizes and colors of soccer balls, all jammed into square cardboard packaging, as well as an assembled miniature soccer goal intended to be set up in a person's backyard, surrounded by boxes of miniature soccer goals not yet assembled, along with assorted soccer paraphernalia such as shin guards and gloves and various colors of shorts and jerseys, which reminded Josiah of Bree's Girls Varsity soccer jersey and the way that she looked in it, but it was not until Josiah looked more closely at the area of the corner of the store in which the soccer balls of various sizes and colors were stacked that Josiah knew that he had found what he was looking for.

o o o

Three days earlier, on the sixth day before Josiah would see Bree again, he had once again gone into the bedroom of Johnson Davis, while Johnson Davis was attempting to install a new hanging bookcase that he had purchased that day, and once again had spent some time looking at the magazine that contained the article with the Ten Tips to Make Her Go Home With You. When Josiah had first taken the magazine from the bedroom of Johnson Davis, several days earlier, Josiah had not been able to finish reading the article. In fact, he had only been able to read the descriptions of the first three tips and part of the fourth before hearing Johnson Davis awaken from his nap and stride heavily into the kitchen to look for something to eat, causing Josiah to place the magazine back onto the top of the stack of magazines and run from the bedroom of Johnson Davis and down the hall into his own bedroom where he had jumped onto the bed and pretended to be taking a nap himself.

Therefore, Josiah had returned, on the sixth day before he would see Bree again, wishing to read the rest of the article, to the bedroom of Johnson Davis, where he spent over an hour and a half reading and then rereading the entire article. As Josiah returned down the hallway to his own room, full of ideas as to how to make Bree go home with him, even though he was still not precisely sure what that meant, though a bit more sure after having read and re-read the article, he looked beyond the door of his own room, in front of which he was now standing, and gazed down the hall toward the door of Bree's room. Josiah listened carefully, and could still hear the sound of the electric screwdriver and the occasional "Goddamnit" coming from the living room below.

Josiah was only in Bree's room for a moment before Johnson Davis began calling his name, needing, as it turned out, for Josiah to go and look in the garage to see if they had any more of these damn screws, and Bree's lights were off and her curtains drawn, making it difficult for Josiah to see the room in great detail, but he was able, with the light emanating from the hallway mixed with the sunlight pushing its way through the thin curtains, to see a series of at least ten to twelve posters of various sizes, all featuring the printed name, in various lettering styles, and pictures of, in various poses and engaged in various activities—usually involving either kicking or holding or chasing a soccer ball—someone named Brent Randolph.

o o o

When Josiah informed his mother that the thing he wanted to spend his one hundred dollars on, or at least a portion of his one hundred dollars, as the thing in question only cost thirty-five dollars, was an official Brent Randolph soccer ball, she looked at him incredulously and asked, "Honey, are you sure you want to buy a soccer ball?" to which Josiah responded, "Yes."

"But dear," Josiah's mother continued, pointing to a different ball on the rack, "you can get this ball, which is nearly exactly the same, except that it is not the official ball of Brent Randolph, for much less money."

"I need this one," Josiah answered quickly.

"But why, dear?" asked Josiah's mother, squinting and waiting for Josiah to respond, which he did not, instead looking down at the ball packaged in cardboard that he held in his hands. "Is it because of Bree? Because Bree has posters of this Brent Randolph in her room?" Josiah responded by nodding in affirmation. Josiah's mother, with a changed tone, asked, "Josiah, are you interested in playing soccer? Do you think that it may be something you'd enjoy doing?"

Josiah again did not respond. Josiah's mother continued, "Would you like me to sign you up to play soccer?"

Josiah raised his head and shook it from side to side. "No," he said.

"Then why do you want to spend your money," Josiah's mother asked, "or at least a portion of your money, on a soccer ball?"

"I'm going to give it to Bree," Josiah responded.

Shortly after Josiah and Josiah's mother returned home from the local mall, Josiah was called downstairs from his bedroom, where he had been admiring the gift he had bought for Bree and also imagining what her reaction would be when he gave it to her, to the dimly-lit dining room, where he found his mother and Johnson Davis sitting at the dining room table. Johnson Davis asked Josiah to please also take a seat, and once he had, Johnson Davis said to Josiah, "Josiah, your mother has told me that you spent a good part of your birthday money on a soccer ball for Bree."

Josiah responded by first turning his gaze from Johnson Davis to his mother and then back to Johnson Davis and then nodding his head in agreement.

"Now, Josiah," Johnson Davis continued, "when I—when we— gave you that money for your birthday, we were hoping that you would spend it on something nice or something enjoyable for yourself. Something that you would want."

"I want to give Bree a gift," Josiah said in response, which seemed to cause Johnson Davis's shoulders to stiffen.

"Josiah, dear," Josiah's mother said, "you shouldn't feel bad, or worry, about getting something for yourself, if that's something you're worried about, because it possibly somehow seems selfish or materialistic, because when someone gives you a gift, they do so because they want you to be happy, or maybe even love you, depending on the situation, but at the very least the person, or people, are getting you a gift because they like you and want you to be happy, unless they are doing it just because they want something from you, which sometimes happens.

"Or," Josiah's mother continued, "if you are worried about receiving a gift when someone else, namely Bree is not, you must remember that everyone has their time to receive gifts, either on their own birthday or on an anniversary or wedding day or in congratulation for landing a new job, the last few of which not really pertaining to you, as much, having just turned sixteen, but the birthday of course, being relevant, especially now, given that you've just celebrated one, and a special one at that, or even something like a high school graduation, as far as occasions for gifts that pertain to you, being sixteen, and something, by the way, that you'll be achieving soon enough, congratulations in advance, and everyone, getting back to your possible worries, has these occasions of their own, gift-receiving occasions, that is, and therefore everyone receives plenty of gifts at those respective times, just as you are receiving a gift, the gift of one hundred dollars, at this respective time, which is your time, but not Bree's, and that gift, just as any gift received by anyone, should be specifically for you, just as theirs should be specifically for them, and should be something that makes you, or them, happy. And then, of course, there are certain holidays, when everyone receives gifts at the same time."

Johnson Davis, who had been staring at his fiancée as she spoke, turned back to Josiah and said, "Why exactly, Josiah, do you wish to spend your money, or a portion of your money, on a gift for Bree?" to which Josiah quickly responded, "I like Bree," which caused Johnson Davis to press his downturned palms against the kitchen table, his fingertips and a portion of his fingers turning red, and say to Josiah, "What exactly, Josiah, do you mean when you say you like Bree?"

"I just like her," answered Josiah after a pause, shrugging his shoulders.

"What do you like about her?" said Josiah's mother quickly, abruptly leaning forward and placing one hand on the table. "Do you think she's pretty?"

"Yes," said Josiah.

"You think she's pretty?" asked Josiah's mother again.

"Yes. And nice," answered Josiah.

"You realize, Josiah," said Johnson Davis, "that Bree is much older than you."

"Actually—" Josiah's mother began before being cut off by Johnson Davis, who continued, to Josiah, "Well, actually, not *much* older, to tell the truth, but, relatively speaking, a fifteen—excuse me, sixteen—newly sixteen-year-old and a seventeen, nearly eighteen-year-old, you understand, can be *much* different, in a number of ways."

"That's very true," Josiah's mother began again, to Josiah, "and also, we must note, she is much more experienced than you, dear."

"That, I would think," said Johnson Davis with a heavy sigh, turning to his fiancée, "goes without saying, given my mention of the difference in age."

"Of course," replied Josiah's mother, "given the mention of the minimal difference in age, but we must take into consideration that Bree is especially experienced for a seventeen-year-old."

"Nearly eighteen."

"Nearly eighteen-year-old, who is especially experienced."

"While we're on the subject," said Johnson Davis, squaring his shoulders to his fiancée, "let's point out that Josiah is a bit less experienced, a bit more innocent, than your average sixteen-year-old."

"Newly sixteen."

"Newly sixteen-year-old."

"Not that that is necessarily a bad thing."

"Not necessarily a bad thing. Not the worst thing, but certainly, as we've discussed, too much innocence, too much sheltering, can be detrimental."

"As can too much experience, obviously."

"Certainly, fair enough, but in the long run, in the larger scheme …"

"What, in the long run?"

"There simply must be a balance, is what I'd like to point out. I think we can agree on that."

"Of course," replied Josiah's mother, "balance is critical."

Shortly after this, Josiah was asked to please return to his bedroom. Johnson Davis and Josiah's mother remained at the table, and from his bedroom Josiah could hear them, though he could not hear specifically what was being said, continue their conversation for nearly another hour.

The next morning, which was the second day before Josiah would see Bree again, Johnson Davis once again woke Josiah up very early and told him to get dressed and meet him in the backyard.

When Josiah reached the backyard, he found Johnson Davis standing on the green grass, his feet spread apart and his fists pressed against his ribs. Johnson Davis led Josiah in the performance of various exercises, including jumping jacks and push-ups and sit-ups and toe touches, all the while berating Josiah for his weaknesses and inabilities—in an attempt to motivate him—as well as orating on the importance and value of proper stretching and exercise, after which Johnson Davis told Josiah to go up and get the ball he had bought and bring it down and they would have themselves a game.

Josiah stood still, other than his heavy breathing as a result of the exercises and stretches he had just performed, unwilling to go and get Bree's gift and bring it down and remove its cardboard wrapping with Brent Randolph's picture and kick it around Johnson Davis's backyard and get it all dirty and grass-stained.

"Go on," Johnson Davis said.

Josiah continued to stand still, looking at Johnson Davis.

"Go on, Josiah," Johnson Davis said, "we'll have a game."

Josiah stood, not moving.

"Come on, Josiah. Get the ball and we'll play a little. I dragged Bree's old goal out." Josiah turned around and looked in the direction that Johnson Davis had pointed. At the other end of the yard was a goal, about Josiah's height, constructed of several connected red pipes and a net made of white rope. One of the poles, the one that constituted the goal's right edge, was slightly bent.

"She took the balls with her," Johnson Davis continued. "Go get yours and we'll play a little."

Josiah turned back to Johnson Davis. He shook his head.

"Why not?" Johnson Davis asked.

Josiah did not answer.

"Why not?" Johnson Davis repeated as he stepped toward Josiah, adding, "Remember our little conversation. About competitive activities? And a healthy body? About the importance? Well, here we are. Now, I'm delighted that you decided to spend a portion of your birthday money on a soccer ball. Let's put it to good use, shouldn't we?"

Josiah stared at Johnson Davis.

"Let's put that ball to good use," Johnson Davis said. "Let's go get it."

Josiah shook his head.

"Let's have some fun with it," Johnson Davis said.

Josiah shook his head.

"Now, why not, Josiah?" Johnson Davis said. "Why shouldn't we?"

"It's a gift," Josiah said.

"A gift?"

"Yes."

"For Bree?"

"Yes."

"Now, Josiah, we've talked about this, haven't we? I thought we'd discussed this. Bree has plenty of soccer balls. She must have taken ten of them out of that garage with her to her mother's. Now, the money I gave you, that was intended for you to enjoy. For you to benefit from. You should be the one enjoying that soccer ball."

Josiah stared at Johnson Davis.

"Why not go up and get your ball and we'll get some enjoyment out of it? Bree has plenty of those balls."

Josiah shook his head. Johnson Davis moved closer to Josiah and placed a hand on Josiah's shoulder. "Now, Josiah," Johnson Davis said, "I must insist that you giving that ball, which you bought with your birthday money, to my daughter, is inappropriate. As Bree's father, I find it unnecessary and inappropriate. I must refuse."

Josiah stared at Johnson Davis.

"I must refuse," Johnson Davis continued. "Now if you don't want that ball for yourself, that's fine. I will take you to the store where you got it and you can exchange it for something else. Otherwise, go on up and get it and we'll play around with it a bit."

Josiah stared at Johnson Davis.

"Either way, Josiah," Johnson Davis said, "I am not allowing you to give that ball to Bree."

Josiah went upstairs to his room and opened his closet door and pulled out the Brent Randolph soccer ball that he had bought for Bree, still surrounded by its cardboard packaging. He then stuffed it back into the closet, hiding it under three coats that Josiah pulled off of their hangers, and went downstairs and out into the backyard where he told Johnson Davis that he could not find the ball.

"You can't find it?"

"No."

"What do you mean, you can't find it?"

"I can't find it."

"Did you look?"

"Yes."

"Everywhere?"

"Yes."

"Are you sure, Josiah, that you're not just telling me that you can't find it because you don't want to play with it because you want to give it to Bree?"

"No."

"No?"

"No. I looked."

"Well, then maybe I should go up and help you look." Johnson Davis then stormed across the yard and into the house and up the stairs, Josiah several steps behind him, and into Josiah's room, where Johnson Davis, after quickly glancing around the room, pausing for a split second to admire the large poster of the man running and sweating, opened the closet door and wiped the three coats away with his hand and picked up the ball and said to Josiah, "Here it is right here. It was right here all along," and then Johnson Davis, with one long pull, removed the cardboard packaging that had surrounded the ball and tossed it aside, saying to Josiah, "I guess you didn't look hard enough. Let's go," before exiting Josiah's room and returning down the stairs and out into the yard.

SEVEN

O N THE DAY that Josiah would once again see Bree, after his morning lesson, Josiah took an especially long bath. Much longer, in fact, than the normal duration of his baths. An hour later, he also took a shower, which itself was also longer in duration than Josiah's normal showers. Tip #1 To Make Her Go Home with You had ordered that Josiah take a bath or shower. Josiah, as it was, regularly took showers, and also regularly took baths. At the age of four, Josiah had informed his mother, one evening at bath time, that because he was Parnucklian, and because Parnucklians, as Josiah's mother had a year earlier begun telling Josiah, did not need to take baths because on Parnuckle there was no dirt, he also did not need to take a bath, to which Josiah's mother responded, after reminding Josiah that he was *part*-Parnucklian, that though Parnucklians did not *need* to take baths, they often did take baths, just for the pleasure of them, usually in beautiful lakes or streams, and that likewise Josiah should try to enjoy his baths, adding that besides, while the planet Parnuckle has no dirt, the planet Earth certainly does, and that Josiah would need to be sure to wash all of the dirt off his body.

Six years later, Josiah's mother told Josiah that while he was part-Parnucklian and Parnucklians often took baths, just for the pleasure of them, he was also part-Earthling, and Earthlings typically prefer to take showers, for reasons pertaining both to time management and to finances, and being that, though he was equal parts Parnucklian to parts Earthling, he spent proportionally more—technically all—of his time on Earth as opposed to on Parnuckle, and the number of days in a week being an odd number, it only made sense that Josiah would take showers for four days of the week and baths for three. Therefore, from that time forward, other than during Josiah's two years in the group home, where he was only able to take showers, Josiah took baths on Thursdays, Fridays, and Sundays and showers on Mondays, Tuesdays, Wednesdays, and Saturdays.

The day that Josiah would once again see Bree, however, being a special day, and one that Josiah had been looking forward to, Josiah decided, just for good measure, to take one of each, and also decided to soap and scrub and shampoo more thoroughly than usual.

o o o

The night before, Josiah had spent nearly two hours in his room reviewing the notes he had made over the course of the last several days. Tip #7 To Make Her Go Home With You had suggested that Josiah prepare for his conversation with Bree, which he had done by creating a list of questions that he could ask Bree, as Tip #5 To Make Her Go Home With You had also suggested that Josiah listen to Bree and ask her questions. The questions that Josiah had come up with were as follows:

-How is your soccer season going?
-How do you like being a senior?
-Do you like the lunches at your school?
-Do you like your classes?
-Which class is your favorite?
-Do you prefer winter, fall, summer, or spring?
-Have you seen any good movies lately?
-What is your favorite movie or TV show?
-What do you like most about Brent Randolph?
-What is your favorite flavor of ice cream?

-Do you prefer cats or dogs?

-Have you ever been to the zoo?

-What is your favorite color?

Over the course of an hour or so, Josiah had memorized each of the above questions and had practiced delivering them to Bree by looking into his bedroom mirror and repeating the questions over and over until they sounded just right. Josiah was beginning to feel prepared, but also knew that the hard part would be listening to what Bree had to say and then making up new questions that corresponded to the conversation.

Josiah had also prepared notes that pertained to Tip To Make Her Go Home With You #4 and Tip To Make Her Go Home With You #6, which were Be a Gentleman and Compliment Her, respectively. Josiah had made notes reminding him to be a gentleman by opening doors for Bree, by allowing her to pass through doors before him, by pulling out chairs for her to sit in, by not sitting until she had sat, and by complimenting her as much as possible, which overlapped with Tip #6, for which Josiah had also prepared a list:

-You look very pretty.

-I really like your soccer jersey.

-You have nice hair.

-I would like to see you play soccer.

-I like your eyes.

-Those are nice socks.

-I like your green bikini.

-Your face is very pretty.

-You have nice clothes.

-You always look very clean.

-I like it when you come into my room.

-I think I'm in love with you.

-I want you to fuck me.

Like the questions he had written, Josiah also memorized this list of compliments, and also practiced delivering them over and over in front of his bedroom mirror. Josiah was especially nervous about the last three compliments, especially the last two, and had decided that he would only use them if the situation seemed right and he felt up to it.

Finally, before turning out the light and going to bed, Josiah once again reviewed the list of Ten Tips to Make Her Go Home With You:

Tip #1: Take a bath or shower

Tip #2: Arrive on time

Tip #3: Give her a thoughtful gift

Tip #4: Be a gentleman

Tip #5: Listen to her and ask questions

Tip #6: Compliment her

Tip #7: Prepare for the conversation

Tip #8: Pay for the date

Tip #9: The Goodnight Kiss

Tip #10: I'll call you

Josiah would take both a bath and a shower in the morning. Arriving on time should be easy, as Bree would be coming to the home of Johnson Davis, where Josiah already would be, and if they were to go anywhere, such as out on a date, they would probably be getting a ride and be in the same car. Josiah had already bought Bree a thoughtful gift, and was pretty sure that Johnson Davis had hidden it somewhere in the garage and he would be able to find it, and he had already practiced being a gentleman and asking her questions and complimenting her, and by doing so, had prepared for the conversation. Luckily, including the tax, Josiah had only spent around forty of his one hundred dollars on Bree's gift, and therefore had plenty of money left over to pay for his and Bree's date. Josiah knew that Bree had a cellular phone, as he had seen her talking on it, but he did not know the number nor did he himself have a cellular phone. If he were to find out the number to Bree's phone, which was pink, he could conceivably call her by borrowing the phone of Johnson Davis, of which there were three in the house. This left the final tip, Tip #9, The Goodnight Kiss, which Josiah was the most anxious about.

o o o

When Josiah walked into his room after his shower, his mother was sitting on his bed, holding the sheets of paper upon which Josiah had copied the Ten Tips to Make Her Go Home With You and had listed his questions and compliments, all of which he had been again reviewing in the time between his bath and his shower and had left sitting on his bed.

Josiah looked at his mother. Her face looked curled up. She wore a white sundress with pink dots. She held the papers in her hand as if about to crumple them into a ball. She stood.

"What is this?" Josiah's mother asked.

Josiah said nothing.

"What is it?"

Josiah said nothing. Josiah's mother held the papers up, shuffled them in her hands, gazing at them.

"Who do you want to fuck you?" she asked. "Who do you think you're in love with?" Josiah did not answer. "Who?" she asked again. She grabbed the collar of his shirt, twisting it in her fingers so that it tightened around his neck.

"Who?"

When Josiah again did not answer, Josiah's mother said, "Well I know who. I know who," and Josiah's mother let go of his collar and brushed past him into the hallway, where she began to call for Johnson Davis, who entered looking dumbfounded and who spent nearly a minute staring at the papers that Josiah's mother had handed him.

"What is this?" Johnson Davis said.

"What does it look like?" Josiah's mother said.

"Dating tips," Johnson Davis said.

"It's her," Josiah's mother said, "your daughter."

"What my daughter?"

"He wants to date her. Wants to fuck her. Thinks he's in love with her."

"None of this says anything about her."

"Oh, come on. The soccer ball. Now this. Keep her away from him."

"Josiah," Johnson Davis said to Josiah, "are these questions, these . . . things . . . for Bree?"

Josiah shook his head.

"Of course he's not going to tell you," Josiah's mother said, "Who else could it be?"

"Dear, I share your concern," Johnson Davis said, "I really do, especially with some of the content here. But none of this proves anything, in regards to Bree."

"We should search their rooms."

"Search their rooms?"

"Yes."

"Now, dear, I'm not saying I'm opposed to searching a child's room. I'm really not. I happen to feel it's the right of every parent to search their child's room—perhaps their responsibility. But as far as we know, Bree hasn't done anything wrong. We don't know what these papers are about. We have no cause. This is America. If you want to know the truth, this actually may be a good thing. What you have to understand about men, dear—about boys becoming men—is that a whole new world is opening up to them. A whole new world is opening up to Josiah, right now, and a bit of fantasizing, a bit of imagining, is natural. In fact, if that's what we're dealing with, I have to say I'm glad to see it."

"Well, I'm not," Josiah's mother said. "I'm not at all. I don't trust her. She's corrupting my son."

"We don't know that."

"Let's search just *his* room, then."

"Would that make you feel better?"

"Yes, it would."

"Very well, then," Johnson Davis said. "Josiah, I'm going to need you to wait in the hall for a moment."

Twelve minutes after Josiah had been sent into the hall, once Johnson Davis and Josiah's mother had discovered the spot between Josiah's mattress and box spring where he kept important papers, such as his notes regarding the Ten Tips to Make Her Go Home With You, which that morning Josiah had accidently left sitting on his bed, and his letters to his father and his drawing of the singer and songwriter and actress Cher, Johnson Davis came out of Josiah's bedroom into the hallway, holding the naked pictures that Josiah had drawn of Bree, which Josiah also kept hidden in the secret spot between his mattress and box spring, and said to Josiah, "What are these, Josiah?" to which Josiah responded by shrugging.

"Are these of Bree, Josiah?" Johnson Davis asked.

Josiah shrugged again.

"I'm afraid, Josiah, that these drawings—these pornographic drawings—are of Bree."

Josiah said nothing.

"Are they, Josiah?"

Josiah again said nothing.

Johnson Davis began to flip through the drawings. "The fact that in this one, Josiah, the subject is kicking a soccer ball, with no clothes on, leads me to believe that all of these drawings—these wildly inappropriate drawings—other than this one of Cher, are of Bree. Is that true, Josiah? Answer me, please."

Josiah nodded.

"They are?" Johnson Davis asked.

"Yes," Josiah said.

"They're naked, Josiah," Johnson Davis said.

"Yes," Josiah said.

"They're naked," Johnson Davis said again.

Josiah nodded. Johnson Davis was going to ask Josiah why on Earth he thought it was acceptable to draw naked pictures of his daughter when Josiah's mother walked through the door of Josiah's bedroom into the hallway, saying to Josiah, "How dare you." Josiah's mother was holding in one hand the letters that Josiah had written to his father on Parnuckle, the most recent on top. She stared at Josiah, who stared back at her.

"How dare you," Josiah's mother said again.

"What, dear?" Johnson Davis said to Josiah's mother.

"I can't believe you, Josiah," Josiah's mother said.

"What's the matter? What the hell is it?" Johnson Davis said.

"He says I'm not his real mother," Josiah's mother said.

"What?" Johnson Davis said.

"Says he wants to marry your daughter and go and live with his father."

"Good God," Johnson Davis said, taking from Josiah's mother's hand the top letter of the stack of letters. "Let me see that."

"How can you say I'm not your mother?"

"You're not my mother," Josiah said.

"What?" Josiah's mother said.

Johnson Davis, who had begun reading the letter, stopped and said, "Josiah!"

"What did you say?" Josiah's mother said to Josiah.

"Dear," Johnson Davis said, "I'm sure he doesn't mean it."

"You're not my real mother," Josiah said, pulling from the stack of pictures in Johnson Davis's right hand—Johnson Davis's left hand holding Josiah's letter—the image he had drawn of his real mother—third from the top, beneath Naked Bree kicking and Naked Bree in bed—and holding it up for both Johnson Davis and his mother to see and continuing, "My real mother is on Parnuckle."

Josiah's mother, with the letters, other than the most recent letter, still clutched in her hand, slapped Josiah on the cheek. One of the papers scratched his skin, but did not cut it.

"Josiah, go into your room," Johnson Davis said, taking the picture of the singer and songwriter and actress Cher back from Josiah and returning it to the stack of drawings. Josiah's mother began to cry. Josiah walked past Johnson Davis and his mother into his bedroom and closed the door. Behind the door, he could hear his mother crying loudly and Johnson Davis talking to her. He could not hear what Johnson Davis was saying.

Two hours later, Josiah heard a knock on his door. When he opened it, Johnson Davis was standing in the hallway. Johnson Davis told Josiah that it was time to go and pick up Bree, and that he thought it would be a good idea if Josiah came along, giving them a chance to talk. Josiah, who by no means desired to discuss with Johnson Davis what had happened two hours earlier—either in regards to the drawings or the letters or to what Josiah had said to his mother—but at the same time could not resist the possibility of seeing Bree even earlier, nodded in agreement. As Josiah followed Johnson Davis down the hallway to the stairs, Josiah noticed that the door to Johnson Davis's bedroom, which was also Josiah's mother's bedroom, was shut.

For the first five minutes of the ride to the town forty-six miles away where Bree lived with her mother, Josiah and Johnson Davis were both silent, other than Johnson Davis's light humming. At the end of the first five minutes, Johnson Davis turned to Josiah and said, "All set?" to which Josiah nodded. After this, the silence, other than the humming, continued for another ten minutes, Johnson Davis concentrating on the road, both hands on the wheel, lightly humming, and Josiah sitting up straight in the front passenger seat, his hands at his side, staring straight ahead at a crack in the windshield. The crack only covered the area of a quarter, or maybe just a nickel. It had a curved center, where something had hit the windshield, and several vines spiking out from that center. The thickness of the crack, especially at the center, revealed the thickness of the glass, which was otherwise not apparent.

Every few minutes, Johnson Davis would take one hand off of the steering wheel—his right hand—and run the hand through his hair, pausing in the middle to scratch, and then place his hand back on the wheel. Likewise, every few minutes Josiah would reach up and touch the latch on Johnson Davis's glove box, not turning it, but just touching it, with one finger, settling the finger's weight on the little knob and then letting that weight both hold the finger against the knob but also pull it downward, sliding the fingertip down the knob until, no longer supported, the finger and hand along with it would drop and Josiah would return both to his side.

At the end of the ten minutes, Johnson Davis turned to Josiah and said, "So, Josiah, how are things?" Josiah took his eyes off of the crack and turned his head toward Johnson Davis, but not far enough to be looking at him, and in response asked, "What?"

"How are things going?"

"What things?"

"Your schooling. New home, et cetera?"

"It's fine."

"How are your studies?"

"Fine."

"Learning a lot?"

"Yes."

"Good."

Johnson Davis and Josiah again remained silent for the next three minutes, Johnson Davis concentrating on the road and the steering wheel and his itchy scalp and Josiah concentrating on the crack and the thickness of the windshield and the glove box latch and the weight of his finger, until finally Johnson Davis turned to Josiah and said, "It must be hard, learning all alone, at home. Do you ever miss going to school, Josiah?"

"Not really," Josiah responded.

"No? Not at all? You don't miss all the people? The friends? The classmates? Being with your group of guys? Your buds? And, of course, the girls. Surely you had your eye on a couple of the girls. A couple of sweethearts? Crushes?"

"No," Josiah answered.

"No? Not at all?"

"No."

"Because if you did, Josiah, if you did have a crush, that would be okay. It would be nothing to be ashamed of. It would be perfectly natural for a boy your age. Take Bree, for instance. Bree, I have to admit, is a pretty girl. If you had developed a crush on Bree, that would be perfectly understandable. Do you have a crush on Bree, Josiah?"

"No."

"Come on, Josiah. Do you have a crush on Bree? Is that why you bought the ball? Why you drew those pictures?"

Josiah said nothing.

"As a father, Josiah, I have to say that I found your illustrations a bit alarming. Seeing that was a bit difficult for me. At the same time, I can understand. I can see, from your perspective, at your age, why such illustrations would come about. I have to say, I did similar things myself at your age, maybe a bit younger, I won't go into specifics, but similar things. All boys do, in one way or another.

"Now your mother, Josiah," Johnson Davis continued, "she's a bit more concerned than I am at the moment. She believes, or is afraid, that you've begun some sort of relationship with Bree. Some sort of physical relationship. Is that true, Josiah?"

Josiah said nothing.

"Are you in any sort of physical relationship with Bree, Josiah?"

"No."

"Because believe me, Josiah, I've had my share of problems with Bree with this sort of thing. More than my share. And I've reacted, in the past, much like your mother is now, worse even. But in this case, I think what we have is nothing more than a crush. An understandable crush, given the circumstances. Is that right, Josiah?"

"I guess."

"Good. That's what I suspected. Now that brings us to this other issue. This issue of mothers and fathers and planets and whatnot, which is what your mother is mostly upset about. I'm sure you're aware that your mother is very hurt by the things that were said this morning. Are you aware, Josiah?"

"Yes."

"Good. And I'm sure you didn't mean the things that you said. And that, deep down, you really didn't wish to upset your mother so badly. You may, in the moment, have wished to upset her, but not so badly. You see, Josiah, all young men, and women, as I've experienced—believe me, I've experienced it, oh, I can tell you—all young men and women, young adults, go through this. Go through this period of viewing their parents—or parent—as oppressively wronging them—justified or not, generally in some abstract way, but not always—and wishing to lash out and even hurt that parent—either emotionally or physically, but more often emotionally, I would hope anyway. You, Josiah, are no different than anyone else. I went through the whole show myself—filled my father's toothpaste tube with mud—as has your mother, no doubt. The problem, Josiah, in this case, is your choice of words, your choice of subject. In this case, the words you've chosen, for your mother, are particularly very hurtful. There may be no worse thing for a mother to hear—a mother who has cared for and raised a child all by herself—to hear from that child that they believe her not to be their real mother. There can be nothing worse—save perhaps hearing that that child has died, or has maybe murdered someone in a rampage. Nothing. You have to understand that while the motives behind your action this morning—namely teenage rebellion and so forth—do not excuse the particular hurtfulness of what you said. Now, Josiah, you don't really believe that your mother is not your real mother. Do you?"

"Yes."

"Yes, what?"

"Yes, I do."

"Yes, you do know that you don't really believe that your mother is not really your mother?"

"No."

"No, what?"

"She is not my mother."

"Now, Josiah. That is really unnecessary. We can just drop that right now. Your mother is not here, and I am not going to be impressed by this little show of yours. You and I both know, Josiah, that your mother is your mother and she loves you very much."

"She is not my mother."

"Josiah, I need you to stop saying that."

Josiah said nothing.

"Stop saying that she is not your mother."

Josiah said nothing.

"I don't want you to just stop talking, Josiah. I need you to say that your mother is your mother."

"She is not my mother."

Johnson Davis immediately pulled his car over to the shoulder of the freeway and sat for several minutes, staring straight ahead and gripping the steering wheel with both hands, at one point lifting his right hand from the steering wheel, holding up his right index finger, slightly opening his mouth, closing it, lowering his index finger and placing his hand back on the steering wheel where it remained for an additional minute before Johnson Davis reentered freeway traffic, carefully employing his mirrors and turn signal and looking over his shoulder and saying to Josiah, "Alright, Josiah. I'll play along. If your mother is not your mother, then where is your mother?"

"On the planet Parnuckle."

"The planet Parnuckle?"

"Yes."

"You know, Josiah, your mother has told me about this planet Parnuckle. She tells me, Josiah, that this planet Parnuckle is the home of your father?"

"Yes."

"Yes. Sort of a strange name, isn't it? Parnuckle?"

Josiah did not respond.

"So then that makes you, Josiah, a Parnuckliite, yes?"

"Parnucklian," Josiah said very quietly, barely opening his lips.

"What's that?"

"Parnucklian," Josiah said, louder.

"Yes. Parnucklian. So tell me, Josiah, what's it like, being a Parnucklian?"

"Fine."

"Fine. It's fine. How much do you know about this planet, Parnucklian?"

"A little."

"A little. Like what?"

"I don't know."

"You don't know?"

"No."

"You don't know. Well, how about this? Your mother tells me that the reason you eat nothing—ate nothing—but chocolate is because the people of this planet eat nothing but chocolate."

"Yes."

"Seems strange, doesn't it? Nothing but chocolate? Strange that they would even have chocolate on another planet."

"They don't call it chocolate."

"Oh, yes. Right. They call it . . . what is it?"

"Boboli."

"Yes, of course, Boboli. How could I forget? What else, Josiah?"

"What?"

"What else can you tell me about this planet, Parnuckle?"

"I don't know."

"Oh, come on, Josiah. Surely you must have more details than eating nothing but chocolate. We're talking about an entire planet. What about the cultures, the architecture, the climate?"

Josiah told Johnson Davis the same details that his mother had often told him as a child, and that he had twice told to his classmates in the first grade, namely that no one on the planet Parnuckle ever has to take baths, or showers, because there is no dirt, and no one ever goes to sleep, because no one ever gets tired, and no one ever has to go shopping, because everyone has everything already in their house, after which Johnson Davis again pulled his car to the shoulder of the freeway, more slowly this time, and turned off the car's engine and turned to Josiah, saying, "Josiah, I am going to ask you a question and I want you to think very carefully about your answer. Actually, no, I don't want you to think carefully about your answer. I don't want you to think at all about your answer. I want you to answer immediately, as soon as I ask the question, without thinking."

Johnson Davis stared at Josiah. Josiah stared back.

"Are you ready, Josiah?"

"Yes."

"Here comes the question."

Josiah continued to stare.

"Don't think. Just answer. Are you ready?"

"Yes."

"Josiah, do you believe that Parnuckle is real?"

"Yes."

"No, Josiah. No. I don't think you're playing the game correctly. Now I want you to think about your answer. I want you to think about it very hard. Do you think that your father, whom you've never met, is a spaceman, from another planet, called Parnuckle, where the only food is chocolate—*chocolate*—which they call Boboli, which is bread, and where there's no dirt and no shopping and whatever else you said, and that your mother, your real mother, whom you've never met—not the mother you've known your entire life, who has loved and nurtured you and is a wonderful woman—your supposed 'real' mother is also on this planet, and is a goddess—a *goddess*—who resembles Cher, who is a concert singer, Josiah, an entertainer. Think about these things very carefully, Josiah."

Johnson Davis and Josiah stared at one another.

"Are you thinking about them, Josiah?"

Josiah nodded.

"Now, I'm going to ask my question again. Are you thinking?"

Josiah again nodded.

"Josiah, do you believe that Parnuckle is real?"

"Yes."

Johnson Davis closed his eyes and opened them again. He asked Josiah, "Do you believe that your real mother is a space goddess that looks like Cher?"

"Yes."

Johnson Davis turned from Josiah back to the road. He started the engine, reentered traffic, and continued driving, not speaking to Josiah for the remaining twenty-seven minutes of the trip.

When Johnson Davis and Josiah arrived at Bree's high school, the soccer field was empty. There was no game being played. Johnson Davis stared at the empty field through his windshield and said, "Son of a bitch," before driving out of the school parking lot and driving up six blocks, over two, and up three more, to the home of his former wife, also the home of Bree on weekdays, where Johnson Davis told Josiah to wait in the car and walked swiftly to the front door, where after knocking he was soon let in. Josiah waited, mentally preparing for Bree to at any moment walk out her front door toward the car, and Josiah planned to get out of the car and hold the door open for her and compliment her on her outfit, whatever it may be, and ask her how her soccer game went, until, four minutes after Johnson Davis went into the house, the door opened again and Johnson Davis emerged. He walked at an equally brisk pace back to the car, got in, and said to Josiah, "Unbelievable," as he started the car's engine.

"Game cancelled," Johnson Davis said, adding, "Went out with the team. Has a ride. Unbelievable, Josiah. This is why I couldn't live with this woman. We drove all this way, for what? Absolutely thoughtless. And allowing her daughter to become exactly the same. Exactly. Says if I would get a cellular phone people could get a hold of me. Provide me the necessary information. I tell you, Josiah, I don't believe in those things. I don't. Thousands of years the world has operated without those damn things. I see that you don't carry one and I admire that. All of a sudden some little contraption comes along and replaces consideration and thoughtful planning." Josiah gazed at the front door of Bree's house as Johnson Davis backed his car out of the driveway.

"Wouldn't tell me where they went, either," Johnson Davis continued, "Knows what I'd do. I wouldn't let this trip be a waste. Wouldn't wait for some *ride*. Would go over there and right in front of her entire team put her in this car and take her home. As it is we drive all the way back, empty handed. 'Has a ride,' she tells me. 'Couldn't get hold of you,' she tells me. You know, Josiah, I'm just going to say it: most of Bree's problems, the root of her problems, stem from her mother. She provides no example. Provides no accountability. None.

"Thank God Bree has soccer in her life," Johnson Davis continued, Josiah barely listening as he pondered where Bree may be at that very moment and who might be giving her a ride. "If it weren't for soccer, Bree would be an absolute mess. No identity. No direction. That is the one thing the youth of this era lack, Josiah: direction. They're just running around like wild monkeys, all of them, even Bree here, every one of them is a wild monkey in a big tree. But the ones without direction, the ones without something to pull them through, those are the ones that fall out of that tree and get eaten by bears or wolves. Soccer gives Bree that direction. If she would just follow it.

"You see, Josiah," Johnson Davis continued, "soccer can only provide her the direction. The path. It's up to her to follow the path.

That's what her mother fails to do. Fails to push her. She needs to be pushed down that path."

Johnson Davis stopped speaking and once again pulled his car to the shoulder of the freeway. "I know, Josiah," Johnson Davis said, "that I was a bit rough with you today. With some of my questions. I know you've been through a lot. An awful lot. And I know that's why you do the things you do and say the things you say. I know you don't mean it, don't believe it. I just don't want to see your mother go through what I've gone through. I know she's been through enough already, and you as well, but I want that to end. To be honest, I'd like to take the burden from her. To be honest, I think all you need is a little male guidance. A male example."

Johnson Davis paused for a moment before saying to Josiah, "Josiah, have you ever driven a car?"

"No," Josiah said.

"Would you like to?" Johnson Davis asked.

"I don't know," Josiah answered.

"Well, Josiah, I think that it's time that you learned to drive. You're sixteen years old, and as a sixteen-year-old young man, you need to learn to drive. That's precisely what I'm talking about. Precisely the kind of thing that you need. I've been telling your mother this. It's not her place, by any means. A man should be taught to drive by his father. And as a man without a father, Josiah, you are going to be taught to drive by me, who hopes to fill a bit of the role. So switch sides and let's go."

Once Josiah was seated in the driver's seat of Johnson Davis's car and had put on his seatbelt, Johnson Davis, now in the passenger seat, said to Josiah, "Okay, Josiah, let's start by putting the vehicle in gear."

When Josiah did nothing, Johnson Davis said, "By putting the vehicle in gear, Josiah, I mean transferring from Park to Drive, which we do by moving this stick. Luckily, Josiah, you have an automatic transmission to work with, which simplifies matters. A manual transmission, Josiah, which is what we call a 'stick-shift,' adds a whole new layer of complexity to the learning process. I had to learn on a stick-shift, Josiah. Do you know what my father said to me when I told him I couldn't do it, told him it was too hard, that I couldn't learn on his truck, which was a five-speed, asked him if we couldn't just use the Lincoln? He said, 'You can count to five can't you?'"

When Josiah did not respond, simply stared at Johnson Davis, Johnson Davis said, "But that's neither here nor there. Go ahead, Josiah, and move us from Park to Drive, which means move the stick here from upper-case *P* to upper-case *D*."

When the stick did not move, Johnson Davis said, "Be sure to push the button, Josiah. With your thumb." When Josiah pushed the button on the top of the stick with his thumb and the stick still did not move, Johnson Davis said to Josiah, "Lesson Number One: never put the vehicle in gear when the engine is not running. It won't let you. We first, Josiah, must turn on the ignition."

After Josiah turned the key in the ignition, which Johnson Davis pointed at until Josiah had done so, starting the car's engine, and Josiah again pushed the button and was again unable to move the stick, Johnson Davis told Josiah that Lesson Number Two was that he first had to push down on the brake, which was the pedal on the right. Josiah pushed down on the brake and pushed the button and moved the stick from Park to Drive and looked at Johnson Davis, who then told Josiah, "Lesson Number Three, Josiah: no driving on the freeway. At least not until after several more lessons," and told Josiah to put the car back into upper-case *P* and switch sides.

Johnson Davis got back into the driver's seat of his car and carefully reentered freeway traffic and drove to the nearest exit, where he exited the freeway and drove past a service station and a supermarket to a quiet residential street where he again instructed Josiah to switch sides and to turn the ignition and to move the stick from upper-case *P* to upper-case *D*. After thirty minutes, at which point Josiah was able to drive forward and to back up and to move to the left and to the right, Johnson Davis instructed Josiah to drive up and down the residential street, Johnson Davis creating imaginary obstacles for Josiah to avoid, such as, "Coal truck on our right, Josiah! Move left. Further left, it's spilling steaming coal! Woman with stroller straight ahead, back to the right. Haven't cleared the truck yet, Josiah, we're being crushed. Okay, there we go. Wait for it. Okay, Josiah, now right. Oops, killed the baby. Mother lived."

Shortly after Johnson Davis and Josiah arrived back at the home of Johnson Davis, Josiah having driven up and down the residential street for one hour before Johnson Davis returned to the driver's seat and finished the trip, Josiah was left alone in the living room as Johnson Davis went upstairs to check on Josiah's mother, who had not left her and Johnson Davis's bedroom the entire time that Johnson Davis and Josiah had been gone.

By the time Johnson Davis and Josiah's mother and Josiah sat down to dinner three hours later—Johnson Davis having spent just over an hour coaxing his fiancée to come out of their bedroom, after which Josiah's mother began preparing dinner, which would consist of spaghetti and meat sauce along with a salad—Bree had still not arrived. Josiah, who had been rehearsing and reimagining Bree's arrival and their meeting once again most of the day, was barely able to eat. As Johnson Davis, once he had finished his meal, left the table to go and call Bree's mother and find out what on earth was going on, Josiah's mother asked Josiah to please help her take the plates into the kitchen. Once Josiah and his mother were alone in the kitchen, with the door shut, Josiah's mother approached the sink where Josiah was standing. She placed her hands on his arms, between his shoulders and elbows, from behind, and said, "Mr. Davis told me about your little talk, Josiah, today in the car. He told me the things that you said, which, essentially, are the same things that you said to me earlier, and I must say, Josiah, that I found what you had to say quite upsetting."

Josiah's mother squeezed Josiah's arms and continued, "Do you know Josiah, what else Mr. Davis told me? He told me that he thinks you don't really mean it, the things that you said, and that you're in need of help. He thinks that you are in serious need of more therapy, or more counseling, but do you know what I think, Josiah?"

Josiah's mother squeezed Josiah's arms even tighter, and pressed her chest against Josiah's back, so that Josiah was held firmly against the kitchen counter, and continued, "Do you know what I think, Josiah? I've had a lot of time, today, to think about these things, Josiah, and I think that when I raised you, Josiah, when you were young, I did the best that I could with the gift that I had been given—yes, Josiah, despite the problems we are having now, you are a gift that I was given—and despite having done the best that I could, I raised you in darkness. I had not yet been bathed in the light of God's love. And I told you stories, Josiah, in the darkness, stories that I hoped would make you feel special, make you feel important, but now, having been bathed in the light of God's love, I know, as I did not then, that none of us are more important or more special than anyone else. What makes us special, what makes us important, is God's love for us, every one of us. We are all humble servants, Josiah, of the one true Lord. We are not the sons or daughters of important officials of far away planets. You are not the son of some celebrity goddess, Josiah, you are a son of God.

"These things that you have been saying, Josiah, the drawings, this is what is called idolatry. Worshipping false gods. This is a sin against the true God. It is the work of the Devil. Though we are all, Josiah, the children of God, and are all loved by Him, we are able to choose our own path. We are able to accept God's love, and walk on the path of humble service, or we are able to walk on the path of the Devil, and what I have realized, today, Josiah, having had time to think very hard about these things, is that you, Josiah, have been pulled onto the path of the Devil, the path of sin, and do you know, Josiah, how I think you got there, what one thing, Josiah, besides your recent exposure to public social services in this country, what one thing has put you on this path? It is Bree, Josiah. This girl Bree walks on the road of damnation, and she is pulling you along toward fire and brimstone."

Josiah and Josiah's mother could both hear Johnson Davis shouting, presumably into the telephone, at his ex-wife, and Josiah's mother leaned in close to Josiah and whispered, "Now, if it were me, Josiah, I would expel the girl from our lives and never allow her back, but that would be tricky, because Mr. Davis loves his daughter very much, understandably so, despite all the trouble she has caused him. This is an issue that Mr. Davis and I will need to deal with over time."

Josiah's mother leaned even closer, her lips just an inch from Josiah's ear, and whispered even more softly, "But until then, Josiah, I don't want to see you having anything to do with that girl, whatsoever. I don't want to see you talking to her. I don't want to see you looking at her. She is a sinner, Josiah; a temptress, and I will not allow her to destroy my only son," and Josiah's mother let go of Josiah's arms, which had begun to hurt, and left the room.

Johnson Davis spent the period of that evening between nine o'clock and around eleven o'clock peering out the front window of the living room, swearing under his breath, or on the phone with his former wife, Bree's mother, swearing loudly, until finally, around eleven twenty, Bree arrived with her new friend Bart. It had been Bart who had given Bree a ride—necessary, once Bree had been unable to reach Johnson Davis after her game had been cancelled and plans had been changed, because, despite being eighteen, Bree had no driver's license of her own. Johnson Davis had refused to allow Bree to take her driver's test as a result of her latest suspension from school. Bart, however, did have a driver's license, as well as a car, a 1992 Camaro, and had had both for several years.

When Bart and Bree entered the living room of Johnson Davis, Bree did not look at Josiah, who had stood when she entered, as a gentleman would, and now stood a few feet away looking directly at her.

"Where the hell have you been?" Johnson Davis said to Bree, to which Bart, standing next to Bree, responded, "Oh, I apologize, Mr. Davis, but it's my fault. We stopped to visit an aunt of mine who lives along the way."

"Who the hell are you?" said Johnson Davis.

"I'm Bart, sir, and it's a pleasure to meet you," said Bart, extending his hand toward Johnson Davis.

"What the hell are you doing here?" asked Johnson Davis, not taking Bart's hand, which remained extended toward him.

"I'm a friend of Bree's," answered Bart. "I gave her a ride."

Johnson Davis turned to Bree, "How do you know this person?"

"From school," Bree responded quietly.

"We would have called," continued Bart, his hand still extended, "but Bree's cellular phone had lost battery power. And I don't carry one."

"Don't carry one?" Johnson Davis asked.

"No, sir," Bart answered, "And this particular aunt of mine has no landline telephone, as she is very hard of hearing. I sincerely apologize for keeping you waiting and worrying."

Johnson Davis looked at Bart and then at Bree and then at Bart again and then finally took Bart's hand, saying, "I suppose so. Come in and sit." As Bart and Bree moved toward the couch in the living room of the home of Johnson Davis, Bree smiled at Josiah's mother, who had just entered the room and was standing near the entrance to the kitchen. Josiah's mother did not smile back, and as Bree crossed the room, she still did not look at Josiah, who was standing only a few feet away from her and was still looking directly at her. When Josiah noticed his mother glaring at him, he sat back down in his chair.

Bart sat down on the couch and then Bree sat down next to him. Johnson Davis sat down in his chair and then Josiah's mother perched herself on the arm of Johnson Davis's chair. Josiah, from his seat, had stopped staring at Bree and was now staring at Bart, as was Johnson Davis, and both Bree and Josiah's mother were looking back and forth from one another to their hands. Bart looked around the room.

"This is a lovely home, Mr. Davis," said Bart to Johnson Davis.

"How old are you, Bart?" said Johnson Davis to Bart.

"Well, sir, I turned twenty-two last month."

"You turned twenty-two last month," repeated Johnson Davis, squinting his eyes at Bart.

"Yes, sir. Twenty-two last month, on the twelfth," replied Bart, looking away from Johnson Davis and looking at Josiah and smiling. Josiah simply stared at Bart.

"And you know my daughter *from school*?" continued Johnson Davis.

"Yes, sir."

"From *school*?"

"Yes, sir. I'm an assistant coach. For the Girls Varsity soccer team."

"And you're giving my daughter a ride home and taking her to see your hard-of-hearing aunt."

"Yes, sir. It was right on the way."

"It was right on the way," Johnson Davis repeated, staring intently at Bart.

o o o

One day Johnson Davis had been cleaning the dirt and dust out of his doormat by standing at the top of his porch steps and smacking the doormat against the concrete steps, creating a small cloud of dust with each smack. Johnson Davis saw, through a small cloud of dust, his next door neighbor Carter Caldwell walking up the walkway. Johnson Davis stopped smacking the doormat and watched Carter Caldwell walk up the walkway, and when Carter Caldwell got to the end of the walkway and was nearly to the porch steps, he stopped and asked if Bree was home. Johnson Davis asked Carter Caldwell what in the hell Bree had done for Christ's sake, but Carter Caldwell responded by telling Johnson Davis that he just really needed to talk to Bree. Johnson Davis responded by asking why in the hell he wanted to talk to her and then Carter Caldwell began to tear up a little bit and repeated that he needed to talk to Bree and then Johnson Davis again asked why in the hell he would need to talk to her and also asked what in the hell is going on. Carter Caldwell began to tear up more and told Johnson Davis that he would simply like to know whether or not Bree was home and if he could please speak with her and Johnson Davis responded by asking Carter Caldwell why in the hell a grown man would need to talk to a fourteen-year-old girl and why in the hell he was crying for Christ's sake. Carter Caldwell then began to scream and he was screaming to Johnson Davis that he could not stop him from talking to Bree and could not stop him from seeing Bree and then

Johnson Davis tried to smack Carter Caldwell with the dirty and dusty doormat still in his hands but Johnson Davis missed and Carter Caldwell began to run backwards away from Johnson Davis so Johnson Davis threw the doormat at Carter Caldwell and the doormat hit him kind of in the side and Carter Caldwell fell to one knee and again began to scream. This time he was screaming, "Please, please I just need to talk to her. Please—" and then Johnson Davis kicked Carter Caldwell in the leg, causing Carter Caldwell to scream and cry more. Johnson Davis then told Carter Caldwell that he had a double-barrel shotgun just inside the door and that he had better get off his Goddamn property, so Carter Caldwell got up and ran back to his house.

When Johnson Davis, who had never and would never own a firearm, went back into his house, he called the police department, but neither Bree nor Carter Caldwell admitted to anything illegal having happened nor had anyone, such as Steven Caldwell or anyone else, witnessed anything illegal nor was there any proof or physical evidence of anything illegal.

A week later, on a Saturday at around four o'clock in the morning, Johnson Davis backed his car out of his driveway and drove his car onto the lawn of Carter Caldwell and spun donuts.

After Johnson Davis's first wife had left him, there was a time period during which Johnson Davis would often drive his car to the home of his first wife's sister, three blocks away, where his former wife was staying until ready to move, and would drive onto the front lawn and spin donuts, usually sneaking back at night to apologetically fill in the holes with a shovel.

A week after he spun donuts on the lawn of Carter Caldwell, Johnson Davis rammed his shopping cart into the shopping cart of Carter Caldwell at the local grocery store and tried to hit him with a baguette.

o o o

"Tell me, Bart," said Johnson Davis to Bart.

"Yes, sir?" said Bart.

"Why would a twenty-two-year-old assistant coach of a Girls Varsity soccer team be driving my seventeen year-old daughter to her father's home an hour away and stopping with her to see his hard-of-hearing aunt?"

"Dad, it's not—it's nothing," Bree said. "He just gave me a ride."

"I am talking to Bart," said Johnson Davis.

"Sir—" said Bart.

"But I'm telling you," continued Bree, interrupting Bart, "it's no big deal."

"I've heard that before," said Johnson Davis.

"Sir," said Bart, "I assure you—"

"What I would like to know, Bart," interrupted Johnson Davis, "is why a twenty-two-year-old soccer coach—*assistant* soccer coach—is giving my daughter—my *teenage* daughter—who, by the way, has *gotten rides*—"

"This is bullshit," said Bree.

"—has *gotten rides* from older men in the past, with less than proud results, a ride home?"

"I can't believe this. Fuck."

"Bree, please. That's inappropriate," said Bart. "This is a conversation between myself and your father. And his concerns are perfectly valid. Especially in this day and age. The truth is, sir, that I see a great deal of potential in your daughter, both as a soccer player and as a young lady. The truth is that Bree has confided in me regarding her past troubles. She has told me everything. The things that Bree has told me, along with the great potential I see in her, have led me to feel the need to help Bree. To guide her. To mentor her."

"To mentor her?"

"Yes, sir. As I said, sir, I see great potential in Bree, both on the soccer field and off. But I feel it is on the soccer field that I can be of the greatest service."

"Of the greatest service?"

"Yes, sir. I feel that Bree's road to recovery, if you wish to call it that, or road to happiness, begins on the soccer field. Soccer is something that Bree excels at. It is something that she can take pride in. But most importantly, it may help to give her direction. And that—direction—is something that young people, especially young people like Bree, really need. Don't you agree?"

"I do. Yes, I do."

As it was eleven thirty at night and much too late for Bart to begin the drive back to the town forty-six miles away in which Bree and her mother lived, Johnson Davis offered to have Bart stay the night on the couch, and if he was free, to have breakfast with the family and spend his Saturday with them, which made Josiah nervous as this could get in the way of his ability to spend time with Bree and possibly implement the steps that would possibly make Bree want to go home with him and that he had prepared for so diligently, but nevertheless Bart accepted Johnson Davis's offer and Josiah's mother brought a blanket from the hall closet and one of Josiah's pillows down to the living room for Bart to use and everyone said their goodnights and went to bed.

As Josiah was changing into his shorts and t-shirt, his mother entered his bedroom, wearing a lavender nightgown and carrying a thick paperback book, and announced that she thought she would sleep in Josiah's room tonight.

"You don't have to," Josiah said to her.

"Oh, I think I will," Josiah's mother said. "Have you brushed your teeth?"

"Yes," Josiah said.

"Good," Josiah's mother said. "Get into bed, then."

Josiah pulled back his covers and got into his bed. Josiah's mother turned off the overhead light by flipping the switch near Josiah's door, got into Josiah's bed, turned on the bedside lamp, and said, "I think I'll read awhile. You go ahead and sleep."

A few moments later, Josiah heard a tapping on his bedroom door. When his mother called out, "Yes," the door opened and Johnson Davis was standing in the hallway.

"Are you coming to bed, dear?" he asked Josiah's mother.

"Josiah tells me he is having bad dreams," Josiah's mother said. "I'll be staying with him tonight."

"Oh, come on, dear," Johnson Davis said. "He doesn't want his mother staying the night with him."

"We'll be just fine," Josiah's mother said.

"He's a bit old," Johnson Davis said.

"We'll be fine," Josiah's mother said.

"I don't think it's necessary," Johnson Davis said.

"Close the door, please," Josiah's mother said.

Josiah was unable to sleep, wondering if Bree would once again come into his room, as she had twice before, an idea that both excited Josiah, in that he very much hoped that Bree would try to come into his room, and worried him, in that he was unsure what his mother might do if Bree *did* come into his room. Josiah spent what seemed like a very long time staring at the ceiling, which in the dark looked like an ocean, or an overcast sky, and reviewing the Ten Tips to Make Her Go Home With You—in particular his questions and compliments—despite the fact that it seemed more and more as if he would be unable to use them.

At around two thirty, as Josiah felt himself finally drifting into sleep, his mother not snoring but breathing loudly next to him, Josiah heard what sounded like footsteps in the hallway, and as the footsteps got closer to the door of his room, Josiah was able to recognize the sound of the footsteps as Bree's, or what he imagined to be the sound that Bree's footsteps would make, light and careful, and Josiah began to feel very excited and very nervous and began frantically reviewing the questions and compliments in his mind, but the footsteps did not stop at the door to his bedroom, but rather continued down the hall and then descended down the stairs until he could hear them no more.

Josiah lay wide awake, waiting for the footsteps to return up the stairs and back down the hall, wondering if he should carefully get up and quietly go down the stairs and see if everything was alright, hoping that Bree had become hungry or thirsty and would soon be returning to her room, wondering what he would see if he went downstairs. Finally, at three forty-four, according to the clock radio on the table next to Josiah's bed, Josiah heard Bree's footsteps come up the stairs, this time faster and less light and careful, and move back down the hallway to her room.

By the time Josiah woke the next morning—his mother having risen earlier than he had and already left the room—and by the time he made his way downstairs to the kitchen, Bart was gone. Josiah found Johnson Davis, wearing light blue pajamas and a dark blue robe, sitting alone at the kitchen table, drinking coffee and reading the newspaper. Johnson Davis asked Josiah if he had seen Bart. Josiah shook his head. Johnson Davis then told Josiah to sit down and to have some coffee. When Josiah again shook his head, Johnson Davis told Josiah to "Come on" and that it would put hair on his chest, after which Josiah's mother entered the kitchen, already dressed for the day in a red and black sundress, and asked Johnson Davis what he was talking about. When Johnson Davis told his fiancée, Josiah's mother, that he was just telling Josiah that drinking coffee would put hair on his chest, Josiah's mother answered that Josiah certainly did not want any hair on his chest and probably did not want any coffee. It was as Johnson Davis remarked that it certainly couldn't hurt him and Josiah's mother answered that fine, if Josiah wanted coffee he could have it and he could get it himself that Bree entered the kitchen, dressed, like Josiah, who had stopped wearing pajamas shortly after he met Bree, in shorts and a t-shirt.

Josiah stood when Bree entered, as he thought a gentleman might, but sat back down when his mother glared at him. Bree's t-shirt was grey and had the words *Phys. Ed.* printed on it. Josiah could see the shape of Bree's breasts beneath the shirt.

"Good morning," Bree said, to which Johnson Davis and Josiah both said, "Good morning," in response. Josiah's mother said nothing. As Bree approached the nearest empty chair and began to pull it out from the table, Josiah again stood, causing Bree to look at him strangely and his mother to again glare at him, causing him to sit down. Johnson Davis did not look up from his newspaper.

"Where's Bart?" Johnson Davis asked.

"Is he gone?" Bree responded, adding, "He must have left early."

"Must have," Johnson Davis said. "Hard at it, I suppose. It's a shame. We could have at least made him breakfast, for all he's doing."

"Anyway," Bree said.

"Yes, anyway," Johnson Davis said, setting his newspaper, still unfolded, down on the kitchen table, "can we get you something? Something to eat?"

"I'm fine," Bree said.

"Not eating?" Johnson Davis asked.

"Just not hungry," Bree said.

"Well, you should eat something," Johnson Davis said.

"I'm fine," Bree said again.

"You've got to have something," Johnson Davis said.

"I'll have whatever you guys are having," Bree said.

"I've eaten," Johnson Davis said. "Had a bagel." Turning to Josiah's mother, Johnson Davis asked, "Dear, what are you having for breakfast?"

"I was going to make some waffles," Josiah's mother said, standing at the kitchen counter, "for Josiah and I."

"How about waffles?" Johnson Davis said, turning to Bree.

"Fine," Bree said.

"I'm not sure there's enough," Josiah's mother said. "Enough batter."

"It's fine," Bree said. "I'll have some cereal."

"Solved, then," Johnson Davis said, picking up his newspaper.

"Actually," Bree said, "there's something I want to talk to you about."

Johnson Davis dropped the newspaper back to the table. "Oh, God, what now?" he said.

"We'll leave," Josiah's mother said.

"No," Bree said. "I want to talk to all of you."

"Oh, God," Johnson Davis said.

"Josiah, go to your room," Josiah's mother said.

"No," Bree said. "Josiah, too."

"Why?" Josiah's mother said.

"I just want to talk to all of you," Bree said.

"But why?" Josiah's mother said.

"You're pregnant," Johnson Davis blurted.

"Dad," Bree said.

"I knew it," Johnson Davis said.

"Dad, for Christ's sake, will you let me talk?" Bree said.

"This is between the two of you," Josiah's mother said.

"Will you please let me talk?" Bree said, "I haven't told you anything yet."

"What is it, then?" Johnson Davis said.

"I'm trying to tell you," Bree said.

"Do it, then," Johnson Davis said. "Say what you need to say."

"I'm pregnant," Bree said.

"Goddamnit," Johnson Davis shouted, standing. Josiah's mother gasped. When Josiah saw Johnson Davis stand, he also stood.

"Dad, sit down," Bree said, and looking at Josiah, "Both of you."

"I knew it, Goddamnit," Johnson Davis said, still standing. "I knew it."

"Sit down, please," Bree said again.

"Dear," Josiah's mother said, "why don't you sit down? You, too, Josiah."

Johnson Davis and Josiah both sat back down. Josiah was staring at Bree. So was Johnson Davis.

"I'm sorry," Bree said to Johnson Davis.

"Again?" Johnson Davis said.

"I'm sorry," Bree said.

"Do you have any idea whose it is?" Johnson Davis asked.

"Dad," Bree said.

"Well, do you?" Johnson Davis asked.

"Dear," Josiah's mother said to Johnson Davis, "I think we all know whose it is."

"What are you talking about?" Bree said.

"What do you mean?" Johnson Davis said.

"Well, I think it's safe to say that it belongs to this Bart," Josiah's mother said.

"What?" Bree said.

"What?" Johnson Davis said, adding, "Bree is not involved with Bart."

"Oh, don't be naïve," Josiah's mother said. "They're clearly sleeping together."

"We are not," Bree said.

"Now, dear," Johnson Davis said to his fiancée, "I admit I had my suspicions when they first arrived, but I truly feel this Bart has the best intentions."

"It's not Bart's," Bree said.

"Then whose is it?" Josiah's mother said to Bree.

"It's not Bart's," Bree said.

"Whose is it?" Johnson Davis said.

"It's Josiah's," Bree said.

EIGHT

A YEAR AND A HALF earlier, when Bree was sixteen years old, she got pregnant. She first suspected she may be pregnant after getting sick at school, throwing up into a clay pot she was making in her first period art class. That afternoon, after school, Bree and her friend Ariel took the bus to the local drug store and bought a pregnancy test and walked to Ariel's house. Ariel's parents both worked and were not home and Bree went into Ariel's bathroom and took the pregnancy test and found out she was pregnant.

Bree ultimately decided that the easiest way to tell her parents, given how nervous she was to do so, was to videotape herself telling them and then play it for them. She pictured herself gathering them together in the living room and putting in the video, which would play her heartfelt and humbly apologetic admission as she stood next to the television set, making pathetic faces and waiting for the video to end, at which point she would begin fielding questions and comments.

Bree later decided, as she began to imagine her parents' reactions to the video—especially her father's—that maybe it would be even better, for everyone involved, if her parents watched the video on their own. Without her there. So on Thursday of that week, Bree passed through the kitchen, where both of her parents were sitting at their solid oak kitchen table, took a packaged pair of toaster pastries from the cupboard, and placed on the kitchen table the VHS cassette that contained the video that she had spent just over three hours of the previous night making—using the Camcorder Johnson Davis had purchased six years earlier—rewinding and refilming numerous times before she felt she had it right—and announced quickly and enthusiastically to her parents as she passed through the kitchen door, "Going to school. Made you a movie. You should watch it."

Halfway through third period, Bree was imagining the various scenarios she might face upon her arrival back at home that afternoon when Johnson Davis walked into the classroom. Bree sunk down into her chair as Johnson Davis, having already spotted his daughter and who was now staring at her, informed the teacher, Bree's Algebra teacher, Ms. Wise, that he needed to see his daughter right away.

"And who is your daughter, sir?" Ms. Wise asked.

"That one," Johnson Davis said, pointing at Bree, who sunk down even further.

"Do you have a visitor's pass, sir?" Ms. Wise asked. Johnson Davis, holding his gaze on Bree—who, though she sunk further and further into her chair, held her own gaze back on her father—pulled his wallet out of his pocket and held it up to Ms. Wise, his driver's license visible in its clear plastic pocket.

"Sir," Ms. Wise said, "you need a visitor's badge. From the front office."

"I need to see my daughter," Johnson Davis said.

"As soon as you've checked in, sir. And received your visitor's badge. That's the policy."

"It's an emergency."

"I'm sure it is, sir. You just need to check in with the front office."

"I'll be back."

"That's fine. As soon as you've checked in."

"Don't go anywhere," Johnson Davis said to Bree, from across the room, finally breaking his gaze as he left.

Johnson Davis did not return by the end of third period, and Bree did not remain waiting in her third period classroom. And when the little neon green slip came during fourth period, calling Bree to the office, she took the slip and walked out of class and down the hall and out the front door and walked down the street and down another and another to the movie theater, where she sat through the first matinee of a movie about two policemen that she didn't pay much attention to but that the other three people in the theater seemed to find pretty funny. When the movie was over Bree walked to the public library, where she told the librarian that she wanted to read a novel about teen pregnancy. When the librarian found and handed Bree a book about teen pregnancy, Bree told her no, she wanted a *novel* about teen pregnancy, and when the librarian said that she would need to check again, Bree told her never mind and began to browse the shelves on her own, picking up lots of books and looking at their covers sort of absentmindedly until finally coming across a book that had been one of her favorites growing up. The book was called *Peter Pan* and Bree and Johnson Davis had read the book together many times when she was a little girl. Bree had especially liked the pictures that illustrated each chapter, though the copy she found at the library did not have those pictures, just a picture on the cover and another one in the first few pages. But the words were the same and Bree recognized them as she began to read, sitting down in a sort of big comfy yellow chair near the back of the library.

As Bree read, she could remember her father's voice reading the same words. She could also remember the things he would add in, always the same things, at the same parts, such as facts about actual pirate life or explaining to Bree, after the first description of Neverland, that Neverland symbolized a perfect place that people could leave and escape to, and when Bree would ask why people wanted to leave and escape, Johnson Davis would respond that people maybe weren't so happy with their lives—something wasn't right about them—and they wanted to change, to make it better, like these children, in the book, who were probably bored with their bourgeois lives. Bree read the entire book one time through, then went back and reread some of her favorite parts before falling asleep in the comfy yellow chair.

She was awakened by the sound of someone walking toward her. When she opened her eyes, she saw that it was her father. The librarian had called the school to report a high-school-age child seemingly cutting her classes, and the school had notified Johnson Davis, who, at the time that the librarian called, was sitting in the school office, having just cooled down after making a rather big scene that ended with Johnson Davis announcing to the entire office staff that his daughter was pregnant and sexually active and how did they like not letting him see his daughter, now? Johnson Davis stood looking down at Bree, in the yellow chair, and asked, "What are you doing?"

Bree looked at the book resting open on her chest and answered, without sarcasm, "Reading." Johnson Davis looked at the book as well, and for a split second, Bree thought that her father, whom she had never seen cry, was going to cry, but he didn't. "I can't believe you could do this," Johnson Davis said, though not in his usual tone. Quieter.

"I didn't mean to," Bree said. Bree was also not crying but her eyes were beginning to tear up.

"I thought you were different," Johnson Davis said.

"Different than what?" Bree said.

"I thought you were better," Johnson Davis said.

"I'm sorry," Bree said.

"What did I do wrong?" Johnson Davis said.

"Nothing. I don't know," Bree said.

"Let's go," Johnson Davis said.

"I'm sorry," Bree said again.

"Let's go."

o o o

Johnson Davis had been thirty-eight years old when he became a father. He was thirty-three years old the first time that he got married, to Bree's mother. Bree's mother was twenty-four when she married Johnson Davis. She had met Johnson Davis two years earlier, as an undergraduate, when she took a class that Johnson Davis was teaching as a graduate student.

Johnson Davis had never thought too much about being a father. When Bree's mother, while they were dating, had asked Johnson Davis if he wanted to have children someday, he had answered, "Yes," but only because that had seemed to be the right answer. Three years later, when Bree's mother, shortly after completing her Master's degree, told Johnson Davis, to whom at that point she had been married for two years, that she wanted to start to try to get pregnant, Johnson Davis again didn't think too much about it, other than that that seemed to be the next step on a path that he seemed to be on. Johnson Davis didn't think too much about it, either, during the year that he and his wife tried to get pregnant, as his wife relayed doctors' advice and read aloud articles she had photocopied from magazines in the library, and he didn't think too much the day that he came home and she was waiting just inside the front door with the biggest smile he had ever seen on her; didn't think too much until she brought home that picture, that grainy black and white and grey picture that looked as much like almost anything else as it did of what it was and that he barely looked at as she held it up to him, wearing that same smile, but that suddenly caught his attention later that night as he closed the refrigerator door—where she had placed the picture beneath a butterfly-shaped magnet—after drinking some tomato juice straight from the bottle. There she was, grey and grainy but his. And after that, he thought of little else.

He began, the next day, by going to an office supply store, where he asked for a daily planner for not that year but the following year, and also for the year after that and the year after that if they had it, the man who owned the store informing Johnson Davis that he could certainly sell him a planner for this year, but that planners for the following year wouldn't be available for several months, and that planners for the years after that wouldn't be available until shortly before those years began, after which Johnson Davis purchased three reams of paper and a ruler. That night, Johnson Davis spent several hours on the floor of his office using the paper, the ruler, a stapler, a pencil, a red pen, a black marker, an old almanac, and math to create daily planners for what would be the first five years of Bree's life.

The planners included books she would read—in pencil—activities she would participate in—in red—and places she would visit—in black. Johnson Davis spent the next four months filling in the planners, and by the end of those four months, the planners were filled with red and black ink and pencil, as well as with notes Johnson Davis had written to himself, regarding the implementation of the planners, writing those notes—with whichever of the three implements he may have been holding at that moment—on small strips of paper that he would then stuff into the stapled seams of the planners.

At the time that Johnson Davis was making the planners, he did not know that he would be having a girl. Luckily, though somewhere deep down Johnson Davis, if given a choice, preferred the idea of a boy, the book and activities and locations that Johnson Davis filled the planners with could just as easily be read or participated in or visited by a girl as by a boy, and when Johnson Davis did learn that he and his wife would be having a girl, it was all he could talk about. He told his colleagues and his friends and his doctor and dentist and sales clerks and complete strangers all about how he had always wanted a daughter, and that he could picture her already, and she was the most beautiful girl he had ever seen, and that she would want for nothing; anything she wanted or needed she would have, he would make sure she had it—to a point, of course, as being grateful for what one has is an important lesson for a child—and that he had had no idea how having a child, even though he didn't have it yet, changed everything, like putting in a new set of eyes, and his child, his daughter, was going places, he would say, would take this world by storm, the skies the limit—metaphorically, though maybe not—and he would show her the world, expose her to everything, that's what it was all about—

child-rearing—he'd decided, making them versatile, accomplished, well-rounded. Like the Greeks.

o o o

Johnson Davis's father had been a minister. Johnson Davis had grown up, with his father and mother, in a different and more humid state than the state Johnson Davis now lived in. The home Johnson Davis had grown up in had had two bedrooms—one for Johnson Davis and one for Johnson Davis's father and mother—and the house had been one block away from the church where Johnson Davis's father had been a minister and wherein Johnson Davis's father would preach every Saturday night and every Sunday morning—Johnson Davis attending every one of those services, sitting in the front row in a tie and blazer next to his mother, from as early as he could remember to the time he left for college.

During the week, Johnson Davis's father remained busy in his second business repairing antique engines in the small garage adjacent to their home. Johnson Davis's father, having learned from his own father, repaired all sorts of antique engines: tractor engines, truck engines, car engines, pump engines, motorbike engines. Though Johnson Davis's father enjoyed repairing antique engines and spent ten to twelve hours of every weekday doing so, the majority of his and his family's income came from his ministerial duties, a meaningful portion of his engine-repair earnings devoted to the perpetuation of that activity through the purchase of junk-yarded engines to break down for parts.

Periodically, upon arriving home from school, Johnson Davis would go into the small garage adjacent to their home and attempt to help his father repair antique engines, but never once from the time Johnson Davis could remember to the time he left for college did Johnson Davis's father allow Johnson Davis to help him repair antique engines, always declaring that his son, by God, was going to be a scholar and an athlete—like the Greeks—just as Johnson Davis's father's father and father's father's father had wanted to be and wanted their sons to be, and each day Johnson Davis's father would send Johnson Davis directly into the house to complete his homework before meeting him back outside before dinner for daily exercises.

One day, a Friday, during Johnson Davis's junior year in high school, Johnson Davis came home from school after baseball practice, and found his father not in the small garage but standing on their front porch with his arms folded across his chest. As Johnson Davis approached, Johnson Davis's father said, "Your mother is gone," and turned and opened the screen door and went into the house. Johnson Davis trotted up the porch steps and into the house. As he pulled open the screen door, which Johnson Davis's father kept very well-lubricated and which never made a sound, Johnson Davis shouted at his father, "Gone where?"

Johnson Davis's father, whom Johnson Davis had never before shouted in the presence of, let alone at, and who had stopped halfway across the large room that incorporated their living room, dining room, and kitchen and turned to face the front door, resuming his prior arms-folded position, implied in his expression disapproval in his son's tone.

"Where?" Johnson Davis repeated, quieter.

"She won't be coming back," Johnson Davis's father said, again turning and walking down the short hallway toward his bedroom and adding, "You won't be seeing her again."

"Why not?" Johnson Davis said, trotting a few steps after his father but slowing to a walk and continuing, struggling to be heard down the hallway without shouting as he asked, "Where is she?" When his father did not respond, Johnson Davis repeated the same, again in a shout.

"That will be all," Johnson Davis's father said as he closed the bedroom door behind him. "See to your homework. Exercise before dinner."

The following evening, Saturday, Johnson Davis sat in the front pew of his father's church, the space next to him empty, looking over his shoulder at every sound of parishioners entering from the gravel outside. Johnson Davis, who had spent the day sitting on their front porch, somewhat sick to his stomach, stopped looking over his shoulder when the sound of individual footsteps crunching the gravel becoming muddled as last-minute arrivals flooded in in the final minutes before his father, who had spent the day working on the engine of a crop duster their neighbor had purchased at an estate auction, emerged from the small door at the front of the church and took his place at the lectern.

His father had only been in place for a moment, long enough to gaze over the faces of his congregation, when he folded his lips into a stilted grin and stepped down from the lectern and past his son and down the aisle of the church. Johnson Davis's father was nearly to the back of the church when Johnson Davis stood and saw his mother, sitting in the back row and watching nervously as her husband approached.

Johnson Davis did not move, only stood, as his father, in a voice that was gentle but could be heard throughout the entire church, said to his wife that she would need to leave, immediately, Johnson Davis's mother responding by shaking her head. Johnson Davis's father repeated, "Leave, immediately," and Johnson Davis's mother again shook her head and Johnson Davis watched as his father grabbed his mother by the left arm, between the elbow and shoulder, and lifted her from the pew, Johnson Davis nearly taking a step as his mother let out a whimper and his father led his mother by the arm out onto the gravel and pulled closed the large door at the back of the church, which up to that point had been kept open, and walked back up the aisle to the lectern, stopping to glare at his son, who immediately sat down.

From the time Johnson Davis's father had left the lectern to the time he returned, no eye in the church had left Johnson Davis's father and not one word had been spoken. A man had stood when Johnson Davis's father had grabbed the arm of Johnson Davis's mother, but had sat back down after only a few seconds. Everyone in the church waited silently, and listened, as Johnson Davis's father squared himself to the lectern, paused with lowered head, as if resetting a tape, and began to speak in his usual Saturday night and

Sunday morning manner, glancing periodically down at his notes, as if what he was now saying had been written there:

"This woman," Johnson Davis's father said to his congregation, who had known their minister's wife quite well, "that you have just seen leave us, was my wife. Was my wife and has fallen. Was my wife and has taken up with another man. Known him. Lain with him."

Everyone in the church was shocked to hear this, but everyone remained silent. When Johnson Davis's father had said that Johnson Davis's mother had taken up with another man, Johnson Davis had looked over his shoulder at the closed door at the back of the church. When his eyes passed back to his father, they found his father's eyes staring back.

"This woman," Johnson Davis's father continued, "sat beside me at the head of a happy home. A family, such as God imagined. A man and a woman, joined together in God's eyes, keeping a Christian home and a Christian child." Johnson Davis's father turned and looked at Johnson Davis. "And we must cast her out," he said, holding his gaze on his son for two long seconds before slowly passing them over the entire congregation and continuing, "To avoid the fate of Adam, who was cast from the Kingdom for the sin of the woman, we must first cast that sin from our sight. We must cast her out, and all like her, lest she destroy *this* house, and all of us."

Johnson Davis's father again passed his gaze, now in the opposite direction, back over the congregation, meeting, in silence, the eyes of many, stopping short of resting that gaze back on his son and hanging his head toward the lectern, resting his hands on its edges.

After another long, silent second, Johnson Davis's father began to cry. His head sunk lower and his hands clenched the lectern tightly, and beneath his crying could be heard whimpers similar to the whimper made by his wife several long minutes earlier. The members of the church, who had not spoken a word nor taken an eye off of their minister, remained silent but began to look around at one another, as if searching for someone who had some idea of what to do. The man who had stood earlier stood again, but sat back down.

Johnson Davis looked at no one but his father, whom he had not only never seen cry, but had never seen behave in a manner much different from his Saturday night and Sunday morning manner, and when Johnson Davis's father began to again speak, in a manner, likewise, completely foreign, all eyes joined Johnson Davis's and returned to his father.

"I did everything," Johnson Davis's father said, his head still hung and hands still clenched and still crying, repeating "Everything" and following it with a whimper.

The following morning, for the first time that Johnson Davis and many of the church members could remember, Sunday morning services were cancelled.

o o o

Johnson Davis, at some point during his wife's pregnancy, remembered having heard on the radio that reading to your child in the womb could increase the child's intelligence—or literacy, or something. So every night, about an hour after dinner, Johnson Davis would sit his wife down on the sofa and bring her a cup of hot chocolate and a plate of cookies—six of them, the store brand version of Oreos—and he would read aloud to his future daughter, in the womb, for two hours. Johnson Davis began by reading aloud some of his favorite books. He read *Treasure Island*, *A Farewell to Arms*, a biography of Jackie Robinson he had traded a pair of sunglasses for when he was a teenager, and several chapters of *Moby Dick*, Johnson Davis's wife stopping him just short of a quarter of the way through the book, specifically at Chapter 32, declaring that the book was ridiculous and that she'd heard enough of it and then suggesting that perhaps it was time that they began purchasing baby books. When Johnson Davis stared back at her, blinking, she announced that they would visit the local bookstore the following day.

The following day, at the local bookstore, which Johnson Davis had been in often, Johnson Davis's wife led him into the children's section, which Johnson Davis had been in never. Within minutes, Johnson Davis was marveling at what he saw.

"Just look at these books," Johnson Davis said to his wife. "Look at this: *The Odyssey* for children. And *Arabian Nights*. And look at this: A pop-up *World Atlas*. Look, honey, the Swiss Alps."

"And look at these," Johnson Davis's wife said.

"Biographies," Johnson Davis said, "for little kids. Little kid biographies. These are great. Abraham Lincoln. Mark Twain. Queen Elizabeth. Jackie Robinson! Look, dear, Jackie Robinson!"

"Haven't you ever been back here before?"

"I thought it was all coloring books and crap."

Johnson Davis spent nearly thirty minutes opening books—sometimes standing, sometimes sitting, sometimes at the one chair at the one table in the children's section, sometimes on the floor—reading about talking rabbits and caterpillars and frogs and trucks, making an ever-rising stack of potential purchases on the one table. He was about to comment to his wife on the brilliant dramatic irony of an Oscar the Grouch story when she said, "I remember this."

"Remember what?" he asked.

"This," and she held up a book titled *The Shortest Giraffe*.

"What do you remember?" Johnson Davis asked.

"My dad read it to me," his wife said. "All the time. It was my favorite."

"That book?"

"Yeah. Didn't you have a favorite book when you were little?"

"I suppose," Johnson Davis said. "We had books. We read the Bible a lot."

"Did you see these?" Johnson Davis's wife pointed out to him a shelf of illustrated books of Bible stories. Johnson Davis picked one up—one with a red cover, titled *Bible Stories for Children: Illustrated Edition*—and began to flip through it, slowly. He then picked up another and did the same, and another, staring at the images of the stories he could now remember his father reading to him and his mother, over and over again, the same stories his father would read, over and over again, to his congregation—which included Johnson Davis and his mother—on Saturday nights and Sunday mornings.

Johnson Davis placed the books back on the shelf and replied, "Yes, I saw these." Johnson Davis paid for the stack of books, over a third of which were biographies, and returned home.

o   o   o

Johnson Davis and Bree did not speak to one another on the drive home from the library. Bree's mother, who had called in sick to work when her husband, after watching Bree's video, had insisted on going to the school to get her, was sitting, again, at the oaken kitchen table when Bree and Johnson Davis came in.

"What took so long?" Bree's mother said.

"It's a long story," Johnson Davis said.

"Where do you want me?" Bree said.

"Living room," Johnson Davis said.

"No, kitchen," Bree's mother said.

"Living room," Johnson Davis said.

Bree walked into the living room, set her backpack down next to the sofa, and sat herself in the chair by the window that had been designated, somehow, over the years, to be her chair. A few seconds later, Johnson Davis walked into the living room and said, "No, your room. Your mother and I should talk first."

After twenty-five minutes, when no one came to Bree's room to retrieve her, Bree walked out to the top of the stairs and listened.

"I'm just not comfortable with that," her mother's voice said.

"Why not?" her father's voice said.

"I'm just not."

"I don't even know what that means: you're not comfortable."

"I'm just not comfortable. I'm not ready to 'decide' that."

"Well, what choice do we have?"

"Are you serious?"

"Yes."

"That's not the only choice," Bree's mother said. As Bree listened, she thought to herself how cliché she was, listening at the stairs, and how cliché her parents were, unable to just say it.

"Isn't it?" Johnson Davis said.

"Why is it?" Bree's mother said.

"Because I'm not going to let her ruin everything. I'm not."

"Has it occurred to you that she's already failed?"

"Failed what?"

"To live up to your expectations. To be whatever it is you wanted her to be."

"Whose fault is that?"

"Oh, of course. Whose?"

"You know."

"And how is that?"

"I told you a million times. A million times."

"And what did *you* do about it?"

"More than you. You did nothing."

"What did you want me to do?"

"Help me. Try."

"How many times did you lock her in her room? How many scenes in front of her friends?"

"I was trying."

"What good did it do?"

"At least I tried."

"Honey," Bree's mother said, "some people just are who they are."

Bree rose from her position at the top of the stairs and went back to her room.

o o o

At the end of Bree's second week of preschool, when Johnson Davis arrived to pick Bree up and take her home, the preschool teacher, who wished to be called Carole, but whom Johnson Davis called Mrs. Harris, informed Johnson Davis that his daughter had hit another student—a boy—that day and in general exhibited aggressive behavior and perhaps would need to find another preschool. Johnson Davis, who initially argued with Carole over what this boy had done and how hard he had been hit and over whether or not those questions were the point, convinced Carole through begging to give his daughter until the end of the month.

When Johnson Davis and Bree arrived home, Johnson Davis told his wife what had happened and that he was very concerned.

"Well," she asked, "Did you speak to her about it?"

"Yes!" Johnson Davis responded.

"Well what did she say?"

"She didn't say anything."

"Anything?"

"No."

"She didn't have a reason?"

"No," Johnson Davis said. "She just said she didn't like him and he's stupid."

"Maybe he is stupid," Bree's mother said.

"This isn't a joke!"

"It's probably nothing. They're just kids."

"They're going to kick her out!" Johnson Davis said.

"Kick her out?" Bree's mother said. "Of what? Preschool?"

"Yes!"

"Who is?"

"The lady," Johnson Davis said. "Mrs. Harris."

"Carole? For what? Hitting a kid one time?"

"She said she's aggressive."

"They're not going to kick her out of preschool," Bree's mother said.

"That's what she said. She has a month."

"We'll tell her that it's not nice to hit and it's wrong and she can't ever ever do it again and that will be that."

"That will be that?" Johnson Davis said.

"Yes," Bree's mother said.

"You think that will work?"

"Yes, I do."

"What if this is a symptom of a bigger problem?"

"It's not."

"What if she needs help?" Johnson Davis said.

"She doesn't," Bree's mother said. "She's three."

"How do you know, though?"

"I just do."

"Are you sure?" Johnson Davis said.

"Yes," Bree's mother said.

"Sure?"

"I'm sure."

o   o   o

The morning after revealing to her parents that she was pregnant, as Bree was dressing for school, no one having ever come to her room the previous afternoon or evening to speak to her, Johnson Davis knocked once on Bree's bedroom door, opened it at a forty-five degree angle, and announced, "No school today."

"Where am I going?" Bree asked.

"You're staying home," Johnson Davis said. "Come down for breakfast."

When Bree came down to the kitchen, she found Johnson Davis sitting at the kitchen table with a bowl of instant oatmeal in front of him and another across from him.

"Where's mom?" Bree asked.

"She's not here now," Johnson Davis said.

"Did she go to work?"

"Yes."

"She left early?"

"Yes."

"Are you going to work?"

"No," Johnson Davis said. "I'm staying home with you."

Bree sat down. Once she was seated, Johnson Davis began to eat his oatmeal. The sight and smell of Bree's oatmeal was beginning to make her feel nauseous. She poked at it with her spoon for several seconds before saying to her father, "I think I want an abortion."

Johnson Davis stopped eating his oatmeal but did not put down his spoon. After a few seconds, he said, "I don't want to talk about it," and continued eating his oatmeal. Bree excused herself to the hall bathroom, where she threw up. She looked at herself in the mirror for a few minutes before returning to the kitchen, where Johnson Davis had cleared the bowls and returned to his seat. When Bree again was seated, Johnson Davis said to her, "I haven't been completely honest with you."

"About what?" Bree asked.

"You're not staying home today," Johnson Davis said. "Neither am I."

"What are we doing?"

"I'm taking you to get an abortion."

"You're just taking me? Without talking to me about it?"

"You just said you wanted to."

"What if I change my mind?"

"Have you?"

"Maybe."

"Well, it's not up for discussion."

"You can't force me."

"Can't I?"

"No. It's the law."

"I'm not trying to force you."

"Then you have to discuss it with me."

"You just told me you wanted to do it."

"But I want to discuss it. What does mom think?"

"I don't know," Johnson Davis said.

"What does she think?"

"She's not sure. She wants time to consider it."

"That's what I want," Bree said. "Where is she?"

"I don't know."

"I thought she was at work."

"I don't know. I'm not sure. I suppose she is."

"What happened?"

"Just a disagreement."

"What happened?"

"Your mother left."

"Left? Left how?"

"Left."

"When?"

"Last night."

"How much stuff did she take?"

"Nothing. Her coat and purse."

"What did you say?"

"That's between the two of us."

"Can we call her?"

"You can. You call her."

o   o   o

It was four days before Johnson Davis saw his mother again, af-ter his father removed her from his church and their home. That Wednesday, as Johnson Davis turned the corner by the General Store on his walk home from school, he found his mother standing in front of the store's never-used side entrance. She was wearing the same clothes she had been wearing when Johnson Davis's father had led her out of the church, but they looked clean. Johnson Davis and his mother stared at one another for a moment before Johnson Davis's mother said, "Hello."

"What do you want?" Johnson Davis answered back.

"Are you okay?" his mother said.

"Where have you been?" Johnson Davis said.

"Close," his mother said.

"Where?" Johnson Davis said. "Who is he?"

"You don't know him. It's nothing."

"What happened?"

"It's a long story."

"Will you come home?" Johnson Davis said.

"I don't think I can."

"We can talk to him," Johnson Davis said.

"I can't."

"Just talk to him."

"I'm going to have a baby," Johnson Davis's mother said.

"A baby?"

"Yes."

"His?" Johnson Davis said.

"Whose?" his mother said.

Johnson Davis paused. "Dad's?"

"No."

Johnson Davis said nothing, simply stared at his mother until finally she lowered her eyes and said, "I won't be coming home, but I'll still be your mother. I'll still be here."

"No, you won't," Johnson Davis said.

"Don't say that," his mother said, lifting her eyes. "We're family."

"No," Johnson Davis said, "we're not."

"The baby," Johnson Davis's mother said.

"No," Johnson Davis said. "If you wanted that, you wouldn't have done it."

"I'm sorry," she said.

"No," Johnson Davis said again, brushing past his mother and running the rest of the way home.

o o o

When Bree explained, on the phone, to her mother, who was vague with Bree as to where she was, about Johnson Davis's plan and her desire to first discuss it, with both of them, Bree's mother returned home, she and Bree and Johnson Davis sitting down in the living room to discuss their options, Bree pulling her chair from the window toward the sofa, where both of her parents sat, though not as close as usual.

"Honey," Bree's mother said, to Bree, "I think you really need to think—very hard—about the consequences of whatever decision you make."

"We make," Johnson Davis said.

"I know," Bree said, to her mother.

"And we want to help you," Bree's mother said, to Bree, "to look at those consequences. To consider them."

"Thank you," Bree said.

"Consider your life," Johnson Davis said.

"What does that mean?" Bree's mother asked Johnson Davis.

"You're sixteen," Johnson Davis said, to Bree, "which means you have sixty to seventy years—God willing—of life left, all of which will be ruined. Right now."

"That's not necessarily true," Bree's mother said, to Johnson Davis. "Her life doesn't have to be ruined."

"No, it doesn't," Johnson Davis said. "Which is why we have no choice."

"Honey," Bree's mother said, to Bree. "This does not mean your life is ruined. It could mean things will be more difficult. But not ruined."

"I'll say, difficult," Johnson Davis said.

"But," Bree's mother continued, to Bree, "you have to be aware that there will be difficulties no matter what. Even with the alternative."

"There is no alternative," Johnson Davis said.

"What difficulties?" Bree said.

"You just have to know," Bree's mother said, "that even if you choose not to keep it. Not to deal with that. It still won't be easy."

"Easier than a baby," Johnson Davis said.

"Why not?" Bree asked her mother.

"Well," Bree's mother said, "think of what you'll have to go through. The pain."

"Giving birth," Johnson Davis said. "That's pain."

"Real pain?" Bree asked her mother. "Or emotional pain?"

"Well, both," Bree's mother said.

"How bad?" Bree asked her mother.

"Which?" Bree's mother said.

"Both," Bree said. "The emotional."

Bree's mother looked at Johnson Davis. "I want to tell her," she said.

"No," Johnson Davis said.

"Tell me what?" Bree said.

"I need to," Bree's mother said.

"No," Johnson Davis said again. "No, no, no, no, no. Absolutely not."

"Trust me," Bree's mother said.

"No," Johnson Davis said again. "No way."

"No what?" Bree said. "Tell me what?"

"Bree, go to your room," Johnson Davis said. "Your mother and I need to talk."

"No, stay," Bree's mother said.

"What?" Bree said.

"I think we should discuss this," Johnson Davis said to his wife.

"You can go," Bree's mother said, "if you don't want to hear it."

"I don't want *her* to hear it," Johnson Davis said. "She won't hear it."

"Hear what?" Bree said.

"I'm telling her," Bree's mother said.

"What?" Bree said. "Tell me."

"No," Johnson Davis said, "I won't allow it. She won't know this."

"She's my daughter," Bree's mother said. "I'm telling her."

"No," Johnson Davis said, "please."

"Honey . . ." Bree's mother said, to Bree.

"Don't."

". . . when I was younger . . ."

"Stop."

". . . older than you, though . . ."

"Stop, please."

"I . . ."

As Bree's mother was about to reveal to her daughter, as she had revealed to her husband, for the first time, the previous afternoon, that at nineteen she had accidentally become pregnant, by her then boyfriend, and had had an abortion, an event that had propelled her into a nearly year-long depression—a fate that she was now fearful of her daughter repeating—she was stopped, mid-sentence, by Johnson Davis's hand over her mouth.

Johnson Davis, who also feared for his daughter, his fear being her taking part in a legacy that as of the previous afternoon—to his shock—came to include his current wife, and who because of that fear found it somehow essential and without question that she remain unaware of the piece of news his wife was about to reveal to her, as if his daughter's hearing it would somehow cement her place in the legacy that he feared, held his hand cupped snuggly over his wife's mouth, bracing his other hand, fingers spread, against the back of her head, commanding frantically over her muffled shouts that his daughter go to her room, go to her room, go to her room.

Bree, first shocked still by her father's sudden action, then momentarily disabled by her mother's wide-eyed, partially irate and partially pleading stare, came to and shouted over her father, "Hey!" as she reached for the same right forearm of her father's that her mother was now clutching, her father twisting away from her so that his right shoulder occupied the space previously taken by the top of his wife's head. Bree began to slap the shoulder, repeatedly, and to shout, "Let her go," as Johnson Davis alternated between "Shh, Shh"s and additional "Go to your room"s, addending one with, "Your mother and I need to talk."

Muffled shouts continued to come from beneath Johnson Davis's hand, and Bree's mother continued to clutch at Johnson Davis's arm. She was able to breathe, her nose uncovered, but her face began to flush red and Bree shouted at her father, "You're hurting her," just before she heard her father's howl of something resembling "Ow" followed by her mother's lunge up from the couch.

"Bree, get in the car," Bree's mother said.

"You bit me," Johnson Davis said.

"In the car," Bree's mother said. Bree hustled through the living room and out the front door, her mother following close behind her.

Johnson Davis did not see either his wife or his daughter for the remainder of that day. Deciding sometime that afternoon that when he did see them again he would sit down with them and discuss the matter properly and respect and honor their decision, no matter how difficult it may be, hoping to make the best of the situation and convincing himself that in the end what really mattered was that they could be together, Johnson Davis drove to the local drugstore and purchased two appropriately apologetic cards, a stuffed koala bear, a plastic rhinoceros, a beach ball, and a small American flag, returning home and assembling these into a sort of shrine that would be immediately visible to anyone passing through the front door.

Later that evening, the phone rang. It was Johnson Davis's wife.

"Where are you?" Johnson Davis said.

"My mother's," his wife said.

"I'm sorry," Johnson Davis said.

"Okay," his wife said.

"I'm ready to talk about it."

"It's done."

"What's done?"

"It," she said. "It's done. We took care of it."

"You . . ."

"Yes."

"Without talking to me?"

"Isn't it what you wanted?"

"You can't just . . ."

"I want a divorce."

"Come home," Johnson Davis said. "We'll talk."

"I want a divorce."

"I'm sorry."

"I know."

"I bought you a card."

"What?"

"And a rhinoceros."

"What are you talking about?"

"Nothing like that will ever happen again."

"I was going to ask you anyway. For the divorce. I decided last night."

"Can we talk about it?"

"I don't want to. Not now."

"What about Bree?"

"We'll work it all out. I'll call you tomorrow."

"Don't go."

"Talk to you tomorrow. Or Friday."

"Is there someone else?"

"What?"

". . . Someone else? . . ."

"Goodbye."

Johnson Davis listened to the dial tone for a full second before saying, "Wait."

NINE

T HE MOMENT THAT Bree told Johnson Davis and Josiah and Josiah's mother that she was pregnant and it was Josiah's, Josiah's mother, who had been standing at the kitchen counter, passed out. When Josiah's mother passed out, she hit her head against a drawer that she had earlier opened in search of a whisk with which to stir the waffle batter, knocking her unconscious. When Josiah stood and stepped around the kitchen table to a point where he could see his mother, who was lying on the kitchen floor, he saw that she was bleeding from a cut on the left side of her forehead.

"Oh, shit," said Bree, who had also stood and stepped toward Josiah's mother.

Johnson Davis quickly approached Josiah's mother and knelt down beside her, shaking her slightly by the shoulder and calling her name. Bree handed Johnson Davis a paper towel which he then pressed against the cut.

"Call 911," Johnson Davis said.

"Wake her up," Bree said.

"I know what I'm doing," Johnson Davis said.

"Slap her lightly," Bree said.

"I know what I'm doing," Johnson Davis said. "Call 911."

As Bree left the kitchen to call 911, Johnson Davis lightly slapped Josiah's mother twice on the cheek. Josiah's mother still did not wake up. Johnson Davis looked up at Josiah, who was standing over them, watching.

"Kneel down here," Johnson Davis said to Josiah. Josiah kneeled down beside his mother.

"Say something," Johnson Davis said.

"What?"

"Anything. Just talk to her."

Josiah stared at his mother.

"Tell her you love her," Johnson Davis said.

Josiah said nothing.

"Tell her."

Josiah stared at his mother.

"Tell her, Josiah. Tell her you love her."

When the ambulance arrived to take Josiah's mother, who still had not regained consciousness, to the hospital, Johnson Davis, after being told that only one person could ride along in the ambulance with Josiah's mother, handed his keys to Bree and said, "Follow in the car."

"I don't have a license," Bree said.

"Oh, piss," Johnson Davis said. "It's an emergency. Just follow."

"I don't drive," Bree said.

"Josiah drives," Johnson Davis said as he stepped into the ambulance.

Bree and Josiah got into Johnson Davis's car, Josiah in the driver's seat and Bree in the passenger's. Bree said to Josiah, "I didn't know you could drive."

"I just started," Josiah said.

"When?"

"Yesterday."

"Yesterday?"

"Yes."

"Are you sure you can do this?"

"I think so."

By the time Josiah had driven Johnson Davis's car one block, Josiah driving much slower than the driver of the ambulance, the ambulance was completely out of sight, prompting Bree to tell Josiah that it was okay because she knew how to get to the hospital, after which Bree said to Josiah, "I'm sure your mother will be fine."

"When will you have the baby?" Josiah asked.

After a pause, Bree responded, "Eight months. A little more," adding, "It's just a cut. She'll be fine."

When Josiah reached the ramp that led onto the freeway, he stopped. "What's the matter?" Bree asked him.

"I can't drive on the freeway."

"I don't know how to get there any other way." A car pulled up behind the car of Johnson Davis, which was stopped at the entrance to the onramp, and began honking its horn over and over. "You have to go," Bree said.

"People have to have sex to get pregnant," Josiah said.

"I know," Bree said.

"They have to fuck."

"I know." Two more cars drove up behind the car that was behind Johnson Davis's car and began to honk their horns as well.

"You said you didn't fuck me."

"You came, didn't you?"

"Yes."

"And I came?"

"Yes."

"Then we fucked."

"That's it?"

"That's it. That's how it happens."

Josiah pushed down on the gas pedal and entered the freeway.

When Bree and Josiah arrived to the hospital, Josiah's mother, with Johnson Davis by her side, had already been taken to a curtain area in the hospital's emergency room, where her cut had been cleaned and dressed and where the doctors had used smelling salts to awaken her.

Bree and Josiah were told by the nurse behind the desk at the entrance to the emergency room to have a seat in the waiting area and to wait and someone would be right with them. When Bree told the nurse that Josiah's mother had fallen and hit her head and was bleeding and that they needed to see her, the nurse again told Bree to please sit and wait and someone would be with them immediately.

Bree and Josiah were waiting for six minutes when Bree again approached the desk and told the nurse that she had better let them into the emergency room right now, and the nurse, who suddenly looked very annoyed and who picked up the receiver of a phone, was about to respond to Bree when Johnson Davis entered the waiting room and looked at Bree and at Josiah, who had stood when Bree had stood, and at the annoyed-looking nurse and asked what was the matter. The nurse put down the receiver of the phone and asked Johnson Davis, "Are these your children?"

"Yes," Johnson Davis said, and stepping away from the desk, Johnson Davis said to Josiah and Bree, "Everything is fine. She is awake." Johnson Davis then turned and looked directly at Josiah and said, "Your mother will be fine, Josiah." Josiah said nothing.

"Should we go in?" Bree said.

"Well," Johnson Davis said, "no."

"Why not?" Bree said.

"I don't think it's a good idea," Johnson Davis said. "Considering."

"Considering what?" Bree said.

"You know exactly what," Johnson Davis said. "I don't think it's a good idea that she see you now. In fact, could you please stop speaking? I don't wish to speak to you right now."

"Take Josiah," Bree said.

"Please stop speaking."

"Take him," Bree said.

Johnson Davis turned to Josiah and said, "I don't think it's a good idea that your mother see either one of you now, Josiah. Considering. She will be perfectly fine. She is awake and perfectly fine. I just don't think she should see you now." Johnson Davis then turned from Josiah and looked over Josiah and Bree's heads at the wall behind them and said, "They are going to keep her overnight. She may be concussed. They say I can stay until six. Wait for me here. I'll drive you both home. Bree I'll take home—home home— in the morning. Her mother has an appointment for her." Johnson Davis looked down from the wall at Bree and continued, "She is not happy." When Bree said nothing, Johnson Davis turned to Josiah and said, "Everything is fine. Wait here," and walked out of the waiting area back into the emergency room.

Five minutes later, after just enough time had passed for Josiah and Bree to find seats in the waiting room and for Bree to ask Josiah if he wanted to go with her for a smoke, Johnson Davis returned. Josiah's mother, who had been moved from the curtain area to a room of her own, had sent Johnson Davis to retrieve Josiah, not wishing, as Johnson Davis had suspected, to see or speak to Josiah at the moment—considering—but also not wanting to leave Josiah alone with Bree. Josiah, who had been pleased at the idea of having several hours to spend alone with Bree and to discuss what would happen now that they would be having a baby, particularly whether or not they would still be secret boyfriend and girlfriend and whether or not they would now get married, instead sat waiting, as instructed, on a bench outside of Josiah's mother's room for the several hours until Johnson Davis left Josiah's mother's room and drove Josiah and Bree home.

After a ride home that was completely silent other than Bree telling Johnson Davis, who had pulled into a fast food drive-through, that she did not eat hamburgers, and Johnson Davis responding that he couldn't hear a word she was saying and to please stop speaking, Josiah and Bree were sent directly to their rooms, with Johnson Davis once again announcing, as Josiah and Bree ascended the stairs, that he would be taking Bree home—home home—and they would be sorting all of this out first thing in the morning.

Josiah was in his room, alone, for fifteen minutes, sitting on his bed and again wondering if Bree being pregnant with his child meant that they would be married, and if so, would they have a wedding, and what would it be like, and what would their child be like, when Johnson Davis came into Josiah's room and said, "Lights out," and turned out the light.

Josiah continued to sit in the darkness for several more minutes pondering his and Bree's wedding before finally taking off his jeans, leaving him in his t-shirt and shorts, and getting into bed. Josiah would very much have liked to walk down the hallway to Bree's room, or have Bree walk down the hallway to his room, so that they could discuss the things that he was pondering, but every thirty minutes Johnson Davis opened the door to Josiah's bedroom and looked inside, where Josiah was pretending to sleep, and closed it again, and Josiah could hear, down the hallway, also every thirty minutes, Johnson Davis opening and closing the door to Bree's bedroom.

Around two in the morning, nearly forty-five minutes after the last time that Johnson Davis had come into Josiah's bedroom, Josiah heard a very light knocking. When Josiah got out of bed, he found that a note had been passed under his door. The note was written on a piece of paper shaped like a slice of watermelon and said, *Meet Me. 3:30. Garage.*

By the time the digital clock on the table beside Josiah's bed said three twenty-five, Johnson Davis had not come into Josiah's room for over two hours. Josiah pulled his jeans back over his shorts and very slowly opened the door of his bedroom and walked out into the hallway.

The overhead light in the garage was already on when Josiah arrived, causing him to squint as he entered. Bree was waiting for him, sitting on a short bench.

"Sit down," Bree said, and Josiah sat down next to Bree on the bench. "I got you something," Bree said to him, "for your birthday."

Josiah turned and looked at Bree. "Do you want it?" Bree asked.

Josiah nodded. Bree stood and walked to Johnson Davis's work table and picked up a pink box and walked back to the bench. She handed the box to Josiah. On the top of the box, handwritten in black ink, were letters spelling out *Happy Birthday*. The letters were written in the same handwriting as the letters on the watermelon-shaped note. Next to the "y" in *Birthday* was a smiley face, also in black ink, composed of two dots and a curved line.

"Open it," Bree said to Josiah. Josiah lifted the pink lid from the box and inside found something shiny. He reached into the box with his right thumb and right pointer finger and pulled the object out, which consisted of a short chain connected to each end of a small metal plate.

"It's a bracelet," Bree said, adding, "Read it." Josiah placed the object in his left hand, picking it up again, this time with his thumb on the top and his pointer finger on the bottom of the small metal plate. Carved into the plate was the outline of a heart, and inside the heart, in pretty letters, *From B to J.*

"Do you like it?" Bree asked.

"Yes," Josiah answered, still staring at the plate and rereading the message.

"There's a little store near school. They sell all kinds of bracelets and necklaces and stuff. You buy one and then they put the stuff on it. They have a machine."

Josiah was still staring at the bracelet when Bree reached across and lifted it from his fingers. Using the tips of her own thumbs and pointer fingers, she opened a small clasp on the part of the chain farthest from the small metal plate. The chain separated, and Bree, holding it open with both hands, draped the chain around Josiah's wrist, which hadn't moved but rather waited suspended in the air, and re-clasped the chain. Bree took Josiah's hand in hers and turned it in mid-air so that the palm faced the floor and slid the chain along his wrist until the metal plate rested on top.

"Thank you," Josiah said.

"No problem," Bree said. Josiah stood and walked to a wooden, free-standing closet where Johnson Davis kept important tools that he did not want to leave in the tool shed, such as his chainsaw and his new Weed Eater, and opened the door, leaning down and reaching in and pulling out the soccer ball with Brent Randolph's signature stamped onto it, covered with grass stains and tiny splashes of mud that would not go away when Josiah had found the ball and had tried to wash it off, and with its cardboard packaging reapplied, Josiah having taped together the small rip Johnson Davis had created when tearing the packaging off. The tape covered up one of the four images of Brent Randolph's face. Josiah returned to the bench and sat down, handing the ball to Bree.

"Is this for me?" she asked.

"Yes," he answered.

"It's not even my birthday."

"I know."

Bree studied the ball for a few seconds, noticing the stains, and said, "It's used."

"I had to use it."

"What do you mean, you had to use it?"

"Your father made me use it. Play with it."

Bree stared at the ball, running her fingers over the grooves and the lettering, studying the images of Brent Randolph—kicking and running and raising his arms in victory—printed onto the cardboard. "This is my favorite player," she said.

"I know," said Josiah.

"I don't mind that you used it. I love it. Thank you." Bree, who had been holding her new ball in both hands, momentarily removed one hand from the ball and placed it behind Josiah's neck and leaned forward and kissed Josiah on the forehead and then removed the hand from the back of his neck and returned it to the ball.

"Thank you," she said again.

Josiah, not looking at Bree but rather staring at a spot on the floor three feet away from the bench upon which they were sitting, said to Bree, "Will we get married?"

"Do you want to?" Bree said.

"Yes," Josiah said.

"Why?"

"I love you."

"Why?"

Josiah shrugged.

"You don't know why?"

"I think about you."

"When?"

"All the time."

"What do you think about?"

"I don't know. Being together."

"Being together how?"

"Just being together. Like boyfriend and girlfriend."

"We are boyfriend and girlfriend."

"But not secret."

"Why does it matter?"

"I don't know."

"Does it matter?"

"Yes."

"Why?"

"We're going to have a baby."

"That doesn't mean we have to be married."

"We should all be together."

"All who?"

"You, me, and the baby."

"Do you think you're ready to be a father?"

"Yes."

"How do you know?"

"I don't know. I just know."

"How will we make money?"

"I don't know. I'll work."

"What will you do?"

"I don't know."

"Where will we live? I know your mother won't let us live with them. My dad, either."

"We'll go somewhere else."

"Where?"

"I know where."

"Parnuckle?"

"Yes."

"Do you know how to get there?"

"Yes."

"How do we get there?"

"I'll ask my father."

"How?"

"I'll contact him."

"How?"

"I'll write a letter."

"How do you know I'll want to? Want to go there? It's a long way."

Josiah shrugged.

"I may not like it."

"You'll like it."

"How do you know?"

Josiah shrugged.

"Describe it to me," Bree said, "so I'll know if I like it."

Josiah then proceeded to tell Bree the same details that his mother had often told him as a child, and that he had earlier that weekend told to Johnson Davis, namely that no one on the planet Parnuckle ever had to take baths or showers, because there is no dirt, and no one ever goes to sleep, because no one ever gets tired, and no one ever has to go shopping, because everyone has everything already in their house.

"That sounds alright," Bree said. "Tell me more."

"Like what?" Josiah said.

"More like what it will be like, for us. Like where will we live exactly? With your Dad?"

"I guess so."

"What's it like? Where does he live?"

o o o

When Patrick, Josiah's roommate in the group home, had asked Josiah to describe the planet Parnuckle, shortly after Josiah had shown Patrick the picture of his real mother and had explained that his real mother lived with his father far, far away on a planet called Parnuckle and that he hoped to soon be able to move to Parnuckle and live with them in their home, Josiah told Patrick, as his mother had often told him as a child, that no one on the planet

Parnuckle ever had to take baths or showers because there was no dirt, to which Patrick responded, "Cool. Probably the planet's land mass is composed of a self-cleansing substance or something," and when Josiah told Patrick, as his mother had often told him, that no one ever goes to sleep because no one ever gets tired, Patrick responded, "Because of a cellular makeup in which half the cells remain dormant, resting and regenerating until it's time to switch places with the other cells."

After Josiah told Patrick that no one on the planet Parnuckle ever goes shopping because everyone has everything already in their house, to which Patrick responded, "Like the food replicators on *Star Trek*, except they respond to thoughts, not just verbal commands, and they can replicate anything," Patrick began asking Josiah questions about his father, such as what his father's position was, Josiah telling Patrick, as his mother had often told him, that his father was the Keymaster of Gozer, leading Patrick to ask Josiah what the Keymaster of Gozer did, and who Gozer was, and where the Keymaster of Gozer would live, all of which led Josiah to shrug.

Patrick then proceeded to inform Josiah that the Keymaster of Gozer most certainly lived in the Royal Palace of Gozer, which was located in the capital city of Gozeria, specifically in a special wing of the Palace, reserved for each generation's Keymaster, and the Royal Palace of Gozer was so massive and so extravagant that the special wing was almost like a palace unto itself.

o o o

"A palace?" Bree asked.

"Yes," Josiah said.

"That sounds nice. Are you sure we can live there?"

"Yes."

"What does it look like? Describe it."

Josiah proceeded to describe the Royal Palace of Gozer to Bree, as Patrick had described it to Josiah, with its marble and gold columns and its stained glass ceilings depicting important scenes from Parnuckle's history, and the Royal Dining Hall, which covered ten acres and included its own transportation system, and when Bree wanted to know specifically about the special wing, where they would be living, Josiah described, as Patrick had described to him, the three large rooms—an acre each—of the special wing, one being the living area of the Keymaster of Gozer, Josiah's father, and his goddess wife, the room transforming throughout the day based on need, from bedroom to living room to wash room, and the second room, known as the utility area, likewise transforming based on need, from office of the Keymaster to temple where people come to worship Josiah's goddess mother to general storage space.

The third room, reserved for special guests and currently not in use, where Josiah, along with Bree and their child, would be living, like the other two rooms, would also be designed, Josiah explained to Bree, as Patrick had explained to Josiah, to fulfill their every need.

"It sounds amazing," Bree said.

Josiah nodded.

"When will we leave?" Bree asked.

"We should go now."

"No. Not now. But soon."

"You're leaving in the morning."

"But I'll be back."

"We can go."

"Soon. Kiss me goodnight."

Josiah did not move.

"Close your eyes," Bree said, and Josiah closed his eyes and Bree kissed him on his mouth, first making contact, then wetting her lips with the tip of her tongue, applying pressure to Josiah's lips, smacking, and backing away.

"Thank you for my ball," she said.

Josiah nodded.

"Will you miss me?" Bree asked.

"Yes," Josiah said, "I'll wait for you."

"I know," Bree said.

It was just after four in the morning when Josiah got back to his room, and he was still awake at six fifteen when he heard Johnson

Davis walking down the hallway toward Bree's room. Josiah could hear Johnson Davis and Bree speaking, but could not hear what they were saying. After a few minutes, Josiah heard Bree's door close and heard both Johnson Davis's and Bree's footsteps coming down the hall. Josiah quickly got out of bed and opened the door to his room and stepped into the hallway. The hallway was dark, but light enough that Josiah could see Johnson Davis and Bree, who had both stopped when Josiah opened the door, just past his room, nearly halfway to the stairs.

"Go back to sleep, Josiah," Johnson Davis said. In the darkness, Josiah could tell that Bree was looking at him, and that she was smiling at him. Josiah turned and looked at Johnson Davis.

"Go back to sleep," Johnson Davis said again to Josiah as he led Bree toward the stairs.

Once Johnson Davis and Bree were out the front door and the front door was shut and the headlights of the car of Johnson Davis had backed down the driveway and the car had driven away, all of which Josiah watched from the second floor banister, Josiah went back into his room and turned on the light and walked up to the large framed poster on the wall that said BELIEVE and pulled it down and smashed the frame against his dresser. He then dragged the poster out from the broken glass and tore it into five pieces and placed one of the pieces on the dresser and found a pencil and, standing at the dresser, drew a picture of Bree on the back of the torn piece of poster. Like the picture that Josiah had drawn of Bree naked and sitting in a chair, in this picture Bree was sitting in a chair, but she was not naked. She was wearing her soccer jersey, and in the picture the jersey was very tight and very clearly showed her breasts, which, in the picture, were larger than they were in real life, and in the picture Bree's hair was longer than in real life, and was particularly flowing, and most importantly in the picture Bree's belly was very large and very round, as if she were eight months pregnant. Josiah then put the piece of poster aside and grabbed another and drew another picture in which he and Bree and their child, who in the picture was a boy, were all standing and smiling and holding hands, and another in which Josiah and Bree were getting married, Bree in a long dress and Josiah in a tuxedo, and another in which Josiah and Bree and their child were sitting and eating dinner at a large round table with Josiah's father and real mother on Parnuckle. On the last piece of poster, Josiah wrote a letter to his father. The letter went like this:

> *Dear Father,*
>
> *I am writing to let you know that soon I will be a father, too. The mother is the girl that I wrote to you about, Bree. We will be getting married, and have talked about possibly coming to live on Parnuckle right away, if that is okay with you. We can discuss this more, later.*
>
> *Until then,*
Josiah

Josiah left the drawings and the letter on his dresser and walked downstairs and took a carton of chocolate ice cream out of the refrigerator and sat down on the couch, where he fell asleep after half of the carton was gone.

Josiah was awakened by the telephone ringing. As he stood, he saw that the carton of ice cream had tipped over and melted and had run onto his t-shirt and shorts and onto the couch and down to the floor. Josiah walked to the phone and answered it. A woman said, "Is this Josiah?"

"Yes," Josiah answered.

"Hello, Josiah," said the woman. "This is Evelyn. Bree's mother." Josiah said nothing.

"It's nice to talk to you, finally." Josiah again said nothing.

"Is my ex-husband there, Josiah?" Bree's mother asked. "Or your mother?"

"No."

"No?"

"No."

"Can you tell my ex-husband to call me? As soon as you see him? It's very important."

"Okay."

"Will you remember?"

"Yes."

"It's very important."

"Okay."

"Don't forget."

As Josiah hung up the phone, he could hear the sound of Johnson Davis's car pulling into the driveway. Through the window, Josiah watched as Johnson Davis, who had picked Josiah's mother up from the hospital on the way home, walked around the front of the car and helped Josiah's mother out of the passenger's seat.

Josiah opened the front door as Johnson Davis and Josiah's mother slowly walked up the driveway, Johnson Davis supporting Josiah's mother with both arms. Josiah's mother wore a small square of white gauze, held on by tape, over the spot on her forehead where Josiah had seen the cut. Once they were through, Josiah closed the door behind them.

"Thank you, Josiah," Johnson Davis said, and then, seeing the chocolate ice cream-colored stain on Josiah's t-shirt and shorts, added, "What on Earth is all over you?"

Josiah's mother, who had not been looking at Josiah at all, but rather had been staring straight into the room at nothing in particular, turned suddenly to look at Josiah when she heard Johnson Davis ask what on Earth was all over him, and when she saw for herself the chocolate ice cream-colored stain, she asked Josiah, "What is that?" adding, "What were you eating?"

"Ice cream," Josiah responded. "Chocolate ice cream."

"Why?" Josiah's mother asked Josiah.

"Christ, it's all over here," Johnson Davis said, noticing the stain on his sofa and floor.

"What happened?" Josiah's mother asked Johnson Davis.

"It's a mess, Josiah," Johnson Davis said.

"You have a message," Josiah then said to Johnson Davis.

"What message?" Johnson Davis asked.

"From your wife."

"Josiah," Johnson Davis said, "I don't have a wife. Right now."

"Your ex-wife," Josiah said.

"What did she say?" Johnson Davis asked.

"To call her."

Johnson Davis quickly stepped into the kitchen to call his ex-wife while Josiah and Josiah's mother stood facing one another in the living room.

"How are you, Josiah?" Josiah's mother asked.

Josiah shrugged.

"I'm going to be fine," Josiah's mother said.

Josiah nodded.

"We have some things, Josiah," Josiah's mother said, "some issues—troubling events—that we need to discuss. We need to have a very serious, very grown-up, discussion."

As Josiah was again nodding, Johnson Davis reentered the living room and in one quick breath ordered Josiah upstairs and his fiancée with him into the kitchen.

Ten minutes later, Josiah was called down from his bedroom, where he had changed out of his stained t-shirt and shorts into a clean t-shirt and a pair of jeans, to the dimly-lit dining room, where, as he had been before, he was asked to sit at one end of the dining room table, across from Johnson Davis and Josiah's mother, who sat, as they had before, perpendicular to one another at the other end of the table, with Johnson Davis's hands placed, as before, palm down against the table's surface and Josiah's mother's hands, likewise, in her lap, and proceeded to tell Josiah, first of all, that despite the scare they had all had and all the problems that had been caused—hospitals and what-not—Johnson Davis had spoken to Bree's mother and it turned out that, according to Bree's pediatrician, Bree was in fact not pregnant.

"It appears she made the entire thing up," Johnson Davis said, "which still leaves a major question unanswered. A question that concerns your mother and I very much, Josiah."

Johnson Davis stopped speaking and Josiah's mother leaned forward and said to Josiah, "Do you remember, Josiah, the talk that we had, when you were younger, about men and women and the things that they do to one another?"

"Yes," Josiah said.

"You remember?" Josiah's mother said.

"Yes."

"What do you remember?"

Josiah shrugged.

"Do you remember what I showed you?" Josiah's mother said. "With the bottle? And the cup?"

Josiah nodded.

"And what a man's penis does to a woman's vagina?"

Before Josiah could answer, which he was about to do by nodding, Johnson Davis cut in, saying to Josiah, "Josiah, look at me," and when Josiah looked at Johnson Davis, Johnson Davis added, "Have you and Bree done things together?"

"What do you mean?" Josiah asked.

"Have you had sexual relations?" Johnson Davis asked.

"What do you mean?" Josiah asked again.

"Josiah," Josiah's mother said, "do you remember how I took the bottle, and—"

Johnson Davis cut Josiah's mother off, saying to Josiah, "Have you had sex?"

"—and put the bottle . . ."

"Yes," Josiah said to Johnson Davis.

Josiah's mother stopped speaking. She began to cry. Johnson Davis stared at Josiah for several seconds, and then asked again, "You've had sex together?"

"Yes," Josiah said. "We fucked."

Josiah's mother began to cry louder. Johnson Davis said nothing, simply stared at Josiah. Finally, he said, a bit quietly, "Why would you say it like that, Josiah?"

Josiah's mother, who had been sitting with her head down, crying, lifted her head and said to Johnson Davis, "I told you," and then said again, a bit louder, "I told you," and slapped at Johnson

Davis's face, causing Josiah to flinch and mostly making contact with Johnson Davis's shoulder, which he had lifted in defense.

"I told you," Josiah's mother said again as she again slapped at Johnson Davis. Johnson Davis caught Josiah's mother's hand, saying, "Don't, damnit. Stop."

Josiah's mother stood, Johnson Davis remaining seated and holding her hand by the wrist. Josiah stood as well.

"Keep her away," Josiah's mother said. "Keep her out of here."

"Don't," Johnson Davis said. He let go of Josiah's mother's hand, which Josiah's mother let drop to her side.

"She'll ruin our lives."

"She's my daughter."

"She's a whore."

"Don't say that," Johnson Davis said, standing. "Goddamnit, don't say that."

"It's true," Josiah's mother said.

"Please, Goddamnit," Johnson Davis said.

"She's not a whore," Josiah said.

Both Johnson Davis and Josiah's mother turned to look at Josiah. "What did you say?" Josiah's mother asked.

"She's not a whore," Josiah said again.

"You shut your mouth," Josiah's mother said to Josiah.

"Dear," Johnson Davis said.

Josiah said nothing.

"Shut your mouth," Josiah's mother said again.

"Dear," Johnson Davis repeated.

"You'll never see her again," Josiah's mother said, "Never," and Josiah's mother began to walk, quickly, along the side of the dining room table toward Josiah, who moved around the other side of the table toward Johnson Davis.

"Go to your room, Josiah," Johnson Davis said.

"Never," Josiah's mother said, and she began to move back along the table the way she had come, toward Johnson Davis and Josiah. Johnson Davis, who was standing between Josiah's mother and the entrance to the dining room, again told Josiah to go to his room, and as Josiah passed behind Johnson Davis and through the living room and up the stairs to his bedroom, he could hear his mother chanting, "Never. Never. Never."

At around eleven thirty that morning, Josiah walked out of his room, leaving the pieces of the torn poster with the drawings and letter on their back and the broken pieces of glass and empty frame all lying on the floor, none of which Johnson Davis or Josiah's mother had yet found, neither of them having come into Josiah's room since returning from the hospital, and both having come to the decision, after Josiah had been sent to his room—that decision having been reported to Josiah by Johnson Davis through the closed door of Josiah's bedroom—that for the time being, until a different or alternate arrangement could be made, Bree and Josiah would be kept separated, Johnson Davis going to see his daughter on Friday afternoons and taking her to dinner or perhaps a movie and returning home, without Bree coming to stay in the home of Johnson Davis, and Josiah, about an hour and a half after hearing this news, walked out of his room and along the hallway and down the stairs and through the living room and out the front door to the driveway, where Josiah got into Johnson Davis's car, having picked the keys up from the coffee table on his way past it, and backed out of the driveway, seeing Johnson Davis and his mother, out of the corner of his eye, step through the front door, and Josiah, remembering the way from his and Johnson Davis's trip two days earlier, began the forty-six-mile drive to Bree.

TEN

T HOUGH THE HOME, on weekdays, and now possibly for all days, of Bree, as well as of Bree's mother, was only forty-six miles from the home of Johnson Davis, it took Josiah nearly an hour and a half to arrive there, having had to first drive to Bree's high school, as Johnson Davis had done, before making his way to Bree's home, where, once he had parked Johnson Davis's car in the driveway, which at the time contained no other cars, Josiah walked up to the front door and knocked. When no one answered, he knocked again and pushed the button for the doorbell. Bree opened the door. She looked like she had been sleeping. Her hair was not as shiny and not as straight as it normally was, but Josiah still liked the way that it looked. She was wearing pink sweatpants and a grey t-shirt. It was not the grey t-shirt that had *Phys. Ed.* printed on it—this shirt had nothing printed on it—but like the grey t-shirt that had *Phys. Ed.* printed on it, Josiah could see the shape of Bree's breasts beneath it.

Bree stared at Josiah for a moment and then said, "Come in." Once Josiah had stepped inside, Bree closed the door. Though the home of Johnson Davis was quite large, especially in comparison to the home Josiah had lived in with his mother, the home of Bree and Bree's mother was even slightly larger. The room that Josiah and Bree were standing in, just inside the front door, was very tall. The ceiling reached high over Josiah and Bree's heads, and above them were large windows that allowed in wide beams of sunlight.

"You came for me," Bree said.

"Yes," Josiah said.

"You're getting good at driving."

"Yes."

"We have to go soon," Bree said. "My mom will be back. She went to yoga."

"We can go now," Josiah said.

After a pause, Bree said, "We need to think. Sit down." Bree led Josiah into the living room and they sat down, Bree sitting sideways on the couch, Indian-style, facing Josiah.

"They'll be looking for the car," Bree said. "We should ditch it. In fact, they'll probably come here first. Probably they're on their way. Probably called my mom on her cell, which will be in her bag. But she'll be done soon."

Bree stood and walked out of the room. Josiah could hear her running up the stairs, which from the couch Josiah could not see, and running back down. Bree returned holding her cell phone, which like her sweatpants was also pink. She pushed several buttons and then held it to her ear.

"Hey," she said, "come get me. At home. Like, right now. And Josiah. We have to get out of here. Five minutes. Kay."

Bree lowered the phone from her ear and pushed another button. She then turned and left the room and again Josiah heard her run up the stairs and back down, and Bree returned holding her purse and sat, as she had been, facing Josiah, on the couch, and reached into her purse and pulled out a pack of cigarettes and a lighter. Bree set her purse on the floor and lit a cigarette and began smoking it. Josiah watched as Bree slowly and smoothly blew the smoke out of her mouth.

"Did they tell you I'm not pregnant?"

"Yes."

"Do you believe them?"

"No."

"Why?"

"Their machines couldn't see it."

"The doctors' machines?"

"Yes."

"Because the baby is Parnucklian."

"Yes."

"Part-Parnucklian."

"Yes."

Bree took a long drag from her cigarette, blowing the smoke out especially slow and smooth.

"How will we get there?" she asked.

"I wrote a letter," Josiah said.

o o o

Earlier that day, between the time that Johnson Davis reported to Josiah he would not be seeing Bree again and the time that Josiah drove away in the car of Johnson Davis, just after Josiah made the decision to drive to the home of Bree's mother, Josiah had written a letter to his father. It went like this:

> *Dear Father,*
>
> *This is Josiah. I will definitely not be able to live with my other mother any longer. There's a lot to explain, but she is very upset and does not want Bree, the girl I told you about, and I to be together with our son or daughter (I hope son). I am going to steal her father's car and go and get Bree right now. We will need to move to the planet Parnuckle today. It is very important that you send a ship for us. Please send a signal or a message so we will know where to meet it.*
>
> *Looking forward to seeing you and my mother (and showing you your grandson or granddaughter).*
>
> *Love,*
> *Josiah*

o o o

"Where's the letter?" Bree asked.

"In my pocket," Josiah answered.

"Read it," Bree said. Josiah took the folded-up letter out of his pocket and read it to Bree. When Josiah had finished, Bree walked into the kitchen. Josiah heard water running. Bree came back without her cigarette.

"How will you send it?" Bree asked.

"I just write them," Josiah said.

"Does he ever respond?"

"He used to."

Josiah then heard a car in the driveway, and Josiah watched as Bree, who had also heard the car, turned and walked to the front door and opened it. Josiah, having followed Bree, could see through the open front door Bart's 1992 Camaro parked behind the car of Johnson Davis, and as Bart stepped out of the car, Bree said to Josiah, "Let's go."

Bree was crossing the driveway several steps ahead of Josiah, and when Bree reached Bart's car and Bart hugged Bree, Josiah stopped, still several steps away. Bart and Bree, their hug finished, both turned and looked at Josiah.

"We've got to go," Bree said, to both Josiah and Bart. Bart stepped toward Josiah, his hand held out.

"Good to see you again," he said. Josiah shook his hand.

As Josiah and Bart released hands, Bart said, "What's the big rush?"

"Josiah stole my Dad's car," Bree said.

"Seriously?" Bart said, looking at Josiah.

"Yes," Bree said.

"You stole his car?" Bart said to Josiah.

Josiah nodded.

"Where're we going?" Bart said, turning toward Bree.

"Let's just go," Bree said.

"Get in," Bart said.

As Bart got into the driver's seat of his car, Josiah and Bree walked around to the passenger side, and as Bree reached for the handle, Josiah reached past her and opened the door himself and held it open for her. "Thank you," Bree said, smiling but not looking at Josiah.

Bree tilted her seat forward for Josiah to climb into the back, and as Josiah buckled his seat belt, Bart, who had begun to back out of the driveway, turned to Bree and said, "Where to, Babe?"

o   o   o

Though he would hear it numerous times subsequently, through the years, on various television shows or in various movies, even hearing it occasionally used by Johnson Davis, who clearly preferred the term "Dear," toward his mother, and by Dutch Lucas, who used the word, as part of his only-partly-authentic-chauvinist-tough-guy persona, in addressing a number of the women who populated his various adventures, Josiah first heard a man call a woman "Babe" when he was seven years old and his mother was dating, for three weeks, a man named Dave, who talked very loudly and who began every sentence, as every sentence Josiah ever heard Dave speak had been addressed at Josiah's mother, with the word "Babe."

o   o   o

When Bart asked Bree where they were going, which he had done by asking her, "Where to, Babe?" Bree answered that they could go to her friend Ariel's, which was back in the town where Bree had grown up, and where Josiah now lived with his mother and Johnson Davis and from which Josiah had just come, and where Bree declared, from the front passenger seat of Bart's car, that none of them, referring to her mother and father and Josiah's mother, would be looking, at least not for a while, and especially not for Bart's car, which they could keep hidden, just to be safe, in the parking garage of Ariel's apartment complex, Ariel not having a car of her own but still having been assigned a parking spot as a condition of her rent, and they could stay there, in Ariel's apartment, for several hours if need be, though it eventually would become a possibility, once Bree's parents had found Bree missing as well, that Johnson Davis would suspect that they possibly were with Ariel, and Johnson Davis would somehow find out where Ariel was now living, and at that point they would need to find someplace else.

Josiah watched, from the back seat, as Bree verbally ran through these scenarios, smoking a cigarette, blowing the smoke out smoothly and slowly, as Bart drove along the freeway. When Bart asked Bree, "What about the cops?" Bree responded that it depends. If they tried to report either her or Josiah missing, the cops wouldn't do anything for twenty-four hours, which Josiah also knew to be true, from television, but if Johnson Davis, and he just might have, had reported his car stolen, the cops might be involved, even though the car was now sitting in Bree's mother's driveway.

Just over thirty minutes later, Bree directed Bart off of the freeway and down several streets, most of which Josiah, who had spent a portion of the just over thirty minutes wondering how the ship his father had sent for them would find them with all of this driving around, had never seen before, until finally Bart and Bree and Josiah pulled into the parking lot of an apartment complex. The building was two stories, with a row of apartment doors along the bottom floor and a matching row above. The upper row of apartment doors had a metal railing, which was bent in two spots, in front of it. The building was painted white, but some of the paint had fallen off.

Josiah, having spent the other portion of the just over thirty minutes wondering what it meant that Bart had called Bree "Babe," followed Bart and Bree up the thick concrete steps leading to the door of Ariel's apartment, which Ariel, Bree's friend, had lived in since shortly after she had graduated from high school—the same high school that Bree had attended until moving forty-six miles away—Ariel paying for her rent with money earned selling marijuana, and shortly after Bree rang the doorbell, the door was opened by a girl who was taller than Bree and who had darker hair than Bree, brown but almost red, but not as straight and not as shiny as Bree's, wearing a black t-shirt and blue jeans that were not as tight as the blue jeans that Bree was wearing and under which Josiah, standing one step down from Bree, could see the shape of

Bree's Thomas Magnum very well. The girl, who was Bree's friend Ariel, and whom Josiah had heard Bree speak to on her pink cell phone on their way to the apartment complex, said "Hello" and led Bree and Bart and Josiah into her apartment, specifically the living room, which consisted of a couch and a chair, both with torn upholstery and both facing a TV set that was sitting alone on the floor. From the living room, Josiah could see straight into Ariel's kitchen, which consisted of a counter and a refrigerator and a few cupboards and a sink filled with dirty dishes.

"This is Ariel," Bree said to Bart and Josiah.

"Hi," said Ariel to Bart and Josiah.

"Hi," said Bart. Josiah said nothing.

"So what's new?" Ariel asked.

"Josiah stole a car," Bart said.

"Who's Josiah?" Ariel said.

"This is Josiah," Bart said.

Ariel looked at Josiah. "Why?" she asked.

"He had to escape from my father," Bree said, "and his crazy mother."

"Makes sense," Ariel said.

"We're on the run," Bart said.

"Cool," Ariel said.

"We need to stay," Bree said.

"Okay," Ariel said. "Want to get high?

o o o

During the summer before their freshman year, Bree and her childhood friend Jessica had attended a weekend soccer camp at the local high school. At lunch time on the second day, three girls named Ariel, Marlena, and Maria, whom Bree and Jessica had not yet met but knew of—as these three girls were members of the Girls Varsity soccer team at the local high school and were helping to administer the weekend soccer camp—approached them and asked if they wanted to come with them to get some pizza, which Bree and Jessica quickly agreed to, throwing the bag lunches that Jessica's mother had made for them in the trash on the way to the parking lot. Ariel and Maria were both going to be juniors, but Marlena was going to be a senior, and as the five of them sat in Marlena's car, Ariel and Maria in the front seat with Marlena and Bree and Jessica in the back, Ariel turned to Bree and Jessica and asked, "You guys ever smoke pot before?" Jessica, taken aback and unsure what to do, looked at Bree, who quickly responded, "Sure we have."

After that day, Bree began spending more and more time with the older girls, in particular Ariel. When high school began that fall, Bree was always at Ariel's side, sitting at the Girls Varsity lunch table and skipping classes to go shopping or to sit in Marlena's car in Maria's long driveway and smoke. Ariel also took Bree to upperclassmen parties and introduced her to upperclassmen boys.

One day, when Ariel was seventeen and Bree was fifteen, Ariel convinced Bree that it would be a good idea, since both girls were very hungry, having skipped fifth and sixth period and smoked a large amount of pot, and since neither girl had any money to spend on food, to shoplift something to eat from the nearby Wal-Mart, which Bree agreed to after Ariel assured them that they would not get caught because she had a plan, which was to take food from the shelves but never actually leave the store with it, eating it as they pretended to browse other merchandise.

Ariel and Bree worked their way through a family size box of Cheese Nips and a standard size box of Whoppers before being stopped in the parking lot by the store manager, who introduced himself as Evan, and as Johnson Davis, looking very upset and very tired, drove Bree home from the local police department at three in the morning, he ordered Bree to never speak to or look at this Ariel again.

o o o

Ten minutes earlier, before walking into Ariel's apartment, once Bree had directed Bart into Ariel's designated spot in the complex's parking garage, Bree had turned to Bart and said, "Let's park for a while," at which point Bart responded, "Awesome," and Bree had lifted her purse from between her feet on the floorboard and, just as Josiah had seen her do two weeks earlier behind the restroom facility at the local fun park, she pulled from the purse the rolled-up plastic bag and the shiny blue instrument and placed the leafy green substance from the plastic bag into the shiny blue instrument and, using a short red cigarette lighter, lit the pipe and breathed in the smoke, holding it for several seconds before blowing it out slowly and steadily. The smell that filled the car, and which Josiah would smell ten minutes later upon walking into the living room of Ariel's apartment, immediately reminded Josiah of that day at the local fun park—specifically the way that Bree had blown the smoke from her mouth that day and her green bikini and David and the mischievous looks—and once Bart had as well taken the shiny instrument and breathed in and blown out the smoke and Bree reached for the pipe and again began to light it, Bart asked, "What about Josiah?"

"What about him?"

"He doesn't get any?"

"He doesn't want any."

"How do you know?"

Bree looked over her shoulder at Josiah and asked him, "Do you want to smoke?"

Josiah shrugged.

Bree turned so that her knees and lower legs rested on the front seat where she had just been sitting and her back was to the windshield. Josiah looked at her, confused and anxious. Bree smiled. Her arms rested on the seatback that separated them, one hand holding the short red cigarette lighter, but the other held open toward him as she gently said, "Come here." Josiah leaned forward. Bree gazed into his eyes. In some way Josiah thought that the gaze felt warm. She gently positioned the instrument into his hand with her hand and said, just as gently, "Put it in your lips," and together, Josiah's hand and Bree's hand softly placed the end of the instrument, which Josiah would soon be hearing—in Ariel's apartment—being repeatedly referred to as a pipe, between Josiah's lips, and as the flame from the lighter approached, Bree gently said, "Breathe in."

o o o

Bart and Bree and Josiah spent twenty to thirty minutes watching TV in Ariel's living room and passing Bree's pipe back and forth amongst them. Josiah, sitting in a yellow recliner chair that Ariel had warned Josiah not to try reclining, twice more smoked from Bree's pipe, as he had done, for the first time, less than an hour earlier in Bart's car. Bart, rather than Bree, now held the pipe to Josiah's lips and lit it for him, as Bart was sitting on the end of Ariel's couch closest to Josiah and the yellow recliner. Bree sat at the other end of the couch, near Ariel, who sat in her own recliner, a brown one that fully reclined. At one point, Bart told Josiah, who had been concentrating on the way that he blew the smoke out of his mouth, that he didn't think Josiah was inhaling properly, and instructed him to hold the smoke in longer and act like he was trying to swallow it, and then Bart held the pipe to Josiah's lips a third time. It took only a few minutes before the outer part of Josiah's face felt like it was squeezing the inner part of his face. Bart and Bree and Josiah and Ariel had been watching a show on TV in which a woman judge was listening to and commenting upon the testimony of a man and a woman, the man and woman having formerly been boyfriend and girlfriend but having broken up, but while they were boyfriend and girlfriend the woman had loaned the man four hundred dollars and had paid his phone bill for seven months and had also paid the man's child support for two different months when the man had been short of money, the man claiming that all of this was a gift and no arrangement had ever been made to pay the woman back and the woman claiming that she helped the man financially out of love, but that her heart was broken when the man slept with her cousin. It occurred to Josiah, around the time that his face started to squeeze itself, that the judge and the man were somehow working together against the woman, and that there seemed to be some kind of unspoken understanding between them and it was all a set up and the woman was falling into a trap. As Josiah considered this, Bree suddenly stood up from the couch and walked out of the room. Josiah assumed that Bree had to go to the bathroom or maybe wanted a glass of water, which sounded good—the glass of water—to Josiah as well, and if Bree was in the kitchen getting a glass of water, this may be a good opportunity for Josiah to talk to Bree about when they would be leaving, as Bart and Ariel would not be in the kitchen, unless they decided that they wanted a glass of water as well.

Josiah stood up from the couch and walked from the living room into the kitchen, which was behind the living room but separated from the living room by a wall. On one side of the kitchen there was a longer but not that long hallway that led to Ariel's bedroom, and on the other side of the kitchen was a short little hallway that led to the bathroom. Bree was not in the kitchen. Josiah picked up a glass from the drying rack next to Ariel's sink and filled it with water from the tap and drank it. Before leaving the kitchen, Josiah peeked into the short hallway and could see that the bathroom door was open and the light inside was turned off.

When Josiah returned to the living room, he saw that Bree was still not there, and that now Bart was gone as well. Josiah simply stood behind the couch, the back of which faced the kitchen and the front of which faced the TV, and struggled to understand what Bart and Bree's absence meant, wondering if they had left, were getting into Bart's car at that very moment, and wondering if he needed to hurry and catch up to them or be stuck there in Ariel's apartment forever, and if they hadn't left, where could they be, and Josiah began eliminating rooms of Ariel's apartment in his mind, having, shortly after they had arrived, been given a brief tour, and Josiah began to be haunted by memories of the fun park and the restroom facility and the feelings associated with them when Ariel, from her recliner, which was positioned askew and therefore had its back to neither the kitchen nor the TV, said to Josiah, "Hey, you okay?"

Josiah, his line of thought broken by Ariel's voice, turned his eyes toward her, but said nothing. She continued, "Why don't you sit down?"

"Where did they go?" Josiah asked. Ariel lifted her head from the headrest of her recliner, looked around the room and, as if noticing for the first time that anyone had left, said, "I don't know," turning her gaze back to Josiah, resting her head back on the head-rest and adding, "But I'm sure they'll be back soon. Sit down."

Josiah slowly stepped around the couch and retook his seat.

"So what are you all about?" Ariel asked Josiah, lifting her head a few inches off of the headrest.

"Did they leave?" Josiah asked.

"Who?"

"Did Bree leave?"

"I wouldn't know anything about it," Ariel said. Pulling a lever on the side of her chair, Ariel dropped the footrest to the floor and propelled herself forward toward the coffee table, upon which sat Bree's shiny blue pipe. "I think she was going to take a nap," she continued, tapping the pipe upside down on the coffee table and leaving a small pile of ash. Josiah, inferring that Bree would be taking her nap in Ariel's bedroom, and also inferring that Bart, who was also missing, would be taking a nap with her, began to feel the emptiness he had felt before and the thoughts that had begun haunting him just moments earlier returned. From her easy chair, Ariel could just reach, slightly tipping the chair as she did so, a small table with a small drawer. Ariel opened the drawer and pulled from it a small orange box, which she opened and dipped two fingers into, her pointer and her thumb, lifting out, pinched between the fingers, the same green substance that Bree kept rolled up in her plastic bags. Ariel carefully placed the substance in Bree's pipe and reached for the lighter, which also sat waiting on the coffee table.

"Josiah, right?" Ariel asked before putting the pipe to her lips and lighting it. Josiah was unsure what Ariel's question meant. In fact, Josiah was unsure about many things. For example, Josiah, even though Ariel had told him where Bree was, began to believe that Bree was gone, out of the apartment, and he didn't know where, and he was supposed to do something, such as go and look for her or catch up to her or something—it was all very unclear and difficult for Josiah to pinpoint—and then he remembered that Bree was in Ariel's bedroom—probably—and probably fuck-ing Bart, and then Josiah began to think about wanting Bree to fuck him, and then began to imagine Bree fucking him, and his

Andre Agassi stiffened, and he imagined Bree on top of him, but
without her soccer jersey, or her green bikini, and Josiah imagined
Bree's breasts, basing his image of them on what he had seen of
them beneath the green bikini, and imagined the noises that Bree
would make, and remembered the noises she had made the time
she came into his room in only her soccer jersey, and then Josiah
remembered that Bree was not fucking him but instead was fucking Bart, in Ariel's bedroom, probably, but Josiah then began to
wonder if maybe Bree wasn't fucking Bart and was just taking a
nap and Bart was off somewhere else, and maybe Josiah should go
into Ariel's bedroom where Bree was taking a nap and take off his
pants but not his shirt and climb onto the bed and on top of Bree
and compliment her and listen to her and ask questions.

"It's Josiah, right?" Ariel asked again after blowing the smoke
from her mouth, which she did differently than Bree, blowing faster and more carelessly. "Your name's Josiah?"

"Yes," Josiah responded.

"Cool." Ariel leaned back and the footrest again popped up,
pointing Ariel's legs directly at Josiah, and she laid her head back
on the headrest.

"So tell me about yourself," she said. Josiah looked at her, unsure
what he should tell her, struggling to think of something about
himself to tell, when Ariel continued, "How old are you?"

"Sixteen."

"That's cool. Do you have a car?"

"No."

"Yeah, me neither. And I'm nineteen." Ariel again leaned forward and dropped the footrest and picked up the pipe and lit it and
sucked in and blew out quickly and carelessly, this time holding
the pipe out in Josiah's direction as an offer. Josiah simply looked
at the pipe, and then Ariel said, "Oh, right. Here," and then Ariel
rose from her recliner and sat down on the couch next to Josiah
and held the pipe to Josiah's lips and said, "I'll tell you when, okay?"
and Josiah, with the pipe against his lips, nodded, and Ariel held
the lighter to the pipe and lit it and then instructed Josiah to suck.

At the moment Josiah realized that Bree was talking, he also realized, simultaneously, that he had known someone was talking, just a few feet away from him, for several seconds, before even realizing it, or even thinking anything about it, as if he heard the voice, even recognized it as Bree's, whom he had been hoping would return, but he had failed to immediately understand what he was hearing, until simultaneously, or so it seemed, realizing both his failure and the fact that Bree was standing behind the couch, at the border between Ariel's living room and Ariel's kitchen, saying, "No, now," evidently not for the first time, as Josiah also realized, subsequent to his initial, simultaneous realization, that this phrase was the phrase that he had been hearing, repeatedly, and not thinking anything about, and as Bree repeated, "No, now," Ariel, still in her recliner, said to Bree, "What are you talking about?" and Bart, whom Josiah suddenly realized, upon hearing his voice and turning toward him, was now sitting on the couch next to him, though Josiah was unsure when Bart had arrived there, said, also to Bree, "*What*, now?" to which Bree responded, a bit more loudly, "Now. We have to go now. Away from here. Now. Gone. Right now."

"What?" Ariel said, as if she was having difficulty hearing.

"Where?" Bart said.

Josiah, looking at Bree and remembering his notes on being a gentleman, stood from the couch.

"Gone," Bree said. "Right away gone. Where there're no phones and no TV and no internet and where they'll never find us."

"What are you talking about?" Bart said.

"No TV?" Ariel said.

"They're on their way right now and I know it and they'll throw us in a van and send Josiah back to the group home and we'll never see him again and he'll never get married or own his own car and they'll lock me in my room forever and I'll never play soccer again and never be a mother or fly in an airplane ever," Bree said.

"Group home?" Bart said.

"Why are you all standing?" Ariel said.

Bree and Bart and Ariel and Josiah then agreed that by now Johnson Davis and Josiah's mother and Bree's mother, as well as the authorities, if involved, would be at the point in their search that they would be looking in places where Bree may have taken Josiah, such as the home of a close friend, like Ariel, and though both Ariel and Bree were confident that Johnson Davis did not know the location of Ariel's apartment, such information could easily be discovered, and the best thing to do would be to drive out into the country, to a remote area, a place that symbolized freedom, with no cell phone service and no freeways, and Bree and Ariel agreed upon a dried-out creek bed that they had several times, during the two years that they went to high school together, gone to to party.

When Bart, on the way out of town, pulled into a strip mall and parked in front of a liquor store, Bree, who was still operating with a defined sense of urgency, though less so than she had been when Josiah had realized she was standing behind the couch repeating, seemingly, the phrase, "No, now," asked Bart what he thought he was doing, Bart responded that he never went to dried-out creek beds without booze.

ELEVEN

Bart—whom, even though he had been very polite to Josiah and always shook Josiah's hand and had helped Josiah hold the pipe to his lips, Josiah did not like that much and wished would go away—drove his car into the farming area outside of town, Bree directing him where to go. It had become dark, Josiah watching as the sun spread pink across the sky before dropping from sight. On a long, straight road with fields on each side and only occasional houses far back from the road, Bree told Bart to begin slowing down, and then to slow down more, and then abruptly ordered him to turn off of the paved road and through a small gate leading them onto a narrow dirt road that ran between two large fields.

"What are those?" Bart asked. "Miniature trees?"

"Grapevines," Bree answered.

Bart drove along this road for several minutes. Josiah thought that it looked quiet out in the dark fields. He also thought—mostly because the fields were dark and quiet—that they would be good fields for a spaceship to land in. The dirt road they were on intersected another dirt road at the edge of a new set of fields, one on each side of the road, each also quiet and dark. Bree instructed Bart to keep going, until finally they could see ahead of them the outline of trees—full size trees—against the dark sky, growing larger until the trees overtook their view of the sky and the road ended and Bree told Bart to stop.

Everyone got out of the car and followed Bree into the trees and down a small slope, Bart carrying a paper bag filled with bottles, and all of them stepping on and over sticks and leaves and rocks, until they were standing in the sand of a dried creek bed, slightly lit by the moonlight coming through the gap in the trees that opened over the tiny creek.

"Here we are," said Bree.

"I need a cigarette," said Ariel.

"I need a drink," said Bart.

"Let's sit down," said Bree, and everyone sat down, forming a skewed circle as they lowered themselves to the sand.

Bree pulled her pack of cigarettes from her purse and pulled from the pack a cigarette for herself and a cigarette for Ariel, and Bart pulled from the paper bag six brown bottles surrounded by cardboard, similar to the cardboard surrounding Bree's ball, and handed two bottles to Bree, Bree passing one to Ariel as they each lit their cigarettes, and Bart passing one to Josiah.

The bottle felt cold in Josiah's hand. It had water running down the side of it. The other members of the circle grabbed and turned the caps of their bottles, removing and tossing them into the sand.

"Cheers," Bart said, and everyone began holding their bottles up and clinking them against each other, Ariel reaching across with her bottle to clink her bottle against Josiah's, which was still un-opened and which he held hovering over his lap. He tried to grab and turn the cap as he had seen the others do but it would not come off, and Bree, who was sitting across the circle from Josiah, was go-ing to tip forward onto her knees and reach across the circle and help Josiah when Ariel, who was sitting next to Josiah on the side opposite, grabbed the bottle from Josiah's hand and quickly twist-ed off the cap, dropping it into the sand and handing the bottle back to him, motioning with her own bottle for him to hold his in the air, as the others had done earlier and which Josiah now did, Ariel then clinking her bottle roughly against his.

Josiah took a drink. He was surprised by the bitter taste. It seemed to Josiah, as he swallowed the beer, that the strong, bitter taste moved over his tongue and through his throat in layers, each layer stronger and more bitter, and he could not help but make a face.

"Try again," Ariel said to him. As Josiah drank from the bottle the second time, he could tell that across from him Bree was watching, and as the layers again passed through his throat and Josiah again made a face—but less of one—Ariel, who had also been watching, asked, "Better?" Josiah nodded, and continued to take drinks from the bottle.

Bart finished his bottle before the others and took and opened one of the remaining two, taking one long drink before pulling another six bottles from the bag and announcing that there was plenty. Bree, finishing her own bottle, reached across Bart to grab two more, again passing one to Ariel, who had also finished, and everyone drank a second bottle as Josiah continued to drink his first. Josiah began to get used to the strong bitter taste, and as he drank the beer his body began to feel warm, and his head felt light, but as he got closer to the bottom of the bottle, the beer began to get warmer, and to taste more bitter, and it was difficult for Josiah to finish the bottle, but he did, as did everyone else.

Seven empty bottles were lying in the sand in the middle of the circle, and five still stood surrounded by cardboard, a small amount of water clinging to their sides. Bree stood, grabbing one of the still-standing bottles as she did, and announced to the group, "We're going for a walk," and she took Bart's hand, who stood up with his hand in Bree's, looking almost like Bree was pulling him up, though she wasn't, and Bart grabbed a bottle himself and the two of them walked away from the circle along the sand into the dark.

Ariel and Josiah sat silently for several minutes, Josiah watching Bart and Bree walk away along the sand until, in the darkness, he could no longer see anything.

"Let's see what else is in here," Ariel said, reaching into the paper bag and pulling out a bottle of clear liquid with a red sticker on it and laying it in the sand, then pulling out a bottle of light brown liquid with a gold sticker and saying, "Perfect," as she twisted off the bottle's cap and took a drink from it.

Ariel passed the bottle to Josiah and told him, "Try some," and Josiah, who was unsure how he would be receiving the message from his father and unsure where the ship that he hoped his father had sent would meet them and who also hoped that Bree would not go too far along the sand, making it difficult for him to find her when either the message or the ship arrived, took the bottle from Ariel's hand. It was heavy, and the hand he held it in dipped in mid-air before adjusting to the weight and rising again. Also unsure how—when either message or ship did arrive—they would explain to Bart and Ariel that they could not come along, Josiah put the bottle to his lips and drank, and he could not keep his entire face from squinting. Inside, it burned.

"Want to take a walk?" Ariel asked, and before Josiah could reply, either by nodding or speaking, Ariel pushed herself up from the sand, dusted her Thomas Magnum with both hands, and stretched out one arm toward Josiah, who took Ariel's hand and allowed her to pull him up, just as Bree had—or appeared to have—just done with Bart. Ariel took the bottle from Josiah, drank from it again, and reached down to retrieve the bottle's cap from the sand below, replacing it. Ariel stepped toward Josiah, placed her hand on the inside of the upper part of his arm, and led him away from the circle in the opposite direction from Bree and Bart, her shoulder bumping into Josiah's as they walked, Josiah struggling to turn and look back in the direction Bree had gone, managing to do so twice before giving up. When Ariel had touched Josiah's arm, his Andre Agassi had stiffened.

Josiah's shoulders felt heavy. His head felt heavy. His legs felt lighter than normal. It was not as easy to walk forward as normal, and with each step some force, a force other than the girl holding onto his arm and bumping into his shoulder, seemed to be pulling him to one side or the other as he tried to move straight ahead. It had become quite dark, and it seemed to Josiah that he and Ariel had come a long way when Ariel poured her weight into Josiah, their legs scrambling them toward the bank, where Ariel let her weight pull both of them to the ground. She laughed, and they each shifted so that they were sitting up on the bank. Ariel held the bottle up to Josiah, asking, "Are you drunk?"

"I don't know," Josiah responded. The bottle in Ariel's hand was still suspended in an offer to Josiah, waiting. She pulled it away, back to her, and took another drink.

"Stand up," she said to him, and Josiah stood.

"Walk over there," she said, pointing to a spot in the sand barely visible to them in the dark. Josiah walked toward the spot, but the same force which had previously made his walking difficult continued to pull him from side to side as he tried to move forward.

"Come back," she said, adding as he returned, "You're drunk." Ariel, looking at Josiah, patted the indented sand where he had been sitting, and he dropped himself back into place.

Ariel removed the cap and took another drink from the bottle. She then passed the bottle to Josiah. Josiah took another drink. His face squinted less. His throat burned less. Ariel shifted in the sand and her leg rested against his. His Andre Agassi stiffened further. Josiah passed the bottle back to Ariel and as she took it she asked, "What's this?" and reached across her body with the hand farthest from Josiah, the hand nearest him holding the bottle, and wrapped her fingers around his wrist, running one of the fingers along the bottom of his wrist between his skin and the metal of the bracelet that Bree had given him. She moved the hand around to the top of his wrist and held the metal plate between her thumb and forefinger, trying to read it in the dark.

"What does it say?" she asked.

"From B to J."

"From B to J?"

"Yes."

"And you're J, I guess?"

Josiah nodded.

"And who's B?"

"It's a secret."

"Is it Bree?"

"No."

"It's not?"

"No."

"Are you sure?"

"Yes."

"Do you want to hear a story?" Ariel asked.

"I don't know," Josiah said.

"I'm going to tell a story," Ariel said. "Do you want to hear it?"

"I guess so," Josiah said.

"Okay. Good." Ariel again removed the cap from the bottle and again took another drink and again passed the bottle to Josiah, who again took another drink and who again felt less burn in his throat and squinted his face less than the time before.

"So," Ariel continued, "this story begins two years ago. There was this guy. His name was Keith Jones. He was a junior. This is when Bree was a sophomore. I was a senior. So I take Bree to this party and she meets this guy Keith Jones. He didn't go to our school, but he went to elementary school with Robbie Thom and they were like best buds and it was Robbie's brother and his friends who were throwing the party so he was there. I knew him. He was always hanging around Steve Bett's garage parties when Steve and I were dating. Anyway, I introduced him to Bree or she met him somehow at this party and she totally fell in love with him. He was really cute. He had this like curly hair but really short. Anyway, she fell in love with him and they hooked up a couple of times, but he was like whatever and never called her or anything. And then we went to this other party and he totally ignored her and she was hella pissed and we were gonna slash his tires or something. But, anyway, like a week later, he calls her and invites her to his school's Winter Formal and she totally freaked and said he was her soulmate and started naming their babies and she bought this dress that was hella expensive and new shoes and makeup and anyway they went to the dance and stuff and then got really wasted afterward and she had sex with him and some random friend of his. But the point is, when he came and picked her up for the dance, she gave him this gift. She had gone out and gotten him a gift. And you know what it was? It was a bracelet. Know what it looked like? Just like this one," and Ariel once again ran a finger along the chain around Josiah's wrist, the finger tracing a line along Josiah's skin, "and she had a message engraved on it. It said 'From Me to You.' I know because I went with her to get it. At this store next to the laundromat. You pay like four bucks for the bracelets—and they have other stuff, too, like dog tags and license plate holders and stuff—and then for another two bucks they engrave whatever you want on it. I got one for my mom once, on her birthday. Anyway, they look just like this. Exactly. The letters and everything."

Ariel reached for the bottle and took another drink, passing it to Josiah without wiping the bottle's lip, which she had been doing, following previous drinks, by placing her palm and fingers over its top and twisting once, removing the excess saliva.

Josiah, still thinking about Ariel's story, picturing Bree giving the bracelet to Keith Jones, who in Josiah's mind looked like a bit like David and a bit like Bart, took a drink from the bottle, a longer drink than before. As Josiah lowered the bottle from his mouth and swallowed, Ariel said to him, "So?"

Josiah simply stared.

"So who's B?" Ariel asked.

Josiah said nothing.

"Who's B?" Ariel asked again.

"It's a secret," Josiah said.

"I already know," Ariel said. "You can just tell me."

"I can't," Josiah said.

"Why not?"

"I promised."

"Who did you promise?"

"I can't tell."

"What did she tell you?"

"It's a secret."

"You can tell me," Ariel said, "and it will still be a secret. I won't tell anyone."

"I promised."

"Bree and I are best friends. We tell each other everything. She wouldn't care."

"I can't."

"Believe me, it's fine. She wouldn't mind. She'll probably tell me, anyway. We tell each other everything."

"I don't know."

"C'mon, it's okay."

"I don't know."

"Look, I know she gave you that bracelet. It's not a secret. I know."

Josiah looked away, staring toward the darkening spot in the sand to which Ariel had had him walk.

"C'mon, it's okay," Ariel said.

"I promised," Josiah said.

"Don't you just want to tell, though? That's the thing about se-crets. As soon as you have one, all you want to do is tell everyone. Anyway, that's how it is for me. When someone tells me a secret, all I want to do is tell the whole world. C'mon. It's fine. I won't tell anyone."

"I don't know."

"C'mon."

"You won't tell?" Josiah asked.

"No," Ariel said. "Besides, she won't care. She'll probably tell me anyway."

"Are you sure?"

"I'm positive."

"Okay."

"Okay?"

"Okay."

"Okay," Ariel said. "So what's the big secret?"

"I'm her secret boyfriend."

"You're her secret boyfriend?"

"Yes."

"That's what she told you? That you're her secret boyfriend?"

"Yes."

"And she's your secret girlfriend?"

"Yes."

"Don't you think that's weird?"

Josiah said nothing.

"Do you like her?"

"Yes."

"Love her?"

"Yes."

"Want to marry her and have babies with her?"

"We're having a baby."

"You're having a baby?"

"Yes."

"You and Bree?"

"Yes."

"Bree's pregnant?"

"Yes."

"Again?"

Josiah said nothing.

"You had sex?" Ariel asked.

"Yes. We fucked."

"You fucked?"

"Yes."

"When?"

"When she came into my room."

"When was that?"

"When we met."

"When did you meet?"

"Three weeks ago."

"Three weeks ago," Ariel repeated. "And she's going to keep it? She's going to have the baby?"

"Yes." Josiah again looked into the darkness in the direction Bree had gone.

"Do you want to be a daddy?"

"Yes."

"You do?"

"Yes."

"Do you want to marry her?"

"Yes."

"Does she want to?"

"Yes."

"She does?"

"Yes."

"So you're getting married?"

"Yes."

"When?"

"Soon."

"Like when, though?"

"We're leaving tonight."

"Tonight?"

"Yes."

"So you met three weeks ago and had sex—fucked—and got pregnant and now you're secret boyfriend and girlfriend and are getting married. Soon. Maybe tonight."

"Yes."

"Hmm," Ariel said, taking another drink from the bottle.

Ariel then told Josiah that she was getting very cold and that they should walk back and sit in the car, where, once Ariel and Josiah had walked to the car, Josiah finding it equally as difficult as walking along the creek bed had been—more so, perhaps, given that reaching the car involved climbing back up the bank—Ariel opened up Bree's purse, which Bree had left in the car, and pulled from it Bree's shiny blue pipe and the rolled-up plastic bag.

"So where will you go?" Ariel asked Josiah as she once again filled Bree's pipe with the green substance, "Once you're married?"

"Somewhere far away."

"But where?"

"It's another planet."

"Another planet?"

"Yes."

"Like Mars?"

"Parnuckle."

"What's that?"

"The planet."

"The planet that you're going to live on?"

"Yes."

"It's called Parnuckle?"

"Yes."

"Parnuckle?"

"Parnuckle."

"Where the hell is that?"

"Far, far away."

"How will you get there?"

"I don't know yet."

"You don't know?"

"I wrote a letter."

"Of course. Why not somewhere closer?"

"It is the home planet of my father."

"Your father?"

"Yes."

"Your father is from another planet?"

"Yes."

"How long have you known this?"

"I've always known."

"How?"

"My mother."

"Your mother told you?"

"Yes."

"Have you ever met him? Your father?"

"No."

"So you've never been there? To Parnuckle?"

"No."

"Never?"

"No."

"You must wonder."

"What?"

"What it's like. What he's like."

Josiah nodded.

"How much do you know?"

"Some."

"Like what?"

"What my mother tells me."

"What does she tell you?"

"That my father is a very important man."

"How important?"

"He is Keymaster of Gozer."

"Keymaster of Gozer?"

"Yes."

"What does the Keymaster of Gozer do?"

"He is second only to Gozer."

"Who's Gozer?"

"The president of Parnuckle."

"Sounds important."

"Yes."

"And kind of crazy."

Josiah said nothing.

"What else?"

"He is very handsome."

"Your father?"

"Yes. Parnucklian men are naturally more handsome than Earthling men."

"Really?"

"Yes."

"Well that explains why you're so cute."

Ariel held the pipe to her lips, lighting it and sucking in. She handed the pipe to Josiah, and asked, "What language do they speak on Parnuckle?"

Josiah, holding the pipe in his hand, answered, "Parnucklian."

"Do you speak Parnucklian?"

"A little."

"Say something in Parnucklian."

Ariel took Josiah's hand, the one that held the pipe, and with her own hand guided it to Josiah's lips. She then lifted the lighter and lit the pipe and instructed him to suck, which he did. As his face once again began to tighten, Ariel held the pipe to her own lips and once again lit it and once again blew the smoke from her mouth—more quickly and less smoothly than Bree—before placing the pipe and the lighter on the dash in front of her and leaning back in Bart's seat. Ariel placed her hand on the back of Josiah's neck and began caressing the short hairs that grew there, moving her thumb and the other four fingers back and forth, apart and toward each other. Josiah's Andre Agassi was now fully stiff, held down only by his jeans.

"Say something?" Ariel said.

"I don't know. What?" Josiah said.

"Anything," Ariel said.

"Boboli."

"Boboli?"

"Boboli."

"That's a Parnucklian word?"

"Yes."

"What does it mean?"

"Chocolate."

"Chocolate?"

"Yes."

"Do you like chocolate?"

"It's the only thing Parnucklians eat."

"Really?"

"Yes."

"So then it means food."

"What?"

"Boboli. It means food. If chocolate is the only food and Boboli means chocolate then Boboli means food."

Josiah said nothing.

Ariel stopped moving her fingers but kept her hand resting against Josiah's seat, her fingertips still in contact with the back of his neck. "Say another one," she said.

"What?"

"Anything."

"Toasties."

"What are toasties?"

"Socks."

Ariel removed her hand from the back of Josiah's neck and placed it on Josiah's jeans, over his Andre Agassi, which further stiffened.

"What about this?" she asked.

Josiah said nothing. His legs began to shake. His teeth were slightly chattering.

"What do they call this?" Ariel asked, lightly rubbing the area of Josiah's jeans over his Andre Agassi.

"What?" Josiah asked, his teeth chattering harder.

"What do they call this? On Parnuckle?"

"Andre Agassi."

"Andre Agassi?"

"Yes."

"Really?"

"Yes."

"Like the tennis guy?"

Josiah said nothing.

"Can I see it?"

Josiah said nothing.

"Can I see it?" Ariel asked again.

Josiah shrugged. "I don't know."

"Can I?"

"Okay."

"Okay," Ariel echoed, and she reached down with both hands and flipped open the button of Josiah's jeans and pulled down his zipper. His legs began to shake even more. His teeth chattered loudly. She then grabbed the jeans and the shorts beneath them at his hips and pulled them down just far enough to allow his stiffened Andre Agassi to lift into the air, once no longer restrained by the jeans.

Josiah and Ariel both stared at it.

"It's nice," Ariel said. "Can I touch it?"

Josiah said nothing. Ariel placed one finger on the tip of Josiah's Andre Agassi and then ran that finger down its side, resting the fingertip in place at the Andre Agassi's base. Josiah clenched his jaw in an attempt to keep his teeth from chattering.

"It's nice," Ariel said again. "Put it away." Josiah pulled his pants back up and zipped and buttoned his jeans.

"Follow me," Ariel said.

"Where?"

"I want you to show me something," Ariel said, and she and Josiah both crawled out of the driver-side door and into the rows of grapevines.

Ariel led Josiah what seemed like a long way down one row of the vineyard, the dirt of the vineyard being much thicker and more powdery than the sand of the creek bed, so that Josiah's feet seemed to both sink and form a cloud with each step. Ariel stopped. She turned to Josiah, who also stopped, and said, "Show me."

"What?" Josiah said.

"Show me how she did it."

Josiah said nothing, simply stared back at Ariel.

"Show me how she fucked you. How you got her pregnant."

Josiah continued to stare.

"When she came into your room," Ariel said. "Show me. Where were you?"

"I was lying down," Josiah said.

"Lay down," Ariel said. Josiah bent his knees and lowered onto his Thomas Magnum, then laid back into the dirt, extending his legs.

"Were you under the covers?" Ariel asked.

"Yes," said Josiah. Ariel took off her jacket and draped it across Josiah's arms and chest.

"Like this?" she asked.

"Yes."

"Then what?"

"She came into my room."

"Were you asleep?"

"Yes."

"Close your eyes." Josiah closed his eyes. "Then what?" Ariel continued.

"She climbed on top." Josiah felt Ariel step over his chest and then lower herself so that her Thomas Magnum rested upon the area of his Andre Agassi, which had lost its stiffness as Josiah had followed Ariel down the row of vines, but now stiffened again.

"Like this?" Ariel asked.

Josiah, his eyes still closed, responded, "Yes."

"Then what?"

Josiah opened his eyes and said, "No."

"No, what?"

"She had no pants on," he said.

"Okay," Ariel said with a smile. She rolled off of Josiah and sat in the dirt with her legs extended, pulling her pants and underwear off. She got up on her knees and knee-stepped back over to Josiah, stopping at his side to remind him to close his eyes, and once again straddled him.

"Did you wake up? When she got on top?"

"Yes."

"Open your eyes." Josiah opened his eyes.

"Then what?"

"Her hair brushed over me. Over my eyes." Ariel removed the band that held her hair in a ponytail, letting the hair fall around her shoulders, and leaned down over Josiah just far enough so that the hair brushed over his eyes and cheeks.

"Then what?"

"She told me to be quiet."

"How?"

"What?"

"How? Did she say, 'Shh'?"

"Yes."

"Shh," Ariel said, leaning down farther to whisper into Josiah's ear, also whispering, "Then what?"

"She said she couldn't sleep," Josiah said.

"I can't sleep," Ariel whispered. "Then what?"

"She started to rub." Ariel began to slide her Thomas Magnum back and forth over the area of Josiah's Andre Agassi.

"Like that?" she asked.

"Yes," he responded.

"Then what?"

"We came."

"You came?" Ariel stopped moving.

"Yes. Both of us."

"Did you take your pants off?"

"No."

"You were under the covers?"

"Yes."

"Then you didn't fuck."

"We both came."

"You didn't have sex."

"She's pregnant."

"You can't have sex without taking your pants off."

Josiah said nothing.

"You must be remembering it wrong," Ariel said. "Do you want me to show you? How it really happened?"

Josiah said nothing.

"Do you want me to show you how she fucked you?"

"Yes," Josiah said.

"Take off your pants."

Ariel stood and pulled her jacket away from Josiah. Josiah lay still. "Take off your pants," Ariel repeated, and as Josiah unbuckled and pulled off his pants, Ariel said to him, "When she came into your room, you had no pants on."

Josiah sat in the dirt with his pants off. It was cold.

"You were sleeping naked," Ariel continued. "Take off your shirt."

Josiah took off his shirt. He began to shiver.

"Lay back down," Ariel said, and as he did, Ariel covered Josiah's chest and shoulders with the jacket.

"Close your eyes," Ariel said.

Josiah closed his eyes.

"You were sleeping naked," Ariel said, "and she came into your room. Very quietly. She was naked, too."

Josiah opened his eyes. Ariel was standing up on her knees, next to him. She had taken her shirt off. Josiah had been unable to see, beneath the t-shirt that Ariel had been wearing, the shape of Ariel's breasts, but now, looking at them, Josiah thought that Ariel's breasts appeared to be bigger than the shape of Bree's breasts had appeared to be beneath Bree's t-shirt. Josiah's Andre Agassi, already stiff, stiffened further.

"Close your eyes," Ariel said. Josiah closed his eyes and felt Ariel again pull the jacket away, saying, "She pulled off your covers."

Josiah, his eyes closed, could then feel Ariel once again straddle him, the skin of her legs, this time, touching the skin of his, causing his legs to shake.

"She climbed on top," Ariel said.

Ariel then reached down toward Josiah's side and picked up his hand from the dirt and guided it to the area of her vagina. It felt wet.

"What do they call this," Ariel asked, "on Parnuckle?"

Josiah said nothing.

"What do they call it?" Ariel asked again.

"There is no word for it," Josiah answered.

"No word?"

"No."

"What would you call it?"

"I don't know."

"Do you like it?"

"Yes."

"Do you want to fuck?"

Josiah said nothing.

"This is the part where she asks you if you want to fuck her. Do you want to fuck her?"

Josiah said nothing.

"How did you answer her? What did you say?"

Josiah said nothing.

"Did you want to fuck her? What did you say?"

"Yes," Josiah said.

As Ariel lowered herself onto Josiah's Andre Agassi, Josiah opened his eyes. Ariel placed her hands on Josiah's chest and began to move her hips and Thomas Magnum back and forth. Josiah came almost immediately. Ariel did not stop.

"Fuck her," she said. She began to move faster. "Fuck her." Ariel sat up straight and removed her hands from Josiah's chest. She grabbed his wrists and lifted his hands to her own chest, holding his palms against her breasts. "You like that?" she asked. "You like fucking her?"

Josiah did not respond. He lay still. The stiffness was almost completely gone from his Andre Agassi. Ariel had not stopped.

"Fuck her," she said. "Make her come."

Ariel leaned forward, laying her chest against Josiah's. She began to lick his right ear and the side of his neck. "Make her come," Ariel whispered into his ear. The stiffness was now completely gone, but Ariel continued.

"Fuck her," she said again. "Fuck me. Fuck me with that Andre Agassi."

"Stop," Josiah said.

"Fuck," Ariel said.

"Stop," Josiah said again.

"Fuck me," Ariel said again. Josiah grabbed Ariel by the arms, both arms in the same place, directly between the shoulder and the elbow, and pushed her off of him into the dirt.

"What the fuck?" Ariel said.

Josiah said nothing. He sat up, leaning forward to pick his pants up from the dirt.

"What the fuck?" Ariel repeated.

Josiah stood and pulled on his pants, nearly falling as he fished his left leg in.

"Don't push me," Ariel said, still sitting where she had landed in the dirt. Josiah said nothing. He simply stood, staring down at her. "Did you hear me?" she said. "I said don't fucking push me."

"You wouldn't stop," Josiah said.

"Don't ever push me."

"You wouldn't stop," Josiah said again.

"I wasn't finished."

"I wanted you to stop."

"Didn't you like it?"

"No."

"Are you a fag?"

"I wanted you to stop," Josiah said again.

"Fucking fag," Ariel said. She stood, picked up her pants and pulled them on.

"I want to stop," Josiah said.

TWELVE

JOSIAH AND ARIEL walked—separately—back to the creek bed, where Bart and Bree were asleep in the sand, Bree's head on Bart's chest. It had begun, just lightly, to rain, and Bree, with sleep in her eyes, declared that they should just head back to the apartment, and Bart, with sleep in his eyes, asked her, "What about your Dad? You said he would look there," and Bree answered that she had been stoned when she had said that and that Johnson Davis wouldn't have any way of finding where Ariel lived and it would be fine, none of which Josiah listened to as he stared at Bree lying beside Bart in the sand.

When Bree and Bart and Josiah and Ariel arrived back at Ariel's apartment complex, Johnson Davis was waiting for them, the headlights of Bart's car landing on his figure standing in the middle of the driveway, directly in front of the stairs to Ariel's apartment, his clothes and hair visibly soaked as he stared straight back into the headlights and lifted his hand in a recognizable signal for the vehicle to stop.

"Oh, shit," Bree said.

"What should I do?" Bart said.

"Stop," Bree said.

Once the car was completely stopped, Johnson Davis walked to the driver-side door. Bart rolled down the window and said, "Good evening, sir."

Johnson Davis leveled his head with the now open window and stared—one by one—into the faces of Bree and Ariel and Josiah, each of whom simply stared back. Johnson Davis then looked at Bart and said, "Get out of the car."

"Pardon me, sir?" Bart said.

"Get out of the car," Johnson Davis said again.

"It's raining," Bart said.

"Exactly," Johnson Davis said. "Get out."

When Bart stepped out of the car and stood in the rain in front of Johnson Davis, Johnson Davis said, "All of you."

"Dad," Bree said from the passenger seat.

"All of you," Johnson Davis said again. "Out."

Bree and Ariel and Josiah all got out of the car and stood in the rain. "Dad," Bree said again.

"No Dads," Johnson Davis said. "Inside."

"Excuse me, sir?" Bart said.

"Inside," Johnson Davis said again.

"Inside where?" Bree said.

"Inside the apartment," Johnson Davis said.

"What apartment?" Bree said.

"What apartment, sir?" Bart said.

"Ariel's Goddamn apartment," Johnson Davis said.

"Ariel doesn't live here," Bree said.

"I don't live here," Ariel said.

"Look," Johnson Davis said, "I have been standing here in the Goddamn rain for two hours and I know Goddamn well that Ariel lives here in that Goddamn apartment right there and if someone doesn't let me inside of it to have a discussion in out of this Goddamn rain about what happened tonight I'm going to call the police for grand theft auto and contributing to delinquency and statutory rape and whatever the hell else and then I'm going to have them search that Goddamn apartment and we know Goddamn well what they're going to find."

Once Bree and Bart and Josiah and Ariel and Johnson Davis were all inside Ariel's apartment, Bart began to try to explain to Johnson Davis what was going on and what his involvement in it consisted of, but Johnson Davis silenced Bart by pointing his finger into Bart's face, the tip of his finger only an inch from Bart's nose, and Johnson Davis held the finger there as he turned to Bree and Josiah and said that they were coming with him, right now, and then turned to Ariel and said, "Never. Never again. No contact. Nothing," and then turned back to Bree and said, "She does not exist," and then continued, his face changing from one of anger to one of confused disappointment, to ask Bree what in the hell was going on, what in the hell, and then turned to Josiah and stared at him for several seconds with that same look of confused disappointment before turning back to Bart and lowering his finger as his face turned back to one of anger and Johnson Davis told Bart to wait for him, right there in that apartment, that they had some items they needed to discuss, and not to leave that apartment until he returned if he had any interest in or notions of freedom, to which Bart nodded and answered, "I'll be here," as Johnson Davis led Bree and Josiah out the door and down the stairs.

o o o

Josiah had walked out of the rows of the vineyard and back to the creek bed several minutes ahead of Ariel, who had still been pulling on her pants as Josiah walked away, and Josiah had found, in the sand, Bart and Bree sleeping. Josiah had kneeled in the sand and stared at Bree, her head on Bart's chest, for several seconds, nearly a minute, before Bree opened her eyes and stared back at Josiah.

o o o

As Johnson Davis and Josiah and Bree approached Johnson Davis's car, which Johnson Davis had retrieved from the home of his former wife, Johnson Davis instructed Bree to wait outside for a moment so he could speak to Josiah, to which Bree protested that it was raining, Johnson Davis responding that it would be just for a moment and instructing Josiah to get in the passenger's side as Johnson Davis got in the driver's side.

"You took my car, Josiah," Johnson Davis said to Josiah, once they were both inside the car.

Josiah nodded.

"Stole it, really."

Josiah nodded.

"Why would you do that?"

Josiah shrugged.

"Josiah, you must understand," Johnson Davis said, "despite the aptitude you've shown in our lessons—despite the fact that I'm certain someday you'll be an excellent driver—you are by no means ready—by no means—to begin driving on your own."

Josiah said nothing.

"You don't even have a license. You could have been seriously hurt."

Josiah nodded and then looked over his shoulder at the sound of the driver-side rear door opening. "Did I mention it's raining?" Bree said through the open door.

"Shut it," Johnson Davis said, without attempting to look back at her, which would have been difficult from his position.

"Look, I'm sorry," Bree said. "I'm getting soaked."

As Bree finished saying the word "soaked," Johnson Davis, still looking forward, again said, "Shut it," this time shouting it—loudly—causing Josiah to flinch. Bree shut the door.

"You could have been seriously hurt," Johnson Davis said again, to Josiah, at his usual volume. "Your mother nearly died."

Josiah nodded.

"Really, Josiah," Johnson Davis said. "She could have died. She was injured."

Josiah looked at Johnson Davis.

"She ran across the lawn after you and it was wet and she slipped and twisted her ankle. She can't stand on it."

Josiah said nothing.

"Between that and her head, you're literally killing her, Josiah. You have to stop."

Josiah said nothing. Bree again opened the passenger-side rear door and sat down in the back seat. Her hair and face and clothes were all wet. Josiah liked the way that her hair looked, all wet.

"Out," Johnson Davis said.

"This is ridiculous," Bree said.

"Out," Johnson Davis said again.

"No. I'm not going to stand out there in the rain. I know I fucked up but I'm not going to just stand out there. We have to talk."

"I'm talking to Josiah at the moment," Johnson Davis said.

"We have to talk," Bree said again.

"Five minutes."

"No, now."

"Rock-Paper-Scissors," Johnson Davis said.

"No."

"Five minutes, then."

"Two."

"Three."

"Two."

"Fine," Johnson Davis agreed.

"I'm counting to one twenty." Bree got out of the car and shut the door. Josiah could hear, even through the sound of the rain hitting the top of the car and the windshield, Bree counting: "One . . . Two . . . Three."

Johnson Davis turned to Josiah, speaking now with a sense of urgency. "It was her," he said. "She made you do it. Convinced you, somehow. Called you. Told you she was grounded and you had to rescue her. It was all her idea. If you really loved her, you would rescue her, something like that."

Josiah said nothing.

"You can tell me, Josiah."

Outside, Josiah listened as Bree counted, "Thirteen . . . Fourteen . . . Fifteen."

"Tell me, Josiah."

"Twenty . . . Twenty-one . . . Twenty-two."

"Look, Josiah, I can understand being in love. I truly can. I've been in love many times. Dozens of times. I know what it can do. In college, I was in love with a girl named Judy Florence for three years. Madly in love. For three years. Unrequited love, the worst kind. Three long years. You should hear the things I did. I won't bore you with it now, we haven't the time. But I did some ridiculous things. Would I have stolen a car for Judy Florence, Josiah? You're Goddamn right I would have."

"Fifty-one . . . Fifty-two . . . Fifty-three."

"I know what you're going through, Josiah. I know the power she has over you. She's manipulated you. Made you do things that you otherwise would never have done. Women have a power over men, Josiah. They can be very manipulative. Your mother told you the story of Adam and Eve, didn't she? Adam loved Eve very much. So much he would do anything for her. Anything. So what does she do? She manipulates him into eating the apple. The Devil's apple. And look how that turned out. The end of Paradise. Original sin and so forth. Ruined it for everyone."

"Eighty-two . . . Eighty-three . . . Eighty-four."

"I know you're a good boy, Josiah. I know you're a good boy and you don't want to hurt anyone and none of this is your fault. I just want you to tell me. Tell me why you did it. All of it. The drawings, the letters, the sex, the car. Just tell me it was all her. All her idea. Just tell me and I'll understand."

"Ninety-nine . . . One hundred . . . One hundred one."

Josiah said nothing.

"She's bad, Josiah. She's a bad person who does bad things and all you have to do is tell me."

Josiah said nothing.

"One ten . . . One eleven . . . One twelve."

"Don't let her manipulate you, Josiah. She's a sinner. Don't let her destroy you. Just tell me and all will be forgiven."

Josiah said nothing.

"Time's up," Bree said as she again opened the door and again sat down in the back seat.

"I knew it," Johnson Davis said to Bree. "I knew it."

"Knew what?" Bree said.

"Josiah told me everything. Told me it was all your idea."

"All what was my idea?" Bree looked at Josiah. Josiah did not know what to say, but tried to make a face, mostly by using his eyebrows, that would show Bree that he did not know what Johnson Davis was talking about. Bree looked back at Johnson Davis.

"All of it," Johnson Davis said. "Stealing and smoking and drinking and sex. Time after time that's all it is with you. And now you take this perfectly good and innocent boy—this boy whose mother I love and whom I've brought into my home—and you drag him into your world of sin and make him do these things."

"I haven't made him do anything."

"You told him to steal the car. He told me."

"He told you?"

"Yes."

"Josiah," Bree said to Josiah, "did you tell him that I told you to steal the car?"

Josiah shook his head.

"He didn't have to," Johnson Davis said. "He didn't have to say a thing. I know."

"I didn't tell him to steal the car."

"I know you did."

"He showed up at the door. With the car. Right, Josiah?"

Josiah nodded.

"He doesn't know the truth anymore. You have him brainwashed. You seduced him and brainwashed him and convinced him he was in love with you and you were in love with him and you had some special Goddamn relationship and were having a child together for Chrissakes."

"We *are* having a child together," Bree said.

"No, you're not," Johnson Davis said.

Josiah looked at Bree.

"We are," Bree said. "I'm pregnant with his child."

"You're not," Johnson Davis said.

"I am."

"You're not pregnant."

"I am."

"The doctor said you're not."

"So you were told."

"Pardon?"

"So you were told."

"What in the hell does that mean?"

"Mom didn't want to deal with your shit and have it be like last time so she told you I made it all up."

"No she did not."

Josiah, who was unsure whether the things that Bree was saying to Johnson Davis were true or not, stared at Bree as she spoke, but Bree did not look back at Josiah but rather kept her eyes on Johnson Davis as she continued, "She did. She said we'd just take care of it and leave you out of it and it'd be for the best."

"That isn't true."

"Call her."

"You're lying."

"Call her."

"I will."

"Do it."

"Give me your phone."

Bree handed Johnson Davis, after first flipping it open, her cellular phone, which Johnson Davis fumbled with for several seconds before handing it back to Bree and directing her to dial the number for him. As Bree, after dialing, handed the phone back and Johnson Davis searched for the "Send" button, Bree smiled mischievously at Josiah. Josiah turned and watched Johnson Davis as he held the phone to his ear and waited for someone to pick up. Josiah could hear the rings and could also tell that Bree was still looking at him and still smiling. Finally, the rings stopped and were replaced by an automated voice reciting the numbers of Bree's mother's phone. Johnson Davis flipped the phone shut. "No answer."

"Leave a message," Bree said.

"You want me to leave a message?" Johnson Davis said.

"Yes."

"I will."

"Okay."

"I'll leave her a message."

"Please."

After a pause, Johnson Davis, with teeth clenched, said, "That bitch."

"Told you," Bree said.

"How could she?"

"I said why."

"You're pregnant?"

"Yes."

"How could you do this? After the last time?"

"It's different."

"How?"

"I'm keeping it."

"Keeping it?"

"Yes."

"You can't."

"Why?"

"College. Soccer."

"What about them?"

"You're seventeen."

"We're going away."

"Who's going away?"

"Josiah and I are going away."

"What are you talking about?"

"We are going away together to raise our child."

"Now, Goddamnit, I refuse to believe for one Goddamn minute that this child is Josiah's."

"Why?"

"For one, I don't believe you've slept together."

"We have."

"I don't believe you. And I don't believe you're going away anywhere or that you want to keep this child. Do you want to know what I believe?"

"No."

"I believe you've been knocked up by some guy and I believe it's probably this Bart which is Goddamn illegal and you're protecting him and using Josiah to do it."

"I love Josiah."

"No, you don't."

"I do."

"I don't believe that. I know the truth."

"Josiah and I love each other and want to be together."

"No. He may. But no."

"It's true. I love him."

"No."

"It's true."

"Prove it."

"She gave me this," Josiah said to Johnson Davis. Johnson Davis and Bree both looked at Josiah, who was holding up his right arm, the hand, made into a fist, folded back to feature his wrist with the bracelet Bree had given him resting around it.

"What is that?" Johnson Davis asked.

"A gift," Josiah said.

"So what?" Johnson Davis said.

"From me," Bree said.

"For my birthday," Josiah said.

"So what?" Johnson Davis said again.

"Look at it," Bree said. Johnson Davis gently took hold of Josiah's wrist, still held in the air, with his right hand and with his left hand pulled the chain half-inch by half-inch until the metal plate rested on top. Johnson Davis looked at the inscription and the heart surrounding it and said, "This doesn't mean anything."

"We're secret boyfriend and girlfriend," Josiah said.

"We're together," Bree said. "This whole time. We had to keep it a secret."

"Baloney."

"We're going to get married," Josiah said, his wrist still held in the air though Johnson Davis had let go of it, "and we'll all be together."

Johnson Davis looked at Josiah and then looked at Bree. "What have you told him?"

"It's true," Bree said.

"Horseshit."

"Why can't you be happy?"

"Oh, spare me."

"No. Really. Listen to what I'm telling you. I'm telling you that I found someone and we love each other and want to be together. So I got pregnant. I'm sorry. But at least this time we have each other."

Johnson Davis said nothing.

"What did you say the last time?" Bree continued. "We weren't going to flush my future for someone's bastard."

"I never said that."

"You did."

"Not like that."

"Word for word."

"It was an emotional time."

"And here we are again and everything's different and right and you still can't be happy."

"What's right about it?"

"Like I said, we're together. Josiah and I."

"You're children."

"I'm seventeen. I'm basically an adult."

"He's sixteen."

"It won't matter. In ten years it won't matter. In five years."

"It will always matter. You can dress it up but it matters. A fuck-up is a fuck-up."

"I'm not a fuck-up."

"You'll always be a fuck-up."

Bree stared at Johnson Davis, who stared back at her. Neither of them said anything.

"She'll be a goddess," Josiah said.

Johnson Davis looked at Josiah. "What do you mean, 'a goddess'?"

"She will be a goddess," Josiah said again, "like my mother. On Parnuckle."

"Oh, for Christ's sake," Johnson Davis said. "This again."

"It's true," Bree said. "Josiah, tell him. About your mother. Your real mother."

"My real mother—" Josiah began.

"I've heard his story about his real mother," Johnson Davis cut in.

"Listen to him," Bree said. "Go ahead, Josiah."

"My real mother—" Josiah began again.

"I don't need to hear his Goddamn story about his so-called real mother," Johnson Davis said to Bree, then turning to Josiah and adding, "We talked about this, Josiah. I thought we'd been over this. You don't have any 'real mother.'"

"Yes he does," Bree said.

"Knock it off, damnit," Johnson Davis said.

"Knock what off?" Bree said.

Johnson Davis turned to Josiah. "Josiah, get out of the car."

"No," Bree said.

"Josiah," Johnson Davis said again. "Get out of the car."

"No," Bree said. "He doesn't have to."

"You and I," Johnson Davis said to Bree, "are going to have a very serious conversation about what in the hell you think you are trying to do, and Josiah does not need to hear any of it. Josiah, please step out of the car."

"He's not going anywhere," Bree said. "Josiah, don't go anywhere."

"Jesus fucking Christ," Johnson Davis said, again through his teeth.

"Say what you want to say," Bree said.

"Goddamnit," Johnson Davis said.

"Say it," Bree said.

Johnson Davis turned to Bree. "You don't really believe this shit, do you? I know you don't. Maybe he believes—though I'm not completely convinced, I'm not—maybe he thinks he believes in all of these spaceships and chocolate and goddesses and mothers and fathers and whatever other garbage. But you're not going to convince me—not at all, not in a million years—that you believe it, too."

"I do," Bree said.

"Bullshit."

"I do. I believe in Parnuckle and I believe Josiah and I will live there with his mother and father and with our baby and we will be happy."

"Bullshit," Johnson Davis said.

"We will," Bree said.

"Bullshit," Johnson Davis said. "I don't want to hear another word." Johnson Davis started the engine of his car and drove out of the driveway of the apartment complex.

o   o   o

Bree, lying in the sand of the creek bed, her head on Bart's chest, eyes open, had stared back at Josiah, for several seconds, nearly a minute, not lifting her head from Bart's chest, before finally saying to Josiah, "Tell me again."

o   o   o

When Johnson Davis led Josiah and Bree through the front door, Josiah's mother was waiting for them, having placed, unable to stand on her twisted ankle, one of the four-legged wooden chairs normally found in the dimly-lit dining room onto the middle of the large carpeted area between the front door and the living room, the chair facing the front door so that she would be the first thing seen by anyone entering, as she was for both Josiah and Bree, who, upon entering to find Josiah's mother glaring at them, stopped at the small square section of linoleum and stared back at her.

"Come here," Josiah's mother said. Josiah and Bree stood still.

"Shoes," Johnson Davis said, standing between Josiah and Bree and the now-closed front door, and Josiah and Bree and Johnson Davis all three took off their shoes, Josiah and Bree each, in turn, handing their shoes to Johnson Davis, who in turn aligned and placed the shoes in the corner of the square. Johnson Davis then walked to a point on the carpet halfway between the square of linoleum and Josiah's mother's chair, stood at a perpendicular angle to Josiah's mother as well as to Josiah and Bree, Josiah and Bree facing Josiah's mother and Josiah's mother likewise facing Josiah and Bree, and said to Josiah and Bree, "Come here." After a pause, Josiah and Bree stepped forward until they were even with Johnson Davis, who then took two large steps back.

"Why are they standing together like that?" Josiah's mother said to Johnson Davis. "Don't let them stand there next to one another like that."

Johnson Davis stood still.

Josiah reached for Bree's hand and took it in his. "Bree and I are leaving," Josiah said.

"What is he talking about?" Josiah's mother said. "Why is he holding her hand? Stop holding her hand."

Josiah's mother began to get up from her chair, but feeling the sharp pain in her ankle, sat back down. She looked at Johnson Davis.

"Make him stop holding her hand," she said.

Johnson Davis stood still.

o o o

"Think of it," Bree had said to Johnson Davis, from the back seat of Johnson Davis's car as Johnson Davis drove back from Ariel's apartment to the home of Johnson Davis. "Think of how happy we'll be. It's a beautiful place. Tell him, Josiah."

Josiah, sitting in the front passenger seat, his body shifted in the seat to face Johnson Davis, began to tell Johnson Davis, just as his mother had told him, about the beautiful fields and the mountains and the lakes reflecting every color—all at once—and the colorful cities with all of the smiling people, and Bree said to Johnson Davis, "It will be a beautiful place to raise a child. And we'll be able to live with Josiah's mother and father—his real mother and father—in the royal palace," and, at Bree's prompting, Josiah began to describe for Johnson Davis the Royal Palace of Gozer, in the capital city of Gozeria, just as Patrick had described it to Josiah and just as Josiah had described it to Bree when Josiah had found Bree lying in the sand, her head on Bart's chest, and Josiah had kneeled in the sand and stared at Bree, Bree opening her eyes and saying, "Tell me again."

Josiah had said nothing.

"Tell me again."

"I don't . . ." Josiah said.

"Tell me."

"I can't . . ."

"Tell me," Bree had said again, and Josiah told Bree, as she lay in the sand, staring at Josiah eagerly, just as he would tell Johnson Davis, a little over an hour later, at Bree's prompting, about the capital city of Gozeria, just as Patrick had described it, and about the Royal Palace of Gozer, just as Patrick had described it, particularly the special wing of the Keymaster of Gozer, where Josiah's mother and father lived and where hopefully Josiah and Bree would be able to live with their child, and after further prompting from Bree, Josiah described the three rooms of the special wing, focusing specifically on he and Bree's own room, which would transform itself from living room to kitchen to bedroom, always changing, based on need, a detail that Josiah could see had sparked the interest of both Bree and Johnson Davis, from the way that Bree, lying in the creek bed, her head on Bart's chest, formed a small smile and rolled her eyes upward, and from the way Johnson Davis tilted the top of his head toward the driver-side window, with Bree, from the back seat, breaking in near the end of Josiah's description to say to Johnson Davis, "We'll have everything we could ever want. Everything. Think of it."

Josiah then began to tell Johnson Davis, as Patrick had told him, but as he had never told Bree, of all of the important responsibilities that Josiah, as the son of an important government official, and as the son of a goddess, would have on Parnuckle, and all of the important things Josiah would be doing once his father retired or passed on, which would be a long time from now, Parnucklians living much longer than humans, just as Josiah and Bree would, once they became Parnucklians, a detail that once again led Johnson

Davis to tilt the top of his head toward the window next to him. Josiah then said to Johnson Davis that he had been searching for Bree, and that he knew that she was made for him—that she was his soulmate and that he wanted to take her with him to his home. Bree, who, as Josiah spoke to Johnson Davis, had been nodding her head and voicing affirmations, stopped and stared at Josiah, specifically at the point when he claimed her as his soulmate, and continued to stare for several seconds after he finished speaking, finally turning to Johnson Davis and saying, "You see. We'll be happy and we'll be in love. And the baby will be happy and loved and grow up in a beautiful place. And we'll be doing important, wonderful things, and none of the things that have happened here will matter."

Despite the fact that it was dark in the cab of car and despite the fact that Johnson Davis was not looking at Josiah but rather staring straight ahead through the windshield, Josiah could see that Johnson Davis had begun to cry.

o o o

"Let go of her hand," Josiah's mother said to Josiah. Josiah did not move. "Let go right now," she said again.

Josiah did not move. "Bree and I are leaving," he said again.

"What did you say?" Josiah's mother asked. Josiah did not respond. "What do you mean, you're leaving?" Josiah's mother asked, and when Josiah again did not respond, Josiah's mother turned to Johnson Davis to ask him what Josiah was talking about and what his daughter was trying to do, and Josiah's mother was going to tell Johnson Davis, as she already had, to get his daughter away from her son and to stop allowing her to touch his hand, but when Josiah's mother turned to where Johnson Davis had been standing, he was not there, but rather was standing behind Josiah's mother, holding several coils of orange and black rope that he had just taken from the garage, where the coils had been hanging from a makeshift wire hook stuck into a pegboard, Johnson Davis having purchased the rope earlier that year and used it only once, to tie down a new sofa, the sofa that Josiah had since spilled chocolate ice cream on and which Johnson Davis at the time had been moving into his home—his former wife, Bree's mother, who had divorced Johnson Davis shortly after their daughter's abortion, having moved their old couch, which had belonged to her aunt, into she and Bree's new home forty-six miles away—and before Josiah's mother could ask or tell Johnson Davis anything, Johnson Davis, whispering, "Just be patient," into Josiah's mother's ear, wrapped the orange and black rope twice around both Josiah's mother and the chair.

"What are you doing?" Josiah's mother asked Johnson Davis.

"Just be patient," Johnson Davis whispered. "Everything will be better."

Josiah's mother tried to remove the rope by lifting her arms, but Johnson Davis, who had been in the midst of securing the rope with a knot when Josiah's mother had loosened the coils by moving her arms, pulled Josiah's mother's arms back into place by pulling the coils of rope tight.

"You're hurting me," Josiah's mother said.

"I'm sorry, dear," Johnson Davis said, "but everything will be better." Josiah's mother began to scream.

Bree, who was still standing next to Josiah, holding his hand, said to Johnson Davis, "We can't let her scream like that."

"What should we do?" Johnson Davis asked.

"Gag her," Bree said.

"I couldn't," Johnson Davis said.

"Do you have any tape?" Bree asked. "The silver kind?"

"Use a pair of socks," Johnson Davis said.

As Johnson Davis finished securely tying the knot behind the chair and as Bree placed a pair of socks taken from the top right drawer of the dresser in Johnson Davis's—and Josiah's mother's—bedroom into Josiah's mother's mouth, Josiah still standing in the same spot, watching Johnson Davis and Bree and listening to his mother scream, the screams becoming muffled as Bree worked the socks into place, the doorbell rang.

Johnson Davis and Bree immediately pondered whom it could be, quickly agreeing that it was someone who had heard the screams and that they should hide Josiah's mother in another room and that the three of them should just pick up the chair with Josiah's mother in it and carry it into the next room, but Johnson Davis and Bree were not quick enough to stop Josiah, who had remained standing halfway between his mother's chair and the front door, and who, shortly after hearing the doorbell, had turned from that spot and stepped toward the door and opened it.

Outside the door was a man wearing a polo shirt and khakis. The polo shirt had a miniature polo player embroidered onto it, and the shirt was tucked into the khakis. The man looked like he was in his mid-thirties, and after staring at Josiah for several seconds, he said, "Is your name Josiah?"

"Yes," Josiah said.

"You're Josiah?" the man asked.

"Yes," Josiah said again.

"I believe I may be your father," the man said to Josiah. "I received a letter."

Johnson Davis, who had made his way to the door, said to the man, "I'm sorry, sir, but you must be mistaken. This is my son-in-law. Future son-in-law. And he and my daughter, it just so happens, are just now leaving to visit his father. There must be a mistake."

"You have a woman tied up," the man said, looking over Johnson Davis's shoulder.

"Indeed," Johnson Davis said.

"And gagged."

"A bit of role-playing."

"I think I went to high school with her," the man said, staring at Josiah's mother over Johnson Davis's shoulder. "And college."

"Small world," Johnson Davis said.

The man—who earlier that day had received a letter from a woman whose name at the time he did not recognize but that he now was beginning to associate with a girl he had gone to high school and college with whom he now saw sitting tied and gagged in a chair—turned from Josiah's mother and looked at Josiah, then back at Josiah's mother and back again at Josiah.

"I'm your father?" the man said to Josiah.

Josiah said nothing.

"I'm your father."

THIRTEEN

T HE NIGHT BEFORE Josiah moved into the home of Johnson
    Davis—his last night in the group home—shortly after din-
    ner, Patrick walked into his and Josiah's room, inside which
Josiah had been sitting alone—Eli Koslowski and Joey Simms,
with whom Josiah and Patrick shared the room, having gone, immediately after eating, out to the yard to shoot hoops—and Patrick
said to Josiah, "They said you're leaving tomorrow."

Josiah nodded.

"Where are you going?"

"With my mother."

"Which mother?"

"My other mother."

"Your Earth-mother?"

"Yes."

"Where?"

"Home. To her home."

"Are you happy about it?"

"No."

"Why not?"

"I don't want to go there."

"Don't go."

"They said I had to."

"What are you gonna do?"

"I don't know."

"You should write a letter," Patrick said to Josiah. "A letter to your Father. Tell him they are forcing you, against your will, to go back and live with your mother. Say that you really really don't want to go back, and ask if there is any way, any possibility that you could come and live with him, on Parnuckle.

"Say that you really want to see him," Patrick continued, "and want to develop your relationship, and say that things have been real tough here and you could start your life over, with him. What time do you leave?"

"Eleven."

"And ask if he can be here by ten o'clock in the morning to pick you up."

"It won't work."

"Sure it will. It has to."

"He won't get it in time."

"He will. You don't even have to send it. You just write it and he'll know. It's like a dormant telepathic link between father and son."

"I don't know."

"It'll work. Write it."

"I don't know."

"Just write it."

o o o

"You must be mistaken," Johnson Davis said to the man in polo shirt and khakis standing outside his front door. "Josiah has a father. He lives far away."

"Why is she tied up?" the man asked.

"Role-playing," Bree said, repeating Johnson Davis.

"Yes, a bit of role-playing," Johnson Davis said. "Would you mind if I had a look at that letter?"

Johnson Davis grabbed at the letter that the man held in his hand. The man pulled the letter out of Johnson Davis's reach and said, "She seems to be trying to say something. Or to scream."

"All part of the role-play," Johnson Davis said. "Her character is both frightened and indignant."

"I don't know what's going on here," the man said. "I received this letter with this address and I just came to find out what was going on, but now I'm here and I remember her and here's this kid and I really think I should speak to your wife about this. Could you please untie her?"

"Fiancée," Johnson Davis said.

"Excuse me," the man said.

"Fiancée," Johnson Davis said. "Not wife yet."

"Could you please untie her?" the man repeated.

"Again," Johnson Davis said, "this must be a mistake. I assure you. If you'd allow me to have a look at that letter."

"I'm going to have to insist," the man said, "that you untie her. I don't think she should be tied up like that. And I'd like to speak with her."

"Sir," Johnson Davis said, "if I could just have a look at that letter."

"I think I may need to call the police," the man said.

"The police?"

"Yes."

"I'm sure that's not necessary."

"Look," the man said, "if this young man is really my son—and, I think, now that I'm here, that he may be—then I have a right to know that, and I have a right to know him. And he has a right to know me. I need to speak to his mother. And she should really be untied. She looks very upset."

"She's not even his mother," Bree said to the man.

Johnson Davis was about to tell the man that he needed to get off of his property or he—Johnson Davis—would be the one calling the police, and Johnson Davis was also about to tell the man that he had a double-barreled shotgun just inside the door here, when Johnson Davis was interrupted by Josiah, who, as the man and Johnson Davis were conversing, had been staring first at the letter in the man's hand, then at the man, looking closely at his clothes and his nose and the shape of it and his hair but mostly looking closely at the man's eyes and the way that they moved and the way that they looked back into Josiah's eyes when the man looked directly at Josiah, until Josiah heard Bree's voice explaining that Josiah's mother was not his mother, after which Josiah looked at Bree and Bree, whose hair in that moment looked especially shiny, looked back at Josiah and smiled. Josiah smiled back at Bree, then turned to Johnson Davis and said, "Let him in."

"Now, Josiah," Johnson Davis said, "I'm sure the gentleman has places to be."

"No," the man said, "I want to come in."

"Let him in," Josiah said again.

"But, Josiah," Bree said, "we were about to leave."

"Let him in," Josiah said a third time.

Josiah and Johnson Davis and Bree backed away from the door, and as the man entered, Josiah closed the door behind him and flipped the light switches on the wall next to the door to the "off" position. The other lights in the house were already off, other than the garage light and the upstairs master bathroom light, neither being visible from the living room, so that when Josiah shut off the light of the main entry and of the living room, both controlled by the two-switch panel on the wall next to the front door, the house was very dark, and as the man and Johnson Davis and Bree stood about disoriented, Josiah picked up a lamp from a nearby end table in the nearby living room, Josiah having seen lamps often used in television and movies to hit people over the head with, and Josiah took the lamp and, his eyes now becoming accustomed to the dark, hit the man, whose name was Drew Martell and who was Josiah's father, over the head with it.

o o o

As Josiah wrote his letter, in his room at the group home, Patrick described for Josiah what his life, once rescued by his father, would be like. First of all, Patrick told Josiah, he would be living, since his father was Keymaster of Gozer, and his mother a goddess queen, beloved by all, in the Royal Palace of Gozer, in the capital city of

Gozeria. Patrick told Josiah that he and his father and mother—his real mother—would live together very happily, all being finally reunited. And when Josiah reached the age of eighteen, which he would be doing very soon, he would get to choose, as all Parnucklians do at that age, his own profession, and Josiah would follow in his father's footsteps as an important official in the Parnucklian government, possibly even taking over for his father—as Keymaster of Gozer—when his father reached the age of retirement, that age, for Parnucklian males, being ninety-four, Parnucklian males living much longer than Earthling males, and as Josiah would as well, once his body had been adequately exposed to the Parnucklian ecosystem.

o   o   o

After establishing that Drew Martell was still breathing, Johnson Davis lifted the letter from Drew Martell's hand, the letter having been placed back into its opened envelope, which Johnson Davis gazed at for several seconds, his eye catching at his own address in his fiancée's handwriting, beneath her own name, in the envelope's upper left corner. Johnson Davis then read the address at the envelope's center, beneath the carefully printed name *Mr. Drew Martell*, and announced that he knew where this was and it was within walking distance, a few miles, and he would take Drew Martell home in Drew Martell's car and walk back, maybe even take the opportunity for a nice run, and Johnson Davis stood and folded the letter and envelope in half and placed it in his front pocket and looked at Bree and said to her, "I think it'll be for the best," to which Bree nodded and after which Johnson Davis looked at Josiah and said, "Good luck, Josiah," before walking halfway across the room to the chair that his fiancée, Josiah's mother, was tied up in, Josiah's mother's eyes being very red and very puffy and a whimpering sound coming from behind the pair of socks that were stuffed into her mouth, and Johnson Davis kissed Josiah's mother on the forehead and said to her, "Be right back. It'll all be better tomorrow. Just you and I." Johnson Davis then walked back to Drew

Martell, picked him up by the armpits, and dragged him through the front door.

Bree closed the door and turned to Josiah. "Get your stuff," she said. "I'll get my stuff. Meet back here in ten minutes."

Josiah followed Bree up the stairs and turned down the hallway toward his room as Bree turned toward hers. After nine minutes, having stuffed his six t-shirts, four pairs of shorts, and four pairs of jeans into his duffel bag, Josiah walked back down the stairs to the area between the front door and the living room. Bree was not there. Josiah's mother was still sitting tied up in her chair, her head hanging to her side, her chin resting on the front of her shoulder. Josiah set down his duffel bag and walked up to her. Her eyes, now closed, were still red and puffy. Josiah placed his hand on her arm, between the shoulder and elbow. She lifted her head and opened her eyes. She began to whimper again from behind the socks. Josiah, who now stood very close to his mother, could see that saliva was running out from the sides of the socks and down her chin. Josiah reached around his mother, one arm on each side of her, his chest pressed against her forehead, and untied the knot. He then removed the pair of socks from her mouth and dropped it to the floor. Josiah's mother began to gasp and cough. Josiah took a step back.

Josiah's mother coughed several times—more than Josiah could count—in between which were interspersed four long, loud gasps, after which Josiah's mother sat silently for several seconds, leaning forward and rubbing the area of her arms, just above the elbows, where the coils of rope had been, before finally saying to Josiah, without looking up, "Good night, Josiah. I'm going to bed," and standing and walking toward the stairway, pausing just before the first step and saying over her shoulder, "I'm sorry," before walking up the stairs and into her room and closing the door. Josiah walked back to his duffel bag and stood waiting for Bree.

o o o

Most importantly, Patrick told Josiah, Josiah having finished his letter, sitting on his bed and listening to Patrick, Josiah would be able to start a family of his own. Somewhere, on that great big planet full of people, there was someone—a girl—just for him, a girl that he would fall in love with and couldn't live without. Everyone had one, somewhere. Josiah just had to be ready and watch for her. And when he saw her he would know. And he would fall in love and she would fall in love and they would get married and have a baby and then maybe more babies and they would move out of the Royal Palace of Gozer and into their own palace, or maybe a villa, and they would be happy, forever, together, in their home.

o o o

After six minutes, when Bree had still not come downstairs to meet Josiah, Josiah walked up the stairs and down the hallway to Bree's room and opened the door. The overhead light in Bree's room was turned off, but the lamp on Bree's nightstand was on. Bree was lying on her bed, with her eyes closed. Next to her, on the bed, was her own duffel bag, pink with a large white stripe, the zipper open and clothes sticking out of its top. The posters of Brent Randolph that had covered Bree's walls were now rolled up and lying next to the duffel bag.

Josiah walked to Bree's bed and sat down. He leaned over her and kissed her on the forehead, as he had just seen Johnson Davis do to his mother. Bree opened her eyes.

"I closed my eyes for just a minute," she said. "I was so sleepy." Bree looked up at Josiah and smiled. "Are you sleepy?" she asked him.

Josiah shrugged.

"Lay down for a while," Bree said. "We have time."

Josiah lay down on the bed next to Bree. Bree rested her head on Josiah's shoulder and placed her hand on his chest.

"Are you excited?" she asked.

"I don't know," Josiah answered.

"What are you most excited about?" Bree asked.

"I don't know," Josiah answered again.

"Are you excited about seeing your father? And your mother?"

"I don't know."

"About our new home?"

"I have to tell you something," Josiah said.

"What?" Bree asked.

"We can't go to Parnuckle," Josiah said. Josiah felt Bree's head shift against his shoulder.

"We can't?" Bree said.

"No," Josiah said.

"Why not?"

"There is no Parnuckle."

Bree shifted again, her hair rubbing against Josiah's chin. It felt soft.

"There isn't?" Bree said.

"No," Josiah said. "That man. Was my father. And my mother . . ."

"Is your mother," Bree said.

"Yes."

"And there's no planet."

"No."

"And no palace."

"No."

"That's okay."

"It is?" Josiah said.

"It is," Bree said.

Josiah and Bree were both silent, lying perfectly still—other than Josiah's chest moving up and down, lifting and then lowering Bree's hand with each breath—for several seconds before Josiah, staring straight up at the ceiling of Bree's room, said to Bree, "Do you still want to get married?"

"Of course," Bree said. "We still have the baby. Still a family."

"Are you sure?"

"Yes."

"What about Bart?" Josiah asked.

After a pause, Bree answered, "Bart? What about him?"

"Are you . . . is he your boyfriend?"

"My boyfriend?"

"Is he?"

"No. You're my boyfriend."

"Secret."

"Not anymore."

"No?"

"No."

"He calls you 'Babe,'" Josiah said, "and holds your hand."

"So?"

"Your head was on his chest."

"So?"

"Did you fuck him?"

Bree lifted her head and stared at Josiah. "Why would you ask that?"

"Did you?"

"No. Why would you ask that? Bart is not my boyfriend. He's just helping me out with some things. Through some things. Things I don't like to talk about."

"What about David?" Josiah asked.

"Who's David?"

"From the park."

"The park? What about him?"

"Were you fucking him?"

Bree pushed up onto her elbows. Then to her palms.

"Josiah, you're being very rude."

"Were you?"

"Stop it."

"And Keith Jones?"

"Keith Jones? What are you talking about? Did Ariel tell you that? She's full of shit. Forget about what's-his-name and Keith Jones. And forget about Ariel and Bart. I don't care about them. They're probably in her apartment doing it right now."

"Doing what?" Josiah asked.

"Who cares?" Bree said.

"What are they doing?" Josiah asked.

"All that matters, Josiah, is you and me. Nothing else. Don't even think about anyone else. It's just like you said. We are meant for each other. Soulmates."

Josiah said nothing.

"Do you believe me?" Bree asked.

Josiah said nothing.

"We're going to be a family," Bree said. "We'll be able to completely start over. Just you and me and no one else. Like a whole new life. Nothing here will matter. Do you believe me?"

"Yes," Josiah answered.

"Just you and me," Bree said. "We don't need a palace. Or a planet. We can be a family here. Have our own home, together. Here."

Josiah began to imagine the home he would live in with Bree. It was not a two-story home like the home of Johnson Davis or of Bree and her mother, but it was not as small as the home Josiah had lived in with *his* mother, and it had a front yard and a back yard bigger than any of those homes, and the back yard and front yard were filled with grass, and the grass was very green and was freshly-cut, and smelled nice, and the house had lots of windows—big windows—and inside the house was very bright, and also smelled nice, and Josiah imagined living in the house with Bree, and their baby, who in Josiah's imagination was three or four years old and was playing with his toys in the bright, nice-smelling living room, and in the bright kitchen was Bree, cooking food that smelled very nice and warm, all different kinds of food, and with Bree in the bright kitchen was another baby, sitting in a baby chair at the kitchen table, which in Josiah's imagination was made of glass and reflected the brightness of the kitchen so that the baby's face was also bright, and in some moments of Josiah's imagination the baby was eating baby food, and in other moments the baby was smiling and laughing, and in moments of Josiah's imagination everyone was smiling and laughing: Bree and the baby and the other baby in the living room and even Josiah himself. And Josiah imagined himself, wearing nice clothes that one would wear to a nice job, and Josiah imagined himself coming home from his nice job in his nice clothes and walking into the kitchen and kissing Bree, first on the cheek and then on the lips, and then kissing the baby in the baby chair, on the forehead, and then kissing the other baby, who had come running into the kitchen from the living room, laughing and smiling, and Josiah and Bree and their babies would gather around their bright table and eat shiny, colorful, warm and nice-smelling food and laugh and smile.

Josiah imagined he and Bree putting the babies to bed and driving the babies to school and picking them up and having the babies' friends over for dinner, like on TV, and taking the babies to the zoo, which Josiah had never been to but had seen on TV, and taking the babies camping or fishing or to other fun places like the local fun park, and Josiah was thinking about the local fun park when Bree said to Josiah, "First we'll need a place to live."

"I know," Josiah said.

"And clothes for the baby," Bree said.

"And toys," Josiah said.

"Yes," Bree said, "and toys. And we'll need a car. We should get out of town. Somehow. Find a way out of town to somewhere new and find jobs and save our money and find a house. Or an apartment, then a house."

"I have sixty dollars," Josiah said.

"That's good," Bree said. "That'll get us food. Until we can find jobs."

"We should go now," Josiah said.

"Let's rest first," Bree said. "Rest up."

Bree again rested her head on Josiah's shoulder and again placed her hand on his chest. Bree's hair brushed up against the skin of Josiah's cheek. Bree closed her eyes. Josiah laid silent, Bree's hand on his chest, conscious of the quick, deep breaths he was taking and how much they were moving Bree's hand, up and down. Josiah tried to concentrate. After several minutes, as Josiah's breathing finally began to slow, Bree opened her eyes and said to Josiah, "Are you sleeping?"

"No," Josiah answered.

"What are you thinking about?" Bree asked.

"I don't know."

"Come on. What?"

"We should go."

"There's time."

"But we could go."

"There's time. Do you want to know what I was thinking?"

Josiah said nothing.

"I wasn't sleeping either. I was thinking. We can do whatever we want now. Anything. We'll have our whole lives ahead of us, together. Our family. And it will be wonderful. But I was thinking, now that we're free—free to do whatever we want—there are things we should do. Before settling. Settling down. If you could do anything—anything—what would you want to do?"

"I don't know."

"Anything."

"But . . ."

"You know what I want to do? If I could do anything on Earth? I'd want to be someone else. Like, pretend to be someone else. That's what we could do. We could become different people. Create entirely new identities, and travel all over the country—or even the world—and see everything, all the sights, like the Grand Canyon, and the Eiffel Tower, and I could be, I don't know, Sarah, an art student, and you could be Devin, a photographer, and we could travel and see new places and meet new people, and if we get tired of who we are, we can just be someone else, just start over, as many times as we want."

Josiah watched as Bree stood from the bed and finished packing her duffel bag, stuffing the clothes sticking out from its top further in and transferring from her dresser to the bag two handfuls each of underwear, socks, and vials of makeup.

"What do you think?" Bree said.

"I want to go now," Josiah said.

"Where should we go first?" Bree said.

"I want to go home," Josiah said. "To go find our home."

"We have time," Bree said.

"What about the baby?" Josiah said.

"We have time," Bree said.

"Getting married?" Josiah said.

"We have all the time in the world," Bree said.

"Are you sure?" Josiah said.

"Of course," Bree said. "We have our whole lives."

Josiah said nothing, and listened as Bree stopped packing her bag and explained to Josiah that they should just leave everything, leave the bags and the posters, everything but the ball and the bracelet, and just go and start over, travel the world, live in cars and train stations, meet interesting people, get into trouble, have adventures, and Josiah stood and followed as Bree walked out of her room, holding the soccer ball Josiah had given her, explaining again that they could have new names and that they could even dye their hair different colors and they could eat food they'd never even heard of before, and as they walked along the hallway and down the stairs and through the living room, Bree told Josiah about all the different places they would go, like San Francisco or Paris or Baltimore, hitchhiking or riding buses or trains as far as they could and then getting jobs in restaurants or supermarkets and saving enough for a ticket somewhere, anywhere.

Josiah followed as Bree walked out the front door and into the street. They walked for forty-three minutes, Bree six steps ahead of Josiah, cradling the ball in her hands. As they walked and as the sky slowly turned from black to grey, Josiah pictured his life with Bree, from the moment they were now living to the moment he would last see her, and in the picture the bright one-story house and the laughing and the smiling were replaced by a parade, a parade of people who looked like David, and like Bart, and people that looked like Ariel, and a parade of goddesses and palaces and important officials and chocolate and babies that he would never see or meet, and of endless letters the addressees of which would never receive, much less read, and in Josiah's picture Bree was always ahead of him, as she was now, and he always behind, following, her moving steadily toward a destination that from his position he could never see.

As the sun began to rise and Bree walked up the thick concrete steps to the door of Ariel's apartment, Josiah did not follow her, and Bree did not look back. Josiah stared at the closed door at the top of the stairs for only a second before turning and walking away.